SETTING THE RECORD STRAIGHT

CHRIS WORTHINGTON

SETTING THE RECORD STRAIGHT

Matador
9 Priory Business Park,
Wistow Road
Kibworth Beauchamp
Leicester LE8 0RX, UK
Tel: (+44) 116 279 2299
Fax: (+44) 116 279 2277
Email: books@troubador.co.uk
Web: www.troubador.co.uk/matador

ISBN 978 1848767 089

British Library Cataloguing in Publication Data.
A catalogue record for this book is available from the British Library.

Typeset in 11pt Aldine401 BT Roman by Troubador Publishing Ltd, Leicester, UK

Matador is an imprint of Troubador Publishing Ltd

Printed and bound in the UK by TJ International, Padstow, Cornwall

To Wendy V
With all my love
C

With thanks to Julia Hamilton

Prologue

August 1988

Two distinct thunderstorms were visible in the massive sky over the plains of south central Texas, one to the northwest, and the other due south. The distance between them was over twenty miles but at this point, almost equidistant from either storm, the sun was beating down relentlessly, the air was as still as stagnant water, and only the occasional distant rumble could be heard. As the temperature nudged one hundred degrees and the wind picked up slightly from the north, three individuals were converging on a house set back off US-183 a few miles north of Leander. It was a Friday afternoon.

The first to arrive at the property was Danny Stanley, who had just slowed to make a left turn onto the unmarked dirt road in his battered old pickup truck. He was 46 years old, he ran a small building company in nearby Georgetown, the place where he was born and raised, and he had not long left his team of three labourers working on a farm a few miles north of here saying he was going to see his accountant and would be back within the hour. His mouth was dry with nervous anticipation as he weaved his truck slowly past a series of deep potholes towards the house, which was set back nearly a quarter of a mile from the main road among a small cluster of trees that provided much needed shade from the blistering summer sun. The house had seen better days, the paint on the window frames was cracked and peeling, and the clapboard frontage was desperately in need of a coat of weatherproofing varnish. The owners were Frank and Lizzie Dealer. Frank was a rival builder, but Frank and Danny were long time friends and had come to a gentleman's agreement about not poaching work from each other. Danny sighed as he pulled to a halt next to Lizzie's car. How could

Frank have let his house go to rack and ruin so quickly? It was only rebuilt seven years ago after the roof was ripped off by the high winds skirting a tornado that passed a few hundred yards away. But it always seemed to be the way with builders' houses … the maintenance of them had to come second to jobs that earned money and paid the bills. Danny put his hat on the passenger seat, checked his teeth in the rear view mirror, cut the engine, and got out.

Also approaching the house from a different direction was JJ, a 12 year old boy cantering gently on horseback from a nearby creek, where he had been swimming with his friend Jed. He'd last seen his mother, Lizzie Dealer, at 9am this morning and had told her he would be out all day, but then disaster had struck a little while ago when Jed gashed his foot badly on some broken glass under the water and had to gallop off back home. Then there was nothing much left to do but come home. Progress on the tree house they were planning would have to wait until tomorrow … there was no rush … the summer vacation still had weeks and weeks to run. At his current rate of canter he would be back at the stables in around five minutes.

The third person approaching the house was Frank Dealer, also 46, and also born and raised in Georgetown. Frank and Danny literally grew up together, they went to the same kindergarten, they both left the same high school without graduating, and since then neither had travelled much further than a hundred miles from this part of Texas. Frank was currently driving south on US-183, around ten minutes away from his home. He had finished work for the day but stopped in a bar on the way and had a couple of beers to celebrate the early completion of a job. He left after thirty minutes, slightly drunk, and looking forward to getting home for a shower and a nap. It was nearly 2pm.

Lizzie Dealer looked up from a pile of damp washing that needed to go into the dryer when she heard the sound of a vehicle approaching. She was 45 years old, but looked much younger, and was born and raised on this very plot of the land, in the previous house that occupied this space. She was surprised to see Danny pulling up, surprised but excited. She dried her hands, quickly straightened her hair with her fingers, and applied some fresh lipstick from her purse in a nearby mirror. Then she walked through the kitchen to the front door and stepped from the relative cool of the house into the scorching heat outside.

Danny ambled over, the heels of his construction boots kicking up small puffs of dust from the hard baked ground.

"Hey soldier boy, you can't just turn up any time you know? You ever hear of making an appointment?"

He ignored this. "Hey Lizzie, anyone at home today? I saw your man Frank first thing picking up some timber at the yard."

"Yep, he's out doing some windows at Grafton's warehouse."

She looked up at the gathering clouds. "I sure hope he's got it nailed cos that looks like a big old storm over there."

Danny didn't look up; he was now only a few feet away from her. "Uh-huh, and the boss man at Grafton's can be a nasty old son of a bitch sometimes. Hey!"

He grabbed Lizzie around the waist and lifted her clear off the ground. She playfully wrestled herself free but then he nudged his face into her neck and the sandpaper stubble rubbed abrasively on her soft skin.

"Youch," she squealed playfully, "you got a face rougher than a..."

"You want to get it on with old Danny boy then?" He breathed directly into her face and she could faintly smell onions. "Frank will be up to his ass in plate glass until that job's finished."

She pouted. "Oh I don't know. I got a whole bunch of laundry that needs to go in the dryer. Houses don't run themselves you know."

He looked around. "So where's JJ?"

"Swimming at the creek with Jed; they're building a tree house. Well, planning to anyway."

Danny bundled her in through the front door after taking a last glimpse over his shoulder. He would be able to see the dust cloud if anyone was on the approach road. Lizzie broke free again and ran through to the kitchen, taking the phone off the hook as she passed it. Then she stopped at the work surface and quickly reached down to her short skirt.

"Hey, don't you go taking anything off now," he scolded, "that's my job. And how about putting up a bit of a fight for Danny boy this time, huh?"

"You are one sick bastard, you know that?" She smiled provocatively. "I like it ... maybe you can give my Frankie some lessons."

He grabbed her shoulders and they kissed passionately, fumbling and pawing at each others' clothes.

Meanwhile JJ had just tethered his horse in the stable and was walking towards the house. As he approached he saw dust rising out front so he knew someone had arrived in the last few minutes. He paused by the back door, but something told him not to shout as he normally did when he came home. He couldn't see whose car it was ... perhaps his dad had come home early. He sighed. Whenever this happened on a Friday afternoon his dad was usually drunk. From within he could hear muffled sounds. His mum was laughing ... or was it laughing? He could also hear the low voice of a man, but it didn't sound like his dad. He quietened his step and approached the kitchen door from within the outer utility room. He saw the pile of washing by the dryer and he heard his mother's voice again.

As Frank Dealer turned off onto the familiar dirt road that led to his house the walkie talkie under the dashboard crackled into life and he pulled over to answer it.

"Hey Frank, I'm sorry man." The voice was distorted. "You know about the deal earlier. It was a breakdown in the supply chain, what can I tell ya? My man at the warehouse fucked up. It won't happen again."

"Josh, I sure hope you're right. Now I got my windows elsewhere today so it all worked out ok but *no* thanks to you and your man at the *fucking* warehouse! My reputation round here can, *and will*, be permanently screwed if stuff like that happens. Please make sure it never fucking happens again. You want to pay the school fees for my kid? You want to buy my wife the facelift she's planning when she hits fifty? There ain't no room for bad builders round here, ok?"

"Ok, ok, definitely. Look, will I see you down at The Spoke tonight?"

"I don't know. I've had couple of beers already today, not sure I need any more."

"Well I'll be down there at 7pm. Try and make it, I'll buy."

"I'll see what Lizzie says." Frank replied. "Who knows, if I'm back early she might want to hit the mall tonight. Jesus!"

The radio clicked off. His truck was still idling at the entrance to the dirt track road and he reached over to the glove compartment to get his bottle of whisky. He took a long slug … screwing up his face as the clear brown liquid burned the back of his throat.

"Fuck it, fuck it all." He shouted out loud. "I got booze here and it's already paid for."

He drank again, emptying the last quarter of the bottle, and his head swam momentarily as the alcohol hit the spot. A cool shower and an afternoon nap were only a matter of moments away.

Back inside the house JJ had crept silently across to the kitchen door and peered nervously through the gap. He could see the back of a man, his jeans were down and part of his backside was on show under the flap of his shirt. He gulped as the man struggled with the person in front of him. He couldn't properly see who it was from here but then the man's head moved to one side and he saw his mum's face! Her mouth was open and she looked hurt. Then he saw the man rip at her clothes. She gasped and cried out. It sounded like she was in pain. For a moment JJ stood rooted to the spot, trying to understand what he was seeing. Were they kissing? If so why was she shouting like that? But then there was another yelp of pain and something clicked in his mind; suddenly things became clear. His mum was in danger and he knew what he had to do. His dad's hunting rifle was in the cupboard about three feet away. The cupboard was never locked and the gun was always loaded; it was fired only two days ago when a pair of foxes tried to break into the henhouse. His mum's voice cried out again and he heard the man tell her to shut up. He needed to protect her. What if this guy was a murderer? He moved quickly, opening the cupboard door with only the slightest creak of the hinge. He had fired the gun quite a few times before, even though it was heavy and the recoil knocked him sideways. Guns were just a way of life around here and he suddenly remembered what his dad told him the first time he was given it to hold.

"Son, I hope you never need to use this, but if something or somebody is threatening you then you use it! And use it good. Don't give second chances."

He released the safety catch and slowly lifted the gun into position. His young mind was racing but his aim was steady. He heard his dad's voice again.

"Don't give second chances! Use it and use it good!"

This was it. The heavy barrel wavered slightly but otherwise was pointing straight at the man's back. He squeezed gently at the trigger, closing his eyes in anticipation of the noise to come. But he couldn't do it, he just *couldn't.* In his mind he could see the dead fox that his dad recently shot; its head was unrecognizable; a mess of blood and gore. He felt his throat closing up as the saliva drained away. His fingers felt numb on the trigger. His feet were stuck to the floor. He tried to shout out but that didn't seem to work either.

Lizzie threw her head back as Danny pushed her towards a work surface and reached down under her skirt.

"Pull my hair!" She whispered harshly. "Pull my fucking hair, pull it hard!"

Danny obliged and roughly grabbed a handful of her shoulder length hair with his free hand, yanking her head back sharply. Then he roughly pulled off her skirt and underwear in one go and she screamed loudly.

"*Stop it!*" A small voice yelled through the crack in the door. *"Stop it!"*

JJ couldn't hear his own voice as he yelled. The whole scene crashed into slow motion as Danny turned around and suddenly he could see his mum in front of him. She was completely undressed and he could see her bare skin glistening in the afternoon sun. He could see her … he could see…"

"*JJ no!*" she yelled, but the gun went off, spinning Danny around as blood and bone fragments exploded from his shoulder.

JJ recovered from the recoil and ran forward as Danny slumped noiselessly to the floor and lay face down, his shoulders rising in large gasps. There was a haze of smoke in the air and it felt as if the echo of the blast was still reverberating around the room.

"*JJ!*" she wailed hysterically but he couldn't hear her. His ears were buzzing from the explosion of the gunshot, which seemed excruciatingly loud in the confined space of the kitchen, and he started to retch as the hot smoke burned at his throat. Lizzie's face and neck were spattered with blood and she grabbed her discarded shirt to try and cover herself as Danny groaned in agony on the floor; a low grunting moaning sound that came from deep within his chest. Lizzie pushed her son aside and ran to the phone. She pulled the shirt on, dialled 911, and screamed into the receiver.

"Help, help, someone's been shot … I'm at Frank Dealer's place … it's Lizzie Dealer … Oh come on, stop with the questions you all know us! Just get an ambulance here quick!"

She slammed the phone down and ran back over to Danny. "JJ, put the gun down and get out of here. Go wait for the ambulance. It's going to be alright, you'll see."

But JJ was rooted to the spot, his face taut with anger and shock. The blood – he had never seen so much of it! Soaking wet and spreading out onto the stone tiled floor. The gun now felt like a dead weight in his hands and he could feel cramp setting into his fingers.

Suddenly Danny summoned up some strength and heaved himself onto his back, clamping his left hand around Lizzie's ankle, and causing her to stumble and grab the table.

"Lizzie, you gotta help me…" He pleaded, his face contorted in pain.

And then another shot rang out, as JJ aimed for Danny's arm again but hit him in the neck instead. Dark frothy blood gushed and gurgled from the massive wound as Danny's face was fixed with a startled expression. His body convulsed briefly, but he was dead within seconds. This time there were no screams as Lizzie crouched dumbstruck by Danny's body, stroking his hair. She didn't look up as JJ ran from the room.

Frank heard the first shot as he emptied the whisky bottle and tossed it thoughtlessly from the window of his truck. But he ignored it. Gunshots were not unusual round here; it was probably that old bastard at the farm on the other side of the road shooting at the birds again. He started driving slowly along the potholed track, ignoring the larger craters with precise automatic flicks of the steering wheel, but then the second shot pierced the stillness, sending a small flock of birds flapping into the air from a nearby tree. A surge of adrenaline coursed through his chest as he realized it was coming from his house and he floored the accelerator to drive the last hundred yards. Within seconds he had to hit the brakes and the truck skidded to a stop a few yards from the front door in a cloud of dust and stones. He rushed inside, passing Danny's truck as he went.

"Lizzie!" he shouted as he burst into the hallway. "Lizzie, JJ! Is anyone here?"

There was no response until he got to the kitchen and saw the horrific tableau.

"Lizzie, what the hell…" He was aghast.

She turned to look at him, her face dissolved in an expression of utter bewilderment.

"Frankie … I love you." She wept quietly. "Please believe me, I love you."

Her head dropped, but Frank couldn't take anything in. Through the haze of the whisky he tried to assess what had happened. He hadn't even recognized who was lying on the floor. Lizzie's mind was racing too. She needed an explanation fast. Frank walked slowly across the room and stood above the body.

"Jesus Christ. *Danny!*" His mouth hung open.

Lizzie stood up silently and walked past him to retrieve the rest of her clothes. Then she methodically got dressed and tried to straighten her hair with her hands. During the last few minutes JJ had retreated to the utility room, still clutching the gun. He watched his mum through the partially open door as she put her clothes on. He couldn't feel anything. His pulse was still racing but he felt totally empty. He could not comprehend the enormity of what he had done.

Frank turned to Lizzie as she wiped some blood off her face with a dishcloth.

His head was shaking slowly in disbelief. "Lizzie, for God's sake tell me what has happened."

He wanted to feel rage as his mind started to piece together a possible scenario but he couldn't seem to summon any up.

Lizzie swallowed hard. Her voice was trembling but her story was clear. "Now Frank, sweetie, you've got to listen me. Please will you listen to me?"

Frank nodded blankly.

"He attacked me, sugar. He tried to rape me. He made me take my clothes off and stand in front of him. And I did it because I was scared. But then when he took his jeans down and grabbed me I..." her voice cracked, "I managed to break free and get past him. I got the gun from the cupboard and I pointed it at him. I didn't want to shoot him but..."

The sound of sirens was heard in the distance and her voice took on a sudden urgency.

"But he came at me again so I pulled the trigger and he went down."

She put her hands to her face. "And then he moved on the ground ... he tried to get up so I shot him again. I remembered what you told JJ and me. Don't give second chances. I thought he was going to kill me."

Frank was still in a daze. "Where is JJ?"

The sirens closed in outside. "He saw it all Frank, well most of it, he came back early too. He's out back I think. He grabbed the gun off me and I think he's still got it."

Frank closed his eyes. "Jesus, I can't believe my little boy saw all this."

"JJ," he shouted, "are you out there? Get in here and do it now!"

There was no response.

"JJ, come on in here, baby." She tried to sound reassuring. "You're not in trouble, do as your daddy says now."

Voices were heard outside, along with the sound of another siren approaching. Frank went out into the utility room and saw JJ crouching in the corner. His eyes were shut tight.

"Gimme the gun, JJ. Everything's going to be fine. You're mom's fine and I'm fine, just give me the gun."

Still JJ didn't move. Then a car door slammed outside and Frank couldn't wait any longer. He snatched the gun from his son's rigid fingers and sent him sliding across the floor, just as the front door burst open and the ambulance crew arrived. The other siren belonged to a police car that was trying to negotiate the dirt road without grounding its exhaust pipes.

Frank returned to the kitchen holding the gun and the young man and woman from the ambulance immediately froze in terror.

"It's ok, fellas." He put the gun down. "The situations under control, no one else is gonna get hurt."

Then two police officers came ambling in, both knew Frank and Lizzie … and Danny … very well.

Frank held his hands up. "Guys, everything's under control, I just need to…"

But the younger of the two officers stopped him. "Frank, can we establish right away who committed this crime?"

Lizzie opened her mouth to speak but Frank got in first. "It was me officer. I came back early and he…"

"Frank Dealer, I'm arresting you for the murder of Danny Stanley. You don't have to say anything, but anything you do say…"

A huge clap of thunder shattered the calm of the afternoon, and the other officer intervened.

"Let's get everyone out of here; you can finish reading him his rights on the way to the car. I'll call for backup to bring Lizzie in."

Outside huge drops of rain were starting to fall, causing tiny explosions of dust as they hit the ground. The storm was gathering overhead.

1

July 2008
Saturday

A text message arrived on a mobile phone in a cramped apartment on the upper west side of Manhattan, causing a harsh buzz on the glass table top where it was sitting. Christine Hudson was cleansing her face in the bedroom next door when she heard the noise and immediately went through and picked it up, trying hard to avoid getting any lotion on the buttons. This number was not widely known, so unless it was yet another call offering free network time she could probably guess who it was from.

The message read, *"Please can you finish things soon? Mid next wk if possible. Thank you."*

She took a deep breath, walked across to the window, and stared out aimlessly at the street beneath. It was nearly 7pm and after the early evening lull the pavements were now buzzing with tourists and partygoers. For a moment or two she wondered where the day had gone.

Fundamentally Christine was unhappy, and had been so in varying degrees for nearly two years, since making the decision to relocate here from Dallas; the place where she was born and raised. Looking back, the move was impulsive and ill thought out. New York City still seemed drab and hostile, and although her job with the *Garden State Sentinel* Sunday lifestyle magazine over in New Jersey was pretty exciting her personal life was bereft of any real enjoyment. She had tried and tried to make friends, but it wasn't happening. She rarely saw anyone on the landings and stairwells of her apartment building, and most of her work colleagues fled for the suburbs at 5:30 every evening and spent their precious weekends taking the kids to ballet or basketball practice. There were other means of course, but the prospect of joining some club or society to be forced into other people's company definitely didn't appeal. Somehow it was difficult to mix here, unlike back home in Dallas. Finding even a sightseeing partner, let alone any other type, had proved virtually impossible and it wasn't long before she began to despair.

Also the emotional scar of her first Christmas here in New York still burned deeply. That New Year's Eve was a night she wouldn't easily forget. Never before or since had she truly felt in mortal danger, and the fact that the perpetrator was never brought to justice still caused her moments of real anger and fear.

She picked up the phone on the worktop by the microwave and dialled. The answer came on the second ring.

"Hey, honey bunch, where are you taking me tonight?" Her voice was playful but masked an underlying nervousness. "It's Saturday night in New York City, are we going to party or what?"

The voice at the other end of the line tried to match her level of enthusiasm, but fell some way short.

"Hey Chris, how's it going?"

"It's going great," she replied. "Now do I need my ball gown or are we slumming in the East Village again?"

There was a brief silence. "I ... I don't know yet, babe. I've been kinda busy today. All sorts of stuff's been happening. Maybe we could..."

"Stuff, what stuff?" She retorted. "Hey it's me you're talking to remember? I'm beautiful and I'll kick you in the balls if you're standing me up."

She laughed but the voice at the other end of the line didn't sound in the mood for humour.

"Hey, I'm kidding, I'm kidding. We could stay in if you like. You could come over here; we could get Chinese food and watch old movies. My sofa's real cozy."

There was silence again. Suddenly Christine was concerned that she had overstepped the mark.

"Hey Don, I'm joking with you, right? You know if you're too busy then we can just talk on the phone a little bit and then we can both get an early night. Maybe that'd be better if you've been busy?

How does that sound? I can tell you about my sexy dream last night, it was…"

The voice resumed. "What I was going to say was … maybe we could have a quiet dinner at Casamiro's first? I'll book my usual table, then we can decide which block of the town we're going to paint red, ok?"

Christine bit her lip and smiled. "Great, sounds good to me."

"I'll pick you up at eight on the dot," he replied.

"Ok, you're the boss. I'll put a nice dress on for you. I know you like me in dresses."

"You bet I do. I'll see you in little while."

They hung up and Christine returned to her bedroom mirror with a definite sick feeling developing in the pit of her stomach. She had nearly an hour to think this one through. Ending the whole thing tonight would be too abrupt, but she needed to put out some definite vibes of dissatisfaction. She applied some foundation and a little blusher to her cheekbones with a well practiced hand. Tonight would be an understated look she thought … no mascara, and just a little eyeliner. She applied it quickly and finished off with a touch of lipstick, choosing a shade only slightly different from her natural lip colour.

She quickly found a brown knee length skirt with matching top, and pulled off her tee shirt and sweat pants to try them on. Then she turned and checked back and front in the full length mirror, scrutinizing her reflection. Pretty damn good by anyone's standards, and some pale brown high boots would finish things off perfectly.

Then suddenly it was 7:45. She knew that Don was always on time for any meeting; he even set out early for the shortest of journeys just in case he hit traffic, and would sit around the corner with the engine running in order to arrive at the precise time specified. She picked up her phone and switched it off. Now all she needed was a plausible reason to dump him. Not that it had to be plausible of course, it would just make her feel better if it was.

At 7:55 Christine was sitting on the floor in the hallway staring at the front door. From her windows she couldn't easily see the entrance to this building eight floors beneath, so she usually waited here, counting the seconds on her watch and trying to predict when the buzzer would sound to shatter the calm. She could hear the faint sound of a TV upstairs and occasional footfalls, but otherwise this was a very quiet apartment block, particularly at weekends when most of the inhabitants seemed to flee the city for destinations unknown. She contemplated her immediate situation while Don's car was stuck in traffic a couple of streets away. She closed her eyes to think. How was she going to do this? What excuse could she contrive?

With Paul this whole thing had been easy; like taking candy from a baby. She really had wiped the floor with him and hung him out to dry. But Don had turned out to be a completely different proposition. On the face of it he was the perfect gent; very polite, very gallant, and extremely charming. But there was also an edge to him, a hint of nastiness that had shown itself through the veneer a couple of times. Not to her directly so far, but occasionally his phone would ring when they were together and he would always excuse himself and leave the room. Then she often heard the muffled sound of him barking orders; like the person at the other end of the line was being threatened. And then he would come back into the room smiling and saying, 'Forget about it, it's only business'. Just like nothing had happened. It gave her the creeps. She would definitely have to tread much more carefully this time.

And for a few brief moments her thoughts turned to Geoff Dealer and their last meeting in Austin two years ago. This was all down to him; her current situation, every aspect, facet, and detail of it, even her move here from Dallas, was entirely down to him and his crazy idea. Although she alone had been responsible for making it happen. There was no way she would be seeing a guy like Don under normal circumstances; he just wasn't her type. Why, oh why had she listened to anything Geoff had said that day? Right now she wished she'd never even wasted her time going back to meet him.

When this situation with Don had been finished up satisfactorily she would have to give some serious thought to cutting her losses and getting out of here. Maybe she wouldn't move back home to

Dallas, but now she'd worked for a big circulation newspaper she could probably relocate to any major city. It would have to be somewhere south this time though; somewhere with plenty of sun and a proper party scene; maybe Miami or New Orleans? After two freezing winters it was becoming more and more apparent that she just wasn't designed for cold weather.

Suddenly the buzzer sounded sharply, causing Christine to almost jump out of her skin. She got up, straightened her skirt, and pressed the button causing a loud crackle of static that almost masked Don's disembodied voice.

"Hey Chris, it's me."

She looked up at the wall clock and saw it was nearly five minutes past. "Hey you're late, that's not like you. I'll come right down."

"No, I'm coming up, I got something for you."

He hung up and walked briskly into the lobby, brandishing a huge bouquet of flowers. Within a matter of moments he was at her door and knocked loudly.

He stood in the doorway as she opened it. "Hey baby I got these for you."

She gasped.

"You still wanna kick me in the balls, huh? You still wanna kick Donny in the balls?" He had a huge beaming smile on his face as he stood with his legs slightly apart pointing at his groin.

Christine pouted. "I'm sorry, I can't believe I said that. I would never do anything to hurt you! You know that don't you?"

"Here they are," he continued, "kick 'em if you want to." He was still smiling, but there was an edge to his voice.

"Those flowers are gorgeous." She looked sheepishly down to the ground. "Are they for me?"

"Neah, they're for my wife, I was wondering if you could put them in water 'til later when I can take them home."

He laughed again. "Hey Chris, you look gorgeous tonight. And you know what? I deserve a good kick in the balls for not paying you all the attention you deserve."

They hugged and she took the flowers from him. "I'll just put some water in the kitchen sink for now then I can put them in a vase later."

"Great idea, then let's get out of here," he said. "Our table at Casamiro's is booked for 8:15."

They arrived fifteen minutes late but a reserved parking space and a warm welcome awaited them at the intimate family run restaurant on a back street in the Little Italy district of Manhattan. He collected the car keys from his driver and told him to take the rest of the evening off, stuffing a twenty dollar bill into his hand for a cab.

Don hugged the proprietor as they made their entrance. "Carlo, I'm sorry we're late; the traffic midtown was a bitch. You know me … am I ever this late? Me! Am I ever late?"

Carlo beamed at them. "Hey, forget about it, your table's ready, the wine's at room temperature, you have a pleasant evening now."

They sat.

"You having your usual?" he asked.

Christine's stomach was turning cartwheels. The thought of eating anything right now made her feel like heaving.

She sighed. "Yep, the usual is fine."

He looked concerned. "You ok?"

"Yeah, I'm fine. Perhaps it's the pollen from the flowers. They're gorgeous but…"

"You never said you were allergic to flowers."

"It's ok, it's only sometimes. It must just be certain types. C'mon let's eat, I'm starving."

He called out to a waiter who was nearby attending to a party of diners. "Our usual, when you've got a minute."

The waiter nodded and carried on taking the other order.

"I love it here they do the best pasta." He announced. "You go anywhere in this town and you won't get pasta like they do here."

Christine smiled. This was one of their regular dining haunts and the food was excellent, but one night she would like to dine in style. This was like sitting in someone's front room.

The meal arrived quickly and they started to eat. Christine picked at her food but Don dived in, shovelling huge forkfuls of pasta into his mouth.

"Man this is good stuff."

He called out to Carlo, who was doing the rounds of the tables.

"Hey, give your head chef a kiss on the forehead from me. This linguine is excellent. Excellent."

Carlo beamed a 'thank you' in return but all Christine could think about was the message on her phone. Things need to be finished up by the middle of next week. What could she say? On the face of it her and Don were getting on great ... she couldn't just dump him out of the blue! Five more mouthfuls she'd give it. Five more mouthfuls, and if Don hadn't started a new topic of conversation she would say something.

"Man this food is good tonight. How's your Carbonara? It looks great." Don asked through a mouthful of side salad.

She smiled. "It's good, really good, my compliments to Luigi and his team out there."

He nodded and carried on eating.

Four mouthfuls, five mouthfuls; the last one took an age to pass down into her gullet. Oh well, here goes.

"Don I've been thinking."

He carried on eating without looking up. "What? What've you been thinking?"

"This thing between us ... I mean it's great but..."

"It's great but what?"

"It's great but, but I'm not sure if you're really into the whole thing. I mean, like properly, you know..."

He paused in mid chew. "What do you mean by that?"

His eyes suddenly took on a glint of menace and Christine's heart started to pound.

She stumbled over her words. "Well I ... I wonder what goes on most of the week when I never see you. I wonder where you are when your phone is switched off and there's no one at your office. It worries me ... I wonder if there's something else going on."

Don leaned forward and lowered his voice. "Look, things between us are going just fine. Ok? My business is my business. During the week I have to run my company, do my work, run around like a fucking lunatic keeping everyone happy. I don't need anyone interfering with that. Ok? *Is that ok?*"

Christine looked down submissively as he sat back and carried on eating. Just what was this business he ran? All she knew was that it was based over in New Jersey and that he had some sort of office not far from here. She only ever saw him at weekends and then he was always 'too tired' to talk about it when she occasionally asked. She was suspicious, and occasionally her mind headed off in some unpleasant directions. What if he was doing something criminal? It was an appalling stereotype, but he had a hint of an Italian look about him, even though he said his family name was Murphy. And as much as she tried to ignore it, she couldn't help feeling like she was stepping into a scene from a *Godfather* movie whenever they dined here.

"Man this food is good," he said, returning to his meal.

But Christine decided to bite the bullet. "Have you got someone else? Have you got a wife and kids in New Jersey or something? I mean..."

Don put his knife and fork down and got up slowly.

"*Out the back, now!*" he hissed.

"Out the back ... what do you mean?"

He grabbed her arm tightly and gently lifted her out of her seat. "*Now!*"

Her knife and fork dropped onto to the table with a clatter and the other patrons looked round alarmed.

"Don't worry about it," Don announced to the room, "some food went down the wrong way. Everything's ok."

He patted her noisily on the back and she quickly grabbed her bag while it was still within reach.

Everyone returned cautiously to their meals. For some reason surprises were not well tolerated in this quiet little dining establishment.

Christine struggled slightly as she was whisked along. "Hey, you're hurting me! Where are we going?"

They pushed through the double swing doors into the hot and noisy kitchen, where everyone was too busy stirring vats of pasta sauce to take any notice.

One of the waiters looked up. "Hey Don, how's it..."

But Don stopped him. "We're going out the back, ok? Some food went down the wrong way, everything's fine."

"Get a drink of water." Someone shouted but Don ignored it.

Christine's eyes widened in panic as they hurried past pans of steaming food and dangerously unguarded grills with sizzling hunks of meat on them that heated the surrounding air. Part of her was wondering how anyone could produce meals in a sauna like this? But another part was thinking that whatever happened now she had her excuse. No one had ever treated her like this in a public place. Their relationship was over.

Then they pushed through a nearby door and suddenly were out on the fire escape. Christine felt the chill of the evening air on her face, and she forcibly removed his hands from her arms.

"Now look!" he hissed angrily, moving in close, "You wanna ask me about my life, that's fine. You think I got something going on that I'm not telling you about, that's fine too. But you *don't* ask me when we're out together, ok? Those are my friends in there, and not all of them are good ones. There's business associates in there, rivals, people who are envious of the company I've built up. People who'd love to see me take a fall. You don't ever discuss our personal life when there're other people around. You got that?"

Christine rubbed at her forearm, trying to numb the pain from the vice like grip he had exerted. Her mind was swimming.

He forced a smile. "Now I'm sorry if I hurt you, but I needed to make it look like you were choking on your food. Now let's go back and enjoy…"

But Christine retaliated. "*Hey fuck off* I'm not having anyone manhandle me in public! You embarrassed me in there in front of those people and I don't care who they fucking well are!"

"Hey c'mon…"

"And how come you can just barge your way through the kitchen like that? Do you own this place or something?"

For once Don appeared flustered. "I know Carlo; we go back a long way. Hey, be careful."

He stepped forward as Christine edged towards the top of the nearby metal staircase, gently feeling the contours of her soft leather handbag, trying to locate her personal alarm.

"You leave me alone. I'm going home and I think after this we're finished. All you need to do is call me a cab."

"No Chris, we don't have to finish it. I didn't mean to upset you, it's just that..."

He reached out for her arm but she stepped back again and her heel went over the edge of the metal walkway. She screamed as she toppled backward and tried in vain to grab the handrail.

"Jesus Christ, no!" Don yelled as he reached out to try and save her but he was too late and she fell down the flight of metal steps with a noisy clatter, plunging into a pile of garbage bags that had been left on the floor of the concrete yard beneath.

"*Oh, fucking Jesus Christ, no!*" He jumped down the stairs three at a time to get to her, lying dishevelled like a rag doll in a pile of discarded food bags, one of which had burst open. Her left cheekbone was cut and a trickle of blood was visible from behind her ear.

"Oh, fuck me, no!" he gasped again in a strangled whisper.

He reached down to her, then stopped abruptly. She was totally still. He delicately pulled her skirt back into place to protect her modesty and then stepped around the corner, retrieving his phone from his jacket pocket. He called 911.

"Yeah, emergency ... I need an ambulance ... round the back of Casamiro's ... yeah the East Village. It's a woman ... looks like she's fallen down some stairs or something. She's unconscious. No, I just walked round the corner to take a piss and I saw her. No, I don't want to get involved, I don't know her. No, I don't want to give my name, just get here quick. I think she's hurt bad."

He rang off.

As he walked around the corner to his car a voice shouted out from across the street.

"Hey Don, hey, how's it going this evening?"

Don Borello's heart sank because he had seen this guy before. He was a local reporter. This was bad.

"Hey, any news you can give me? Anything going down tonight? You got the latest Yankees score?"

Don ignored the questions but his heart was pounding and his mouth was dry. It would have taken some amount of good will to clear what just happened with Carlo, but now he was potentially in big trouble. Still, he walked calmly to the car and got in.

"Ok, you have a good evening now." The reporter shouted, quickly noting something down on the back of the newspaper he was carrying.

As Don started the engine his phone rang and when he checked the display he saw his wife's number. He ignored this too and drove off, heading east for Brooklyn, where he could get some advice on how to proceed.

Around five minutes later the reporter heard the sound of sirens and was close enough to follow them to their destination on foot. He stopped on the opposite corner when he saw the red and blue lights flashing outside Casamiro's, and then as he waited another siren started whooping a few blocks away. Within a minute a police squad car had arrived and two officers climbed nonchalantly out and wandered into the darkness of the alleyway. The reporter hopped anxiously from one foot to the other because he was absolutely bursting to take a leak. But he was excited too. Maybe, just maybe, this was a mob hit and he had seen Don Borello walking away from the crime scene. This could be the big one! Within another minute a stretcher was dispatched from the back of the ambulance and returned quickly with a body on board and a saline drip being held aloft by a paramedic.

"Taxi!" he yelled, stepping out into the street and virtually forcing one to stop. He needed to find out who the victim was to have any chance of making a story out of this.

"Can you follow that ambulance, home boy?" he asked through the reinforced grill, "That's my buddy in there."

"Sure thing," was the muffled reply.

As the ambulance drove away, Brodie Murnaghan flipped through the numbers on his phone and called Rick, a detective for whom he was an occasional informant. He had a positive ID on Donal Severo Borello; there was no mistaking it.

The phone only rang a few times before the answering service cut in. "Rick, hey it's Brodie … it's around 8:45pm and I've just seen some of you guys stretchering someone from round the back of Casamiro's in the East Village. I didn't see anything, except a few minutes before, Donny boy Borello came out from the same alleyway. I shouted to him but he ignored me. I know it was him so

I think you guys need to check this one out. Ok, later."

The cab bounced across the uneven streets of Lower Manhattan and it was soon apparent that the ambulance was heading for the Brindley hospital on the lower East side.

"Hey buddy," the reporter shouted through to the driver, "you can drop me off at the next intersection."

"But what about your friend?" The driver seemed disappointed that the chase was being called off.

"You know what?" the reporter replied, "I never liked him that much."

The cab drew to a halt and the reporter climbed out. Quickly he reached for his phone again and scrolled through his list of contacts. He dialled.

"Hey Rodriguez; Brodie … hey listen … there's an admission coming your way in a couple of minutes … well get *off* your tea break for God's sake! I need to know who it is … yeah, yeah … usual game rules and procedures apply … yeah, I know I owe you from before, just make triple sure you get this one, ok … I'll tell you why when you get me the name, ok … ok, ok … just get to it man, you've only got a couple of minutes! Ciao."

Brodie ended the call and disappeared quickly around a darkened corner to empty his bladder.

2

Sunday

Geoff Dealer sat on the apron of his driveway waiting for the large electric gates to swing gently closed behind his pickup truck. He knew they would close successfully … they always did … but he had to wait until he heard that reassuring mechanical clunk of the dead bolt before he could move on.

He felt deeply troubled. It had been three days now since he had received the message to end his relationship with Hannah, but he really didn't want to go through with it.

Unfortunately, though, he had given himself little choice in the matter.

The pieces were slowly falling into place; he already had enough of her money, he had a sure fire way of getting her fired from her job ready and waiting; all he needed now was to think up an excuse; a way to break her heart. Then his client would be pleased, and he could think about relocating to a new address as quickly as possible. Dumping her was going to be difficult though, mainly because he'd had some of the best and most frequent sex of his entire life; but also they had become surprisingly close over the last month or so, which wasn't the way this was supposed to work. He had already fallen for her, and he could tell she had strong feelings for him too. But he couldn't lose his nerve now. Nothing must get screwed up, not for the next few days anyway. He had to bring her down. He had to finish this off.

The gate clunked closed and he pulled away.

Then yesterday afternoon when he'd visited his PO Box he'd found a letter that, according to the postmark, had been delivered over two weeks ago. The mere sight of it shook him, because he immediately recognized his mom's handwriting. But the content made him feel sick in the pit of his stomach:

Son, I sure do hope you get this. I know we haven't spoken in a long while but I need to talk to you. To see you if possible. The doctors have told me I have cancer. It's a malignant melanoma (skin cancer), but they don't think it's going to kill me. I've obviously spent too long baking in the Texan sun! They've got to operate to see how bad it is, so hopefully when they do that they'll find out it's not gone too deep. I'm going into hospital in Georgetown in a week from now. I know it's very short notice, but I've only just found out myself. I'd love to see you before they operate son because this is scaring the hell out of me. There's things I need to say to you face to face. I'm not going to write them down in case you don't get this letter.

Anyway that's all for now. Please let's forget the past. Try to get here if you're not too busy. Lots of love Mom.

Geoff stood still for several minutes as people pushed by him to get to their mailboxes, surprised, staggered, horrified! He read the letter over and over, studying the spidery handwriting closely. She would have been into hospital by now and would have gone in thinking, for sure, that he didn't want to see her again. His mind immediately raced in all possible directions. What if she never came round after the operation? What if she was given the wrong dose of anaesthetic and left in a coma? What if they operated and found the cancer had spread and she was now in intensive care plugged full of tubes and hooked up to a life support machine?

Since reading the letter an extra layer of gloom had descended, leaving him wandering around in a daze. The Danny Stanley shooting came back to him as clearly as if it had just happened, as did the way he felt on hearing the news of his father's horrible death in jail a few days later. He didn't know what to think; his perception was that his mother had totally deserted him after that horrible day all those years ago … and he could have understood it if he'd been an adult at the time, but he was just a kid. His own mother abandoned her only child, so why should he be there for her now? Where was it written that an illness, however serious, mysteriously wipes the slate clean? He settled on this option for a while, but the thought that she could quite possibly be dying kept stabbing at him. He must go and see her, he decided eventually, but not for a few days yet. Some serious mental preparation and soul searching would be required first. He would call though, and perhaps pretend to be a long lost cousin. Yes, he would definitely call … probably tomorrow.

It was now 6pm on a beautiful summer evening in Los Angeles. The sun was sinking but still hot in the sky, and the familiar faint brown smog could be seen from up above by various police and traffic helicopters as they flitted between isolated scenes of unpleasantness in the vast urban sprawl beneath. At the lower end of Benedict Canyon Drive, though, it appeared neither smoggy nor unpleasant as Geoff's brand new Toyota flat bed pickup threaded its way down towards Beverly Hills. Every day his route took him past a jaw-dropping display of real estate; past garish pink stuccoed houses, huge mock Spanish villas, and equally mock English Tudor mansions. But he paid very little attention to this blatant display of wealth because, amazingly, this was now his neighbourhood.

As a place to live, Los Angeles left a lot to be desired compared to back home in Austin, Texas. It felt soulless, it sprawled endlessly; it had no centre, no heart, and bizarre extremes of wealth and poverty. It was a constant assault on the senses and, most of all, the city and everyone in it felt totally fake. It was a place he would never, *ever*, have chosen to live. The only real selling point was the ocean, which he visited daily. It was the one place where he could confront the mixed up emotions that constantly raced around his brain; the one place where he could find some tangible sense of perspective and calm.

Eventually Benedict Canyon Drive intercepted Sunset Boulevard and Geoff made a left turn, driving for a while until he reached one of the less salubrious districts of West Hollywood, where he turned off into a slightly down at heel side street and pulled up outside a semi dilapidated building that housed his recently acquired, low rent, second residence. He climbed out, walked over to his front door, unlocked it and went in.

Inside the apartment the decor was striking, minimalist, and stylish beyond anything the exterior suggested. It was painted throughout completely in pale cream, with darker cream skirting and door frames, beech hard wood flooring and white canvas blinds at the windows. All rooms were the same. He walked into the lounge area where there was a small battered canvas couch, a coffee table, and a large TV screen with a discreet but very potent hi-fi system nestling beneath.

Over the last few months Geoff had felt a real need to find a second place to live. His life on the edge of the Hollywood Hills was remote and isolated, and during the times he spent there he often went two or three days without speaking to, or even seeing, another person. He needed a pizza joint he could walk to, he needed bars nearby, preferably ones with topless girls, and he needed a grocery store that he could crawl to if he ran out of milk. So he scoured the internet property pages and found this place, which had become free at short notice after the incumbent tenant had broken his lease and skipped town.

But he also felt the need to make some serious decisions soon. Renting two places to live had seemed like a good idea at the time but in reality it was totally absurd, even though at the moment he could easily afford the payments on both. Did he want quiet, remote, and exclusive living? Or did he want inexpensive, downbeat and sleazy? Or was he just kidding himself by flitting back and forth between these two social extremes and being unable to feel at home in either?

What he really needed was someone of value in his life; then the choice of living quarters would be much less important. That was the root of the problem, although up until recently he had stubbornly refused to acknowledge it. Nearly two years he'd been living here, two years in a city awash with beautiful women, and still he hadn't found anyone. Apart from Hannah, of course, but she didn't count for obvious reasons. It was clear now that he had never properly settled anywhere, or to anything, since breaking up with Christine all those years ago. Their relationship had given him a few years of much needed stability. But now he was just drifting.

He sighed heavily. Hannah was such a fantastic girl and so far they'd had a really great time together. Maybe he should suggest they run off to Florida, or Mexico, or Europe; anywhere basically. Forget the arrangement. If she never found out, he was sure they could make a go of it. At the moment he didn't even care what he'd been told about her.

He walked through into the bedroom where he picked up a

small sports holdall from behind the door and then turned to leave.

"Hey fella, you look like the vet's just croaked your dog."

"Yo, Corporal Bill!" Geoff jumped as he stepped outside and almost walked into one of his elderly neighbours who was walking past with a brown paper bag of groceries.

"So what's on your mind?"

"Me? Nothing, I'm fine." Geoff replied. "Is there anything I can help you with this evening Sir?"

"Get outta here," Corporal Bill smiled, "do I look like I need help carrying a bag of washing powder?"

"Sir, sorry Sir!" Geoff barked in response. "You all have a good evening now."

"Yeah, yeah, you too." Corporal Bill muttered as he turned the key in his lock.

Geoff put the holdall on the passenger seat, got in and sat for a while, stretching his neck muscles by circling his head around, and pushing his shoulders back into the seat. As he reached to turn the ignition key his cell phone rang, and Geoff saw it was his client Ken calling.

"Hi Mr Kenneth Kamplann, how can I help you this evening?"

"I just want a progress report, that's all," Ken said in an agitated voice, "after all it has been three…"

"I know it's been three days," Geoff cut in, "I just need to pick my moment; the timing hasn't been quite right."

"Well you'd better damn well make it right soon!" Ken exploded. "I need this to be over with quickly."

"Yes, Sir I understand, and I'm on the case."

"Look, I don't need to remind you what she did, do I?"

Geoff sighed heavily. "No, Ken, you don't need to remind me because you tell me every time we speak. She used your business partner to embezzle money out of your company, she screwed your business partner, and then she dumped you. Right?"

"Damn right, now you said you'd gotten ten grand out of her, is that for certain?"

"Yes Sir, ten grand is invested away so securely she'd need surgical implements to get at it. And soon it will be yours again, minus a small administration charge of course."

"Well that's good." Ken sounded relieved even though Geoff had told him this news three weeks ago.

"How did you *do it* man?" Ken asked, amazed. "I mean *ten grand*, Jesus Christ, isn't she gonna be all over you when this goes down?"

"She'll have to find me first," Geoff replied. He couldn't be bothered to explain that both Ken and Hannah would be getting their money back.

"And what about the job thing?" Ken asked urgently.

"That, my friend, is the best bit," Geoff replied, "the money stuff is boring. We went into her law offices after hours a few weeks ago. She was drunk so I got her to strip off, and I filmed her strutting around stark naked in her boss's office, bad mouthing the firm and saying all sorts of wonderful stuff."

Ken laughed hysterically at the other end of the line. "Brilliant, *fucking brilliant!*"

"And very soon it will be appearing on a popular video hosting website, along with an email to her company informing them of the necessary viewing details."

"Ah shit," Ken gasped, still laughing, "that's the best thing I've heard in weeks. You'd better send me a copy me of that email so I can take a look too!"

"Sure thing, all I need to..."

But suddenly Ken was serious. "Now you just let me know when you've broken that girl's heart and she's crying in a bar somewhere; then I'll sleep a bit easier."

"Will do Sir, it'll be in the next day or so for sure."

"I'm looking forward to it, and you let your boss know next time you speak to him what a fantastic idea this is, ok? You should roll it out nationwide."

"I'll be sure and let him know." Geoff laughed to himself. "Ok Ken, speak to you soon. Bye."

Geoff fired up the engine of his truck and headed due west until he reached a small municipal parking area close to the Santa Monica shore. Then he wriggled and squirmed into the jogging gear from the holdall, got out, and sprinted down to the water's edge.

The sun was now setting out over the ocean. Geoff had lived in several locations in the United States, but none where he could watch the sunset in such spectacular glory; dipping gradually, gracefully, before meeting and merging with its own reflection and sinking slowly out of sight. He drank in the view as the channel of yellow light fell across the placid water all the way to the beach, feeling the life affirming warmth of the last few rays.

He breathed deeply and tried to clear his head. There were important things he needed to focus on.

3

On the opposite side of the continent, a plain clothes detective stood near Christine Hudson's hospital room in lower Manhattan. While he waited he read the accommodation section of the notice board for something to do. He laughed at one of them;

Luxury penthouse … available soon … quick before ex wife gets her filthy hands on it … It's a joke!! 3rd floor apt, upper west side. 90th St. Good neighborhood. Nice doorman. Car owners not welcome. Call for rate.

There were plenty of pets for sale too, although, for God's sake, who would want to keep an animal in an apartment? Animals need places to crap that are not under your kitchen table! Outside a violent electrical storm had just finished drenching the city, briefly deluging the drainage system with many thousands of gallons of litter-strewn water and illuminating the night sky with an almost continual flicker of lightning. Rick Povich was caught in the dying burst of this downpour and was pretty much soaked to the skin just from running 20 yards along the pavement. He quickly drew his hands through his hair, attempting to manually comb it into place, and was conscious that his leather coat was still spilling raindrops onto the spotless tiled floor. Just as he took a side step to start consulting the upcoming list of medical seminars a nurse approached him.

"You can see her, but only very briefly. She's still very groggy from her sedatives so don't push her, ok."

"Ok ma'am, I'll go easy with her; it shouldn't take long anyway."

"I hope it won't," she replied, "you know this is way after regular visiting?"

The nurse pushed the door open and showed him inside to where Christine was lying in bed; her face was bandaged up and there was a drip in her arm. She looked up but didn't give much in the way of a welcome.

"Ok sweetie, this is the detective who needs to talk to you, his name is Rick."

Rick approached the bed. "Hi Christine, how are you doing today?"

Christine's voice was feeble. "You're joking right? How am I? How do I look?"

The nurse spoke as she retreated towards the door. "You look fine honey, now you help the officer out while I go and do the rest of my rounds."

She left the room and the detective stood in awkward silence for a moment.

"I'm serious, how do I look? No one will tell me, and there doesn't seem to be a mirror in the hospital anywhere! Now how about that?"

Rick had seen much worse, and his voice oozed calm. "You look fine ma'am. You've taken a bit of a beating, but you'll be ok. Now can you..."

"Yeah, fine maybe for keeping the kids away from the fire. I'm serious. If my face is messed up I'm going to kill myself. No question about it."

"First off, do you know who did this to you?"

Christine was immediately aghast. "You mean he isn't already in custody for this?"

"Err, no ma'am not yet."

"You mean, like everyone who was out back in the restaurant didn't leap on the guy?"

"No they didn't. Do you have a name for us please?"

"Sure I have his name, it was Don. I also have the worst headache in medical history."

"It's ok Christine, everything is going to be alright; you're safe now."

"Safe, yeah right; this is safe, huh?" Her manner was abrupt. "A tramp could walk in off the street and steal my bag."

There was a brief standoff. Rick dealt with awkward members of the public on an almost hourly basis, but assuming that the perpetrator of this crime was confirmed then a great deal of care would be called for. Other departments would also need to be informed.

"Don who?"

Her tone was sarcastic. "Don Murphy if I remember correctly. You know it's amazing what a bang on the head does for your memory."

"Irish was he?"

"Don't know, he didn't look it or sound it."

"And you know him personally, rather than just knowing his name I take it?"

She nodded.

"So why did he do this to you?"

"I made a bad choice from the wine list! *Jesus* what kind of question is that?"

Christine raised her hands up in a gesture of despair, wincing in considerable pain from the injuries to her back and shoulders.

"We were having an argument in a restaurant, I can't even remember what about, and then he bundled me out of my seat and through the kitchen, out onto a fire escape. I remember wondering why we had gone through the kitchen in front of all the staff, where we shouldn't even have been, and no one seemed to notice or care. Then we argued some more and he started to get threatening. And then I don't know what happened. I think he pushed me backwards ... and that's kind of it really. The nurse told me I was found in a pile of garbage at the bottom of a fire escape. She said if the bags hadn't broken my fall I'd be either dead or paralyzed."

"Well in that sense you were lucky. The thing is though, we have a witness, not to the assault itself, but someone saw an individual named Don Borello leaving the alleyway just before the ambulance arrived. Do you think you could have gotten the name wrong?"

"Not that wrong!" She replied, but as she spoke something twigged in her memory.

"And how come this witness just happened to know who the guy was?"

She paused, this time her colour draining visibly. "Borello, oh my God, don't I know that name? He's Mafia, isn't he? I've seen his name in the papers. *Oh shit!*"

Suddenly all her suspicions about him crashed noisily into place. Jesus Christ, she'd been dating a mobster! He was almost certainly a criminal; he could even be a murderer! Every single Mafia cliché crammed into her head at once, along with a million other questions about Anna, the woman who was paying her to do this.

"Ma'am, is everything ok?" Rick asked gently. "You look like you're about to flatline on me."

"No, it's ok, I'm fine," she lied, "I just went a bit dizzy, that's all."

Rick was cautious. "Obviously we don't know for sure it's him."

"Well how do you work that one out?" Christine sensed his discomfort while simultaneously scanning her memory for a newspaper mugshot of her alleged assailant.

"The evidence is circumstantial, of course. Don Borello could've just gone round the back to take a pee. We can't prove he assaulted you."

"Well what about the eye witnesses then? There were people in the restaurant, people in the kitchens, what about them? What about the proprietor guy, Carlo?"

"Everyone we spoke to said it was a busy night and they didn't see anything abnormal. Said they saw two folks arguing but didn't really..."

"*Bullshit!*" She cut him off in an instant. "They saw two folks arguing, two folks leaving through the kitchen and one of them not coming back! Well what about the waiters?"

"They were busy too ma'am; basically we haven't got a positive visual ID on this guy at the moment. As far as we know, Don Borello wasn't at Casamiro's last night."

Christine's temper flared. "Well that's just bullshit. *Bullshit!* Arrest all the staff! Threaten to shut the place down; they're covering up for him, for God's sake!"

Rick ignored the verbal onslaught. "We can't do that ma'am. Now is there anything else you can tell us at the moment?"

She shook her head in dismay. "Well, what about his home, what about his business, have you actually *tried* to find him?"

"Yes ma'am we have. We went to his house in Queens and the

neighbours said the family had been away for a couple of days. And there was no one at his business address in Alveston, New Jersey; it is the weekend after all."

He looked at Christine with a sympathetic sigh, knowing full well that if Don Borello was behind this he wouldn't exactly make things easy for the authorities to find him. This didn't seem like mob business though, more like some sort of domestic.

Rick suddenly stood; there were many questions that needed answering, but now wasn't the time.

"Ok then Christine, I've gotta fly. Now if you do come up with anything else, anything at all, even really trivial stuff, can you please let us know? I'll leave the number of the station at the front desk."

She sighed. "Sure thing officer, anything to help New York's finest."

Rick was now by the door.

"Say, do I need any protection from this guy?" she asked.

"No, I shouldn't think so…" He was not entirely convincing. "In mob terms Don Borello is small fry. Anyway, we'll catch him sooner than you know it. Now you get some rest and I'll be in touch."

He left before Christine had a chance to respond.

"Unusual time for house calls ain't it Rick?"

The nursing supervisor accosted him as he crossed the corridor. She glanced at her watch and saw it was nearly 10:30pm.

"Hey Betty, how you doing?"

"I'm doing great Ricky boy … you were careful with our new guest I hope."

"Careful, I'm always careful. What time is it anyway?"

"Nearly ten thirty."

"Betty, in my job the hour of the day and the day of the week don't matter. I don't think she cared too much anyway."

"Does she need any special treatment … armed guards at the door perhaps?"

"Get outta here. She's just another patient."

"That's not what I heard."

"Well forget what you heard or else I'll get some of my friends in the traffic department to tow your car from outside your house."

"You get your butt out of my hospital!"

He paused. "So where did you hear whatever you heard?"

"One of the porters seemed to know. Now scram!"

Rick laughed. "I'm going, I'm going. Anyway all these nurses in uniform are bad for my blood pressure."

He disappeared through some nearby double doors and descended the stone steps three at a time. As he stepped out into the warm night air his phone rang.

"Y'ello," he answered.

"Rick, hey it's Brodie … Brodie Murnaghan."

"Hey Brodie, what's happening?"

"Everything's just ducky my friend. So what did Donny bad boy Borello do then? I ain't heard no more news about it. Have you picked him up yet?"

Rick perched the phone on his shoulder and lit a cigarette. "Now why should I tell you anything, huh?"

"Because I bring you stuff, for Christ's sake! I bring you leads. I need to be on your payroll damn it. "

"Ok you got me a lead. I'm grateful, ok?"

"Grateful! You'd have no clue who did this if it wasn't for my help."

"Look, Brodie, I'll buy you a beer next time I see you, and if we can pin anything on Don Borello we'll get you a commendation or something. Now how does that sound?"

"It sucks! So who was the victim?"

"Yeah, the minute you get a name there'll be a story. 'Mobster in brutal assault on innocent woman'. Dream on brother."

"Ah, c'mon Rick, you know I can find out other ways?"

"So find out another way. Catch you later."

"You know what?" he shouted into the phone, "I already know anyway. Just confirm it for me Ricky. C'mon be a pal, I've got a job to do as well."

"Sorry guy, no can do."

"It's Christine Hudson, isn't it?" Brodie gasped in frustration as a truck passed noisily and almost drowned him out.

Rick hung up the phone and descended the stairs into a nearby subway.

4

Monday

It was nearly 7:30am on a beautiful summer morning in the leafy green suburb of Maplewood, New Jersey, and Tara Sassia was in her bedroom, still in her underwear. She was late, however she found the time to stand for a moment and admire herself in the full length mirror in the corner of the room. She stepped into a pair of heels similar to those in the shoe rack downstairs and looked again, noticing the pleasing muscle definition in her legs when forced to move around on tip toes. She bent forward slightly, adjusting both breasts individually inside her bra to attain maximum cleavage, and then turned and grabbed both cheeks of her behind and scrutinized closely for any hint of cellulite. The curtains were all pulled back at the windows and she imagined for a brief moment how great it would be if their neighbour had some high powered optics trained on her from the shrubs at the end of his garden while his fat wife was still snoring in bed. She theatrically adjusted her thong a bit higher over her hips with two insignificant twangs of the elastic and stepped out of the shoes onto the luxurious thick carpet, scrunching her toes into the heavy duty wool strands. Oh, what the hell? Why shouldn't she be undressed in her own room? If people wanted to stare through the windows it was them who were the perverts, not her.

Tara unplugged her mobile phone from its charger and switched it on. As the phone went through its mini start up sequence she searched and searched through a wall of closets for a suitable skirt, cursing her mother for packing too much stuff onto the same rail, but tempering this with the knowledge that she could never be bothered to put her own clothes away. Eventually she found one, along with a white blouse. Her phone bleeped at this point, signalling the arrival of a text message, so she hurriedly went over to take a look. There were actually two messages, one from Becky and one from Gerhard; both asking if everything was still ok for tonight. Tara stared at the ceiling as she contemplated her reply. She had already said yes last time the three of them met, but now she was nervous that things were moving a bit too fast. She took a deep breath, tapped in 'ok looking 4ward 2 it' and hit the send button to both of them. It would be difficult to back out now. She quickly dressed and took another look at herself, making slight adjustments to the length of her skirt, and then walked over to her underwear drawer and rummaged around for some hold-up stockings; her legs looked too pale against this skirt, she thought. Finally she picked up her bag and briefcase, admired herself from both front and back in the mirror, briefly adjusted her skirt up a smidgen, then ran down the stairs. She then collected a lightweight coat from the rack, shouted goodbye to her mom, who was still in the kitchen, and banged the door closed.

Outside it was already hot, even though the sun hadn't fully appeared above the trees bordering the park at the end of the street. She walked for ten minutes, heading towards the centre of this small township, where she would pick up a newspaper, coffee, and a plain bagel from her favourite diner in the main street across from the railway station. Amazingly for a Monday there wasn't a queue of customers when she arrived, and as she emerged she saw a train approaching and darted quickly through the traffic, reaching the platform just as a heavy set train guard yelled at the top of his voice.

"Hoboken, Hoboken, express service to Hoboken."

She managed to climb on board just before it slowly started to move off, and as she looked back she saw a knot of commuters racing across the parking area in their business suits, cursing and lashing out at the accelerating train. This was the last express service that would convey its human cargo on the first stage of their journey into midtown Manhattan for 9am, and as the train rounded the curve she saw phones being retrieved and apologetic calls being made. Tara smiled to herself; for those left behind this was already not a good morning. Once the train reached its terminus on the western side of the Hudson River, Tara would then have to take two subway rides to get to her office. All being well she should be seated at her desk by 9:15. She managed to grab a few sips of her coffee while standing shoulder to shoulder with expensively suited commuters, eventually putting the brown bag with her coffee and bagel down between her feet. She managed a quick scan through her paper, although the proximity of others forced the folded pages within a few inches of her nose, and by pure chance she saw a brief article at the foot of page four that momentarily took her breath away.

"Oh man, oh man, will you take a look at *that!*" She spoke out loud in surprise, but none of the nearby passengers took any notice. She gasped again and then read the article to herself.

"Alleged mob foot soldier Don Severo Borello, 42, of Temple Beach, Queens, is on the run today after being suspected of hurling a young woman down a flight of stairs, causing her severe injury. The woman, Christine Erikah Hudson, 33, is in a serious condition in the Brindley Hospital with spinal problems and facial lacerations. She was found on Saturday night at the base of a flight of metal stairs behind a restaurant in the East Village. No comment has been made by the hospital, but sources believe that the victim was with Borello on the night of the accident. It is understood that if Borello's current parole is violated then he could face a mandatory ten years in jail as a variety of racketeering charges have since been levelled at him. Could this be the incident that finally brings Borello to book?"

As the train snaked its way through the New Jersey suburbs Tara crouched down, retrieved her coffee cup and took several swigs through the aperture in the lid, while pondering what she had just read.

"Well how about that?" she whispered, as her memory was flooded with recollections of her short lived liaison with Paul Herrycke nearly two years ago, and her subsequent dealings with Christine.

She used to see Paul on the train almost every day back in the autumn of 2006; on this very train on many occasions. But to begin with they never spoke. Eventually there was a visual acknowledgement, sometimes even a semi gallant gesture – he gave up his seat for her on one occasion – but still never a word. Until one day in December they happened to see each other on a sparsely populated early train out of Manhattan into the New Jersey suburbs, and in that situation Tara and Paul couldn't avoid speaking to each other when they found themselves in the same nearly empty carriage. So they did speak, and they hit it off immediately. He had been to a concert the previous night and decided to stay over, and she had been to a friend's birthday party at a rowdy restaurant in Greenwich Village. Both had decided to take the day off. Paul seemed like such a gentleman, apologizing over and over for his shyness in not speaking to her sooner. They talked and talked for the whole of the twenty minute journey, and as she disembarked they exchanged numbers and called each other the following evening. That weekend they spent Saturday in New York City on a museum and art gallery jaunt, and in the evening had, from Tara's perspective, a memorably romantic and funny session ice skating in Central Park as the snow fell. Then a few days later he took her to a lovely restaurant near to where they both lived, stopping on the way home at his parents house for coffee. Over the next week or two they travelled in on the train together a couple of times, although it was often difficult to talk during the hubbub of the morning rush hour, and they went out on two more dates together. Although she hid it from Paul so as not to scare him off, Tara began to fall in love very quickly. But it was a big mistake. After only another week he told her he was going to a software convention in Las Vegas and said he'd send her a postcard.

But he never did, and more importantly he seemingly never returned from his trip, and Tara was appalled. From her standpoint he had vanished from the face of the earth. And, assuming that he hadn't actually died somewhere along the way, that made him a bastard, just like so many of her previous boyfriends.

In the days following Paul's mysterious disappearance she vowed to herself to be much more wary of men because there was an aching predictability about their behaviour that made her nostrils flare in anger. They were all the same underneath, she decided, no matter how much they tried to disguise it with varying degrees of personality, intellect, and a sense of humour. And in future she swore to approach all potential relationships with massive amounts of cynicism and mistrust.

And then, while she was travelling home on the train in March of the following year, she saw a very small ad in the personal columns. It read as follows:

"*Set the record straight. Contact me if you've been in a bad relationship. I might be able to help you.*"

It then gave a phone and PO Box number.

Tara couldn't imagine what this could possibly be about, but she had already decided that Paul was in trouble if she ever saw him again. So she snipped the ad and placed it in her purse for safekeeping, knowing, of course, that nothing could be done unless he made another appearance in her life. And then, amazingly, one month later, she saw him at the Hoboken railway terminus, waiting for the early evening commuter express out into the suburbs. She boarded the train at the other end of the carriage and kept her head down, but he got off at the first stop in Newark, and she watched him through the grimy carriage window as he descended the stairs out of view. For the next few days she watched as he took the same train and soon decided to go to the building where he had previously told her he worked. For three nights she waited unsuccessfully, but on the fourth she spotted him emerging with a couple of others and heading for a nearby bar. A few more nights of doing this confirmed the bar as a fairly regular haunt of his, and she didn't wait much longer before calling the number from the ad; just to find out if 'setting the record straight' would live up to its enigmatic promise. No one answered, but she did leave a message, and almost a week later Christine called her back. She could still remember the hesitant sounding voice at the other end of the line and the definite level of uncertainty as to what was actually on offer. But eventually, when Tara managed to tease out the necessary information, she decided that this service was most definitely for her. It was brilliant; paying an anonymous third party to pile emotional crap on someone else's plate for a preset time period, and she was hugely excited at the prospect of Paul being romantically traumatized and strung out in the wind to twist at her behest.

When they met a few days later, Christine stressed to Tara that Paul might not take the bait, but Tara wasn't worried. "You're beautiful," she said to Christine, "Paul might be married with children by now, but I can't imagine him turning down an offer from you. I'd go out with you any day of the week."

So it was all set.

Christine approached Paul at the same bar within a matter of days and he fell for her undoubted charms very quickly. So, from then on Tara sat back and let it all happen, apart from making interim payments on a monthly basis and requesting status reports every once in a while. On one occasion, nearly six months into the assignment, she was delighted to hear a slightly muffled secret recording of an argument where Christine tore Paul to shreds for not paying her enough attention. It was a joy to listen to; Christine was awesome and Paul was a complete pussy. And then, in the November when they had been together around eight months, Tara decided it was time to finish things off. So she sent the message and within a week heard back that the deed had been done. Her final meeting with Christine was just over a week after that, when she learned that Paul had actually left his job and fled to London in an attempt to recover from the head fuck (Christine's words) that she had put him through. Beyond that she hadn't given him, or her, another thought; until now.

Eventually the train crawled into the dead end platform at Hoboken and Tara jumped out among the throng of commuters before it had even come fully to a stop. She headed straight for the subway, holding on tight to her newspaper and bagel; the coffee, still half full, had been left on the floor of the train.

Her mind was racing; she felt energized, determined and, she soon realized, still very angry. There had been no significant relationships in her life since Paul; no special moments when she had looked deep into a man's eyes and felt that wonderful sense of promise and anticipation. As she sat on the subway she recalled them falling over in a tangle of limbs on the ice rink, and the way he gently helped her up and brushed a snowflake from her cheek, their faces only inches apart. There had definitely been something real between them, a connection; a spark of energy. Right up until he vanished without trace.

Ten minutes or so later as she rode the elevator up to her midtown office she decided, somewhat arbitrarily, that whatever the reason for Christine's unfortunate circumstances, this unexpected reminder meant that Paul had no longer heard the last about his despicable behaviour. This had to be followed up; she had to find him, which meant she would need to go and see Christine as soon as possible.

Tara nodded briefly to the receptionist, and walked into a large open plan office, acknowledging several people as she passed. It was now just after 9:20am and she was the last to occupy her desk.

5

In the hours after his arrest, Frank Dealer struggled with his conscience from the confines of his cell. All he had to go on was the blurted out confession that Lizzie had made before the police arrived. But Danny Stanley had been a friend since they were kids … there is no way he would have done this. And even if he were a rapist, why would he choose to attack the wife of one of his best friends? In Frank's mind at the time it just didn't add up. Of course Lizzie and Danny could have been having an affair. But if so, how did it end up with one of them pointing a shotgun at the other? And then, of course, there was JJ, who had supposedly witnessed the whole event. Frank knew that he would serve time if he admitted to the murder … even in Texas, even protecting his wife from a supposed aggravated assault. And that very thought crushed him. But equally he could never send Lizzie to face a trial, even if it was only for killing someone in self defence. He had to see her to get things straightened out.

But Frank Dealer's mental anguish was short lived. The day after his incarceration he was transferred to a nearby State Federal Penitentiary, and on the same afternoon a riot broke out in the wing where he was being kept. The guards managed to contain it for a while, but then a fire was started in one of the cells and an inmate burned to death. His screams for help went unheeded as the available staff struggled desperately to keep order, and as his cries faded away all hell broke loose. Thirty people were injured, ten of them seriously, and two died before the situation was brought under control with tear gas. The supervisor of the wing was shot in the head with his own gun, and Frank Dealer was stabbed in the thigh with a kitchen knife as he tried to prevent two young guys from killing each other. No one came to Frank's aid as he lay there bleeding heavily from a severed artery, and he died in tears as his warm blood flowed onto the concrete floor, not knowing what would become of his family.

The full details surrounding his death were kept from Lizzie and JJ, but the impact on them both was devastating. Their extended family immediately circled the wagons to keep away the press and a whole host of gawkers and onlookers who seemed to materialize out of the woodwork. But for reasons Geoff couldn't comprehend, then or now, he and his mom were kept apart, and as a result the bond that should have held them together, come what may, was irrevocably broken.

The day that Geoff last saw his mother was etched deeply in his memory. It was the afternoon of his dad's funeral, and it was the first time he had seen her since the shooting several days previously. He could remember her bowed head and totally blank expression in vivid detail and how it didn't change throughout the service, even when she raised her head to speak to someone. He never once took his eye off her face as she sat in the row in front, three seats to the right. He noticed every time she dabbed at her nose with a tissue, every time she opened and closed her eyes, and every time her shoulders rose and fell as she breathed.

He remembered thinking over and over again that none of this should be happening and that all of it was *totally* his fault! Why was everyone so calm? Why weren't they all shouting and screaming at him?

She was accompanied by a man and a woman whom Geoff had never seen before, and who seemed determined to shoo away anyone who tried to speak to her. After the service she didn't acknowledge anyone at all to begin with, but at the wake in the local church hall later she managed to contrive a quiet moment to speak to Geoff. He remembered being utterly petrified at what she might say. He even thought she might take him outside and beat him. But she stooped down and stared with expressionless eyes.

Her voice was shaky but strong and she said, very slowly, "Son, we've both been through a real bad time over the last few days…" She seemed to be looking straight through him, "a really, really bad time … and I'm not sure either of us is over it yet."

Then Geoff went to speak but she shushed him up.

"The thing is, I'm not sure how I feel about things at the minute. You, me, everyone, and everything; nothing seems to make much sense right now. So I'm telling you that I'm going away for a while to try and recover ... to try and get things to make sense again. And you're going to be just fine. You're going to live with Gran and Grandpa Dealer in Round Rock, just like you've been doing for the last few days, and everything's going to be ok. You'll see, you'll see."

And then she touched him on the shoulder.

"Everything's been arranged, JJ." She looked around, suddenly distracted. "I'm going away for a while but you'll be ok. Granny Dealer will look after you..."

Then Geoff opened his mouth to speak again, but she shook her head and put her finger to her lips.

"I'll see you soon, Son. It won't be for long, I promise. You're going to be ok. You're going to be fine."

And with that her two unknown minders appeared at her shoulder and she melted away into a nearby crowd of people and was gone. It was the last time Geoff saw her; and it was twenty years ago, almost to the month.

Before that afternoon was done, Lizzie got into her car and drove south to stay with her sister a hundred or so miles away on the outskirts of Houston, and it was during this period that her life gradually came apart at the seams. For days and weeks and months she aimlessly wandered the streets and parks near her sister's house, completely overwhelmed by a stifling, suffocating depression. She just couldn't see a way out ... apart from the obvious ... so eventually she turned to drink and soon became a full blown alcoholic. At her lowest point she slept with a drifter whom she met at her weekly counselling session and became pregnant with his child. She miscarried close to full term after a 'fall' during a violent argument, and then became seriously agoraphobic, until her sister grew weary of the situation and literally threw her out on the street.

Eventually she found her way back to the family home, almost six years to the day after she had left. The doors and downstairs windows were locked and boarded up, but otherwise it appeared exactly the same as she remembered when she looked over her shoulder from the back seat of the police car on that awful day.

It was time to move on she decided, and immediately cashed in one of her long term investment policies, called in some local builders, and had the house redecorated from top to bottom, while she stayed on site in a small caravan. She moved in three weeks later, and for the first time Lizzie Dealer felt that she could begin to close the book on that portion of her life. Years had been lost; totally wasted, but enough was enough. She was still emotionally fragile, but it was time for a new start … and she hoped to be able to find Geoff, who by this time would be nearly eighteen. But when she attempted to make contact with the Dealer family she found that her mother and father in law had sold up and moved away, and no one seemed willing to say where they had gone.

During the time after the shooting, Geoff underwent a huge emotional upheaval that was only made worse by being moved away to a different district and having to start at a new school where he knew no one. It was a truly awful time for him, but his new guardians did the best they could to bolster his spirits by keeping him focused on his education, strongly encouraging him to make new friends, and by involving him in a whole host of community activities that his original parents never seemed to have the time for. They also began a very gentle but calculated brainwashing exercise, to try and remove any lingering thoughts of guilt or culpability for the way things had turned out by never, *ever*, referring to Frank or Lizzie again, or Danny Stanley – whom they were great friends with and who had built part of their house because Frank was too busy. They would only look forward they decided. Also they cleansed their house of the past by quietly packing away all of their family photographs and memorabilia. It was hard for them too, to effectively forget that they'd had a son and daughter in law, but they thought it was the only way to move things forward, and at all costs they wanted to protect Geoff from his mother's descent into what they saw as madness, and of course they regarded her infidelity as the prime reason for the untimely death of their son.

It was almost a year after the event when Geoff unexpectedly told his grandparents the truth about what had happened that day, and the news shook them to the core because it meant that their son was not the murderer that everyone in the county had come to believe. The accepted version of events was even backed up by Danny Stanley's widow, who subsequently found evidence to prove her husband's guilt. It was an old fashioned crime of passion; Frank had discovered his wife and Danny by accident and taken the law into his own hands, with little Geoff always being regarded as an innocent bystander. But the truth turned everything upside down, and also left them with a horrible dilemma. Their son had died in jail with a murder charge hanging over him, but a simple confession from Geoff could clear his name.

After many hours of agonizing they decided to let sleeping dogs lie, mainly because Frank was never convicted of murder so an admission of the truth from Geoff would not even lead to anything as formal as a pardon. What they did do though was shutter up their house and head south for Galveston to spend the rest of the year by the sea in their holiday home. It was one of the best times of his life that Geoff could remember. He swam everyday in the warm waters of the Gulf of Mexico, and there was now nothing around him that could rekindle any memories of the past ... so much so that somehow his mothers disappearance bothered him less and less. He had lost touch with her in the same way as he had with all of his school friends. And that was ok because they were just people. And as his grandfather frequently told him ... people come and people go. At the time he didn't think that he would never speak to her again, but he had new parents now, and although they were quite a lot older they were certainly there for him. And that's what mattered.

During that summer Frank Dealer Senior and his wife Helen kept in touch with Lizzie's circumstances via a series of intermediaries, and by the time the year was almost up they had decided to sell their property in Round Rock and move to the coast for good. This had been in their thoughts to do within the next five years anyway, but the shooting gave things a whole new sense of urgency. And so Geoff spent his teenage years on the outskirts of Galveston, gradually becoming a stronger and more independent person as time passed, and when he graduated from High School he wanted to study in Austin, nowhere else.

And it was several years later, after he had left Austin for Los Angeles, that Geoff decided to try and re-establish some form of contact with what was left of his family. He still didn't think he could face his mother directly. He still didn't want to 'deal' with the Danny Stanley incident. But he wanted to leave a number with someone. Just to show that he had made the first move. Maybe someone would try and contact him. Eventually he managed to track down an aunt in Georgetown, Texas through the directory listings. It was Lizzie's oldest sister, who was now in poor health. Geoff left her his new PO Box number in a brief call from a payphone on Santa Monica beach. That was as much as he could do at the time.

6

In Los Angeles it was nearly midday as Geoff pulled up in the designated spot outside his apartment and shouted a vague hello to Corporal Bill, who was carefully polishing the chrome on his car a few dozen yards away.

He was still battling conflicting emotions over the letter from his mother. On the one hand he couldn't imagine facing her after all this time, and yet he couldn't even think about ignoring her letter. He was torn. What if she needed care? What if she'd been given six months to live and there was no one to look after her? Would she really expect him to give up his life for an indeterminate period after all that had happened? He shuddered that he could even think like this. Surely a normal person would help their family, come what may?

As he stepped into the relative cool of his apartment he heard his mobile phone ringing.

"Hannah, hi, I've been…"

"JJ, honey, I rang you a whole bunch of times. Where are you?"

"I know, I heard, I was driving."

"Hey, you want to go to the mall this afternoon?"

Geoff winced in horror. "Err, I guess, shouldn't you be at work though?"

"Shouldn't you?" she replied excitedly, "Anyway, yes I should, but you know what? I've built up a bunch of extra hours over the last month so I'm taking the afternoon and tomorrow morning off."

"Well, that's great … you know how I love to shop."

Geoff rubbed his forehead anxiously. An afternoon at the mall ranked very highly in his list of things *not* to be doing under any circumstances, but especially now, as he had received official notice to terminate the relationship.

"You don't mind do you?" she asked hopefully, "I mean you might have plans."

Geoff minded immensely. "No, of course not, I'll see you at the usual mall in the usual place. What time?"

"Hmm, I don't know. Two hours from now. Is that ok? I've just got to finish off a few things here first."

"Two hours is fine. I'll see you later."

Nearly two and a half hours later Geoff was in traffic just outside the mall in Santa Monica, crawling in a slow moving line to enter. Then he rang Hannah's phone once to let her know he was in the vicinity before spending a frustrating ten minutes circumnavigating the subterranean parking area. Could he end things today, he wondered as he craned his neck back and forth in the gloom trying to locate a free space? This was crazy, he needed to finish with her but he had scarcely given any thought as to how he would do it, and he felt like he needed a reason; a proper reason that would hurt her. His client Ken would want that.

Before too long they met in their usual place with a kiss and a hug.

"Hey, I'm sorry I took a while in the parking lot." He frowned. "Inexcusable! What I want to know is what are all these people doing here? It's Monday! Haven't they got jobs? And if they haven't, how can they afford to be here?"

Hannah shrugged.

"Oh man, you're looking great today." Geoff tried his best to be upbeat, but in the next few days this would all be over. And a large part of him really didn't want it to be.

"So, torture me, take me clothes shopping until they switch the lights off and throw us out."

"Ok," she said excitedly, "but let's get some coffee first. Mine's the largest latté on the menu."

"Deal!"

They headed for a nearby coffee shop and Geoff shouted an order as they stepped through the door. As they sat down, Hannah reached over the small table and gently grabbed his hands.

"You know JJ, I've been thinking recently how much you've

turned things around for me over the last few months, and I want you to know that I really appreciate it."

Geoff was dismissive. "Aw shucks, it was nothing."

"No, really, I mean it. After everything that went on with the bastard I was going out with before; I'm just amazed that I stayed with him so long before dumping his sorry ass out on the porch. But you, I don't know, you seem to have a different outlook on things; your approach is so laid back and I think it's rubbing off on me. I used to be so uptight about things but now I want to get mellow, just like you."

"In other words you wish to strive for mellowosity."

She leaned over and kissed him. "Yes Sir, I do."

A fabulous looking waitress brought their order and Geoff smiled a brief thank you.

"Ok then, let's approach the nirvanic state of mellowdom together. Cheers."

They clinked their coffee cups together and drank.

"You know, I was thinking back the other day to when we first met. You remember that?"

"Sure do," Geoff said.

"It was almost like you knew I was down and looking for someone else. It felt like you knew where to find me."

"That's me," he replied smugly, "I can sense the vibes from a couple of hundred feet."

He had known where to find her, as it happened. He had a location, an approximate time, a verbal description and a small photograph. There really wasn't much room for error.

"You know, I was thinking we could go on vacation together, if you'd like."

Geoff shrugged casually but inside nerve ends were twanging. "I guess…"

"Well, I know it's a bit early. I usually don't go on vacation with a man until the summer of the second calendar year, but…"

He put on a smile. "Well, in that case I feel honoured to be asked so soon."

"You darn well should! The thing is, a friend of mine at work has just asked if anyone wants to rent out her condo in St Thomas next month. One of their holiday rentals has fallen through and she's anxious to keep the place filled all summer. What do you say?"

Geoff was caught off guard. "Err, well, I guess. I'll have to check, obviously, if I have anything booked, any major surgery scheduled, but, well, if not then sure let's do it."

Hannah was suddenly defensive. "We don't have to, I mean, if it's too soon. But the offer came up and it seemed a pity to waste it."

"Yeah, no, great, I mean … honestly, it's a lovely thought, and I haven't been to the Caribbean in years so why not?"

Defensiveness turned to glee in an instant. "So we'll go then? I can tell her it's ok?"

Hannah was clapping her hands in excitement and didn't notice the extended pause.

"Yes … yeah, why not."

They drank from their coffee cups again and Geoff watched her closely as she smiled. God she had a beautiful smile. Then his thoughts drifted. Why didn't he have the guts to just forget this arrangement? They could be out of here and away on a plane in no time.

"JJ, are you ok?" Hannah asked after a while. "I've just been watching you. You've finished your coffee but you look like you're in a daze."

He shook his head and breathed out heavily. "Hey, I don't know what happened then; I was miles away."

"Dreaming of the Caribbean, huh?" She smiled.

"Yeah, yeah, I'm looking forward to it. Let's hit the shops."

As they paid the bill and left, Hannah squeezed Geoff's hand. "Hey, how do you fancy spending tomorrow morning with me as well?"

Geoff gulped silently and managed a smile. "Yeah, why not, I'm working from home this week, so who's going to know? And anyway, I've got a very understanding boss."

7

"Do you and your friends want a coffee honey?"

In New Jersey it was 11pm and Tara's mother shouted loudly up the stairs to the back bedroom from where the muffled sound of music could be heard. Inside Tara and Gerhard, an athletic blonde man, were sitting on the bed. Both were naked, but Tara had now gathered up the thin top sheet around herself to protect her modesty. They had just finished having sex a matter of moments ago. Becky was sitting over by the TV, wearing only stockings and suspenders, trying to hear the news against the sound of music from the stereo system. She was drinking from a can of coke and looked generally hot and sweaty. A very faint voice was heard from outside and Becky called over to Tara.

"Hey, I think I can hear your mom calling. What do you want to do? Will she come in?"

Unperturbed she got up, walked over to the bed, and started to sort through a pile of clothes.

Tara shrugged and ran one hand through her hair while playfully stroking Becky's thigh with the other. Her forehead was glistening with sweat and her breathing was still coming back down to its normal level.

"Don't worry, she hasn't the faintest idea what goes on in here, and she would never, ever, come in."

Becky found a bra, fastened it under her breasts, and then quickly twisted it around into place and pulled the straps over her shoulders. Then she found a tiny stretch dress and pulled it over her head.

"Anyway you guys, I gotta go. Let me know when you want to hitch up again, ok?"

At this point Gerhard spoke out. "Oh come on, no time for another one?"

"Not tonight horny boy. Say, Tara, if you find my undies can you bring them to me? Perhaps not direct to the office though."

"Sure, do you want me to wash them first?"

"Neah, waste of time, anyway they're so small you could wash them in a coffee cup."

Becky stopped in the doorway. "Are you glad we got together then?"

Gerhard smiled and went to speak.

"No, not you," she laughed, "I think I know your answer."

"Sure I am," Tara looked away, "I still can't believe all this has come from talking to a stranger in the ladies' bathroom at work."

As Tara's mom returned to the front room, where her husband was watching a late night talk show, Becky slipped quietly down the stairs, out of the front door, and headed for the train station and the last service back to New York City. It was a warm and sultry evening and she thrilled to herself as she walked along this quiet suburban street, past dozens of closed curtains illuminated with either the gentle flicker of a TV screen or the dull glow of a bedside lamp. Had anyone else in this desperately dull neighbourhood had three in a bed sex in the last hour, she wondered?

Tara got up and walked naked across the room, then picked up some clothes and started pulling them on. Gerhard looked on admiringly as she did this.

She turned to him. "Hey, we don't know each other very well right?"

He shrugged.

"You see, I've got this problem that's come up in my life at the moment and I'm not sure what I'm planning to do is the right thing."

She pulled a vest top over her head and struggled into a pair of jeans; she didn't bother with underwear. "How are you on the subject of getting revenge on people?"

Gerhard shrugged again, it was a vague but leading question. "It depends on what you mean; physical revenge, as in injuring someone or destroying their property, no, never."

"No it's nothing like that. But I feel the need to get this guy back for what he did to me…" her voice dropped to nearly a whisper, "even though it wasn't really that much."

"I don't know," he replied in his clipped European accent, "revenge is an ugly word. I try not to get involved unless it's something serious."

Tara nodded. "Hmm, I know what you're saying."

"Do you want to tell me about it? Get a second opinion."

"Yeah, maybe…" She stopped. "No, not now; anyway, it's late and I need to get up for work in the morning. Get your clothes on and get out of here."

"Ok," he said, "I had a great time tonight, I'd…"

"I'll bet you fucking did!" she replied, cutting him off.

He pulled on a pair of boxer shorts, jeans, a sweat top, and some socks and training shoes.

"Ok, I'll catch up with you soon," he said, "and if you want to talk about this thing then I'm working from home tomorrow. Call me and I'll give you an alternative perspective."

"Ok," she said casually, "I might just do that."

He left, gently closing the bedroom door and stepping carefully down the stairs and outside into the warm night air. He had parked his car around the corner, so he started to jog to it.

Sometime later, in Los Angeles, Geoff was lying on the bed in his apartment wearing only a pair of boxer shorts, after just having taken his second shower of the evening. The first one at the gym was under a pissy showerhead and had scarcely managed to rinse the soap from his body. It had been a tough workout this evening, he had pushed himself beyond his normal level of endurance, and he grimaced as the excess lactic acid caused deep, gnawing, unpleasant aches in the muscles of his arms and legs. Maybe he was getting a little old for all this macho posturing down at the gym? Most of the guys there seemed at least five years his junior, and everywhere he looked in the changing area there were tanned torsos and finely honed pecs. Everyone seemed super fit and there were times when he felt distinctly out of his depth. He slowed his breathing and managed to measure his pulse rate by watching the bedside clock. If his counting was correct it was currently ninety beats a minute – a little on the high side for lying flat he thought.

He sat up as he felt acid reflux in the back of his throat; almost certainly as a result of eating a deluxe quarter pound double cheeseburger with onions, pickle and ketchup in slightly over four mouthfuls on the way back.

It was nearly midnight as he stared at a small crack around the central light fitting on the ceiling. It had definitely got larger in the last few days. Perhaps there had been an earthquake and no one had told him. A more likely option, though, was his upstairs neighbour, who for some reason dropped heavy things on the floor at random hours of the day and night. Some of them sounded immensely heavy – like last week, when Geoff was awoken in a state of shock at nearly 4am by a massive crash directly above his head. Perhaps that was why the previous tenant had vacated at such short notice.

After a further few moments the acidity got the better of him and he got up and walked a few paces into the bathroom in search of an indigestion remedy, switching on a row of spotlights above the mirror to flood the washbasin area with light. Geoff squinted at his face for a few moments, but what greeted him was not a pretty sight. He had shaved unevenly earlier on and his stubble was now reappearing in patches, and there were other areas where his skin was red, blotchy, and lined. After taking a brief slurp of bright pink liquid from the medicine cabinet he walked back into the front room, rolled up the window blind and stared out onto the sparsely lit parking area. He could see his truck two spaces across to the right and an old beaten up Lincoln saloon parked right up against it. He cringed, imagining a pair of fat sweaty slobs and their brood of ugly kids repeatedly battering the paintwork on his door as they all squeezed out with a bucket of fast food each. Maybe moving here wasn't such a bright idea after all.

He rolled down the blind before returning to the bedroom, where he lay staring at the ceiling for a while, listening hard to the unusual stillness. For the first time in ages he actually felt afraid of going to sleep. Eventually he closed his eyes but his mind was very much alive and racing in all directions. Last night he'd had a grisly dream which woke him in a cold sweat. He and Christine were in his old car down a rough track at Mount Bonnell in Austin; a popular lover's lane, and a place they used to frequent regularly in the early part of their relationship. The air was hot and damp after a mid evening thunder storm, but Geoff was somehow watching from outside the car. Inside he could see a faceless individual on top of Christine, dressed in a white hat and white suit. Also he could see clearly that Christine was slowly changing from a young beauty into a gnarled and wrinkly old woman. Then suddenly he was in the car, and there was blood everywhere, all over his clothes, and all over the seats, and all over Christine who now appeared to be dead. He yelled and scrambled out, blood dripping from his hands. There was a shotgun on the ground nearby, just like the one his dad used to have, so he picked it up and ran along a line of nearly twenty cars, systematically gunning down the occupants, all of whom were copulating inside. When his bullets were spent he was exhausted and delirious, but it was then that he saw his mother, wrapped in a shawl and with a wooden crate of ammunition by her side. Geoff stared into her grey featureless eyes until she reached into the crate for a box of bullets. Then he looked around and swallowed hard in dismay as suddenly he could see many other lanes radiating out from this central point, all lined with cars, and all similarly full of young people.

"Reload then kill them all," his mother croaked in a harsh whisper, "all of them. And when you're out of bullets come back to me and get some more to finish the job."

Geoff opened his mouth to speak but no words came out.

"*Kill them all!*" This time she was shrieking and Geoff had to cover his ears. "Kill them you worthless piece of shit! Shoot the man in the back, let his sweetie watch him die and then kill her! Do it! *DO IT!*"

It was at this point that Geoff woke up, terrified and gasping for air. He breathed deeply, desperate to calm himself down, but in the end he had to get up and go for a drive down to the ocean, where he sat on the beach until nearly 5am, shivering and clutching his mother's letter in his hands.

Now he sat up, conscious that he was sweating again. Being alone in this frame of mind was no good for anyone. He contemplated going out to a bar, or maybe a movie. Eating was definitely out. But he desperately needed to sleep. He was no good as a human being without it. He lay back and closed his eyes tight, desperately trying to think positive thoughts. For the moment any thoughts of his relationship with Hannah, and how to end it, had not entered his head.

8

Tuesday

"So JJ, what is it you actually do? We've been together nearly three months now and all you'll ever say is that you're in finance; that you work for a bank."

Hannah and Geoff were sitting out in the early morning sunshine on the patio in Benedict Canyon. She had arrived at 9am and they had just finished eating fresh fruit and some pancakes that Geoff had rustled up from a ready mix pack.

"That's because I really, actually, am in finance," he replied casually.

"Ah c'mon, on our first date, the very first time you came over to me in that bar, I asked you what you did for a living and you said you were in finance, and that you worked for a bank, and that's been the story ever since. At some point are you actually going to tell me what your job is, and how you got this fantastic house? And, how come I keep calling you up during the day and you never seem to actually be at this bank you supposedly work for?"

Geoff sighed, oh what the hell, a few white lies wouldn't hurt at this stage.

"Ok, here's the thing," he replied, "I am in finance but I don't work for a bank. Well not yet anyway."

"Right, so what have you been doing while we've been seeing each other?" Hannah looked mildly concerned. "And what about yesterday when you said you had an understanding boss?"

"I do have an understanding boss; it's *me*. I've been working for myself, in finance, just like I said."

Hannah shook her head in confusion. "So..."

"Ok, I'll tell you, I've been working for myself as a trader on the foreign exchange markets for the last couple of years. Currency trading, you know, foreign exchange, buying and selling. I read about it in a magazine article. It's a piece of cake, as long as you know your limits and stick to them."

"But ... don't you need ... I mean..." She shook her head. "Well how does it work? What do you actually do?"

"I choose an exchange rate ... I don't know, the French franc against the dollar, the peseta against the yen ... one that's volatile is good. I look which way it's changing then I buy some yen or some English pounds or whatever, then I watch the exchange rate, making sure my investment is growing. Then when I can't stand the excitement anymore I get the hell out. I sell my share at its new value, then I lose a bit on tax, but the rest is mine; like I said a piece of cake. To start with I used to sit by the phone and watch CNN business desk for 22 hours a day, but now it's a whole heck of a lot easier with a fast Internet connection and some trading desk software. That cost me a couple of thousand bucks, but I can pick a set of exchange rates and monitor them in real time. It's money for nothing really. A couple of weeks back I made fifteen grand in two hours. I was watching five different currency values and..."

"*Fifteen thousand dollars!*" Hannah was visibly staggered.

"Yeah, but my stake was eight grand in total. You can't just bet fifty bucks ... you've got to take a big risk."

"Eight grand! You risked eight grand?"

Geoff shrugged and poured them both some coffee.

"And this is how you make a living, right? Is it legal?"

"Of course it is! That's how the world of commerce works. People buy things and then sell them for a profit. Don't make out like I'm some sort of white collar criminal, for God's sake."

Hannah smiled. "Well, well. I have to say I'm impressed."

"You see this house?" he continued, "two years ago when I moved here from Texas I decided I didn't want to live in some crappy two bed apartment in Santa Monica, so I devised myself a short term really, *really* high risk trading strategy to buy and sell my way up to two and a half million dollars so I could get someplace decent to live."

He paused for a swig of coffee. "And amazingly it worked, although for a few weeks I didn't sleep more than a couple of hours at a time in case the markets dropped and I lost everything."

Hannah's mouth was now hanging open. "Wow, I've heard about guys like you making millions on the stock market. That's awesome!"

"The trouble is, though, I'm never more than a handful of mouse clicks away from total financial ruin. As a way of earning a fast buck its fantastic, but..."

She didn't seem to hear this, and bit her lip seductively. "Fuck me JJ, here, *now!* Finding out that you're a millionaire risk taker is such a *massive* turn on."

"Hi sugar, how are you doing? You've been out for the count since I came on duty."

It was early afternoon at the Brindley Hospital in New York City and Christine turned awkwardly to face the door and attempted a smile, although all forms of expression were still painful due to severe facial bruising, which was changing colour almost by the hour. More pressing by a considerable amount, though, was the spinal injury sustained from bouncing down a flight of metal stairs. Christine only had limited feeling in her legs at the moment, and she struggled to turn in the opposite direction to see the wall clock. The pain in her face as she squinted upwards was intense, and there seemed to be a slight blurring of her vision as she tried to focus on the display mounted high on the wall. She was fairly sure that it read almost 1pm. One thing she *was* sure of, though, was that she needed to speak to Geoff urgently. If she hadn't have agreed to go back to Austin and meet him two years ago and, more importantly, if she hadn't listened to his stupid, stupid, *stupid* idea, then she wouldn't be lying here now in a hospital bed seriously injured and many hundreds of miles from home. That was an inescapable fact and she intended laying the entire blame at his feet. How could she have been so...

Suddenly she realized that the staff nurse was speaking to her.

"What can I do for you, sweetheart?" Louise had a million administrative things to do in the next hour.

"Can you bring me a phone so I can make a call?"

"Sure thing, I'll go and get one for you directly."

"And can I get some fresh water; this tastes of washing up liquid."

"Oh I'm sorry about that hun," the nurse gasped. "Ok, I'll be right back."

Staff nurse Louise Thurmann disappeared for a couple of minutes before returning, carrying an old style phone with the cord wrapped around it wedged under her arm, and a fresh pitcher of water plus glass. She poured some water and then fussed around for a moment connecting the phone to an outlet by the side of the bed.

"Here you go babes, I bet you want to call your folks, huh? Are they in the area? I think we need to get them here to see their precious daughter a.s.a.p. Now I guess you're gonna need me to dial for you, so you just read out the number."

Christine struggled to remember Geoff's number. "No, it's ok I can do it, and no I'm not calling my folks; A, because they're in Dallas, and B, because my mom would drag me back home by my hair if she saw the state I'm in."

"I'm sure you know best." Louise placed the phone on the bed. "There you go, sweetie, you push the button again when you need me."

In Los Angeles a phone in the breast pocket of a shirt draped over the back of a chair on the patio began to ring, but it was scarcely likely that anyone would hear, let alone answer, because Hannah and Geoff were making love in a large wooden gazebo in the garden below. Both were naked and she was thrashing around noisily, close to her climax. Geoff, though, was very hot and very much out of breath. He concentrated hard to stay focussed on the task at hand, but random thoughts were distracting him. Principally the fact that this relationship should not still be in existence.

He adjusted his position and managed to up the pace slightly, causing Hannah to cry out.

"Oh yeah, come on, *fucking well come on!*"

"Ok babe, ok!" he gasped.

"Talk to me JJ, you can make me come in seconds."

At length the answering service on Geoff's phone kicked in with a very brief message.

"Sorry, I'm not here. Please leave a message and I'll get back to you".

In the short time spent waiting to leave her message Christine had become angry and almost tearful, but made sure to speak clearly.

"Geoff, I need to speak to you. I followed your stupid crazy suggestion, about setting the record straight, and now I'm in hospital in New York. Some guy attacked me and I'm seriously hurt, so I want you to call me as soon as you get this, ok? Please Geoff."

She tried to hang up the phone, but the receiver slipped from her hand and off the side of the bed beyond her reach. She shouted out anxiously for the nurse who fortunately was nearby at the time.

"Hey sweetie, let me help you with that."

Christine tried to turn slightly and cried out with pain.

"Are you getting this Geoff? *Are you fucking getting all of this?*"

The nurse looked confused. "Who is he sugar? Do you want us to try and contact him for you? Is it your husband"?

Christine managed to fake a slight laugh. "No … I don't really know what you'd call him."

As she slumped back awkwardly and grimaced in pain Louise reached behind her with practised hands and lifted her forward.

"C'mon, let me help you, let's rearrange these pillows to make you a little more comfortable, then you must try and get some sleep. Are your legs feeling any better today?"

Christine shrugged. "I don't know. I guess I can feel them slightly more. I had an itch earlier on."

"An itch, why that's wonderful! Itches are good, especially in places you didn't expect to get them. My mom always used to say when something started to itch it was getting better. I'll catch you later hun, you just buzz if you need me."

Christine lay back on her newly plumped up pillows and sighed loudly as the nurse fluttered out of the door. Her face then cracked into a sob. Just what did she expect this phone call to achieve? What *did* she want Geoff to do about this? Did she want him to drop everything and rush to her side? Take leave from his job? Abandon his family, assuming he now had one? What would she say to him if he turned up in the doorway? Nothing immediately sprang to mind. After all, the only thing he did was to make a stupid suggestion and then disappear. She had been the one to put it into practice.

She fixed her gaze on the wall clock as the seconds ticked by, struggling to work out what time it was on the west coast. But after a few moments the mental effort of attempting elementary arithmetic had drained her, and she drifted off as sleep overcame her in great crashing waves.

Back in Los Angeles, Geoff and Hannah were now walking back up to the patio. He was wearing shorts, she was topless but wearing a sarong around her waist with bikini bottoms underneath. She appeared triumphant, but he looked hesitant.

"JJ, is something bugging you? I've just had the best fucking climax in about three months and you're looking like someone's just torn up your Super Bowl tickets."

"No, I'm fine, just thinking about stuff."

"What's on your mind, is it something I can help with?" She sounded concerned.

"Oh it's nothing really," he hesitated, "well I'm not sure about the vacation."

Hannah's concerned expression evaporated. "Oh, why damn it? You were up for it yesterday."

"I know but..."

"But what? Come on, I already wrote my friend a cheque out. She needed the money to pay her rent this month."

Geoff's brain felt it was about to explode. He absolutely had to end this whole thing soon. He smiled weakly. "Yeah ok, I'll see how I'm fixed. No problems."

Her smile returned in an instant. "That's what I wanted to hear my fantastic little millionaire risk taker."

Later, in New York, Tara left her office building at 5:15pm, well before her normal departure time, skipping a 5pm editorial meeting in the process. She descended into a nearby subway, forging her way through a crowd of commuters, and boarded a downtown train heading for the hospital where the article had said Christine

Hudson was staying. It was not her intention to visit in person, just to confirm Christine was still there, and maybe try and wheedle some information as to the severity of her injuries; and from that infer a possible length of stay.

As the train moved forward she frowned as conflicting thoughts entered her head. A large part of her wanted to let this go; it was all in the past and probably she should just chalk it up to one of life's bad experiences. But another part of her screamed, *no!* Paul had to be made aware of the emotional distress he had caused. The journey passed while she was deep in thought, but after alighting from the train and resurfacing at street level she decided she couldn't let it drop. Things had to be taken further. Paul was still very much in trouble! So she picked up a small bouquet of flowers from a nearby street seller and breezed off in the direction of the hospital.

"Hi, I'm a friend of Christine Hudson. I heard she was staying here, so I just wanted to leave her these flowers."

The receptionist at the main front desk tapped away briefly at her keyboard.

"Sure, and who shall I say they're from?" She replied without looking up.

"My name's on the card," Tara replied.

"Thank you ma'am, I'll see she gets them," the receptionist replied vacantly and turned to walk into the back office.

"Err, excuse me, do you mind me asking? Is Christine badly hurt, I mean..."

Suddenly the receptionist was paying attention. "I'm sorry ma'am, we can't give out that sort of information."

"Oh, I know, I know." Tara replied earnestly. "It's just that I'm an old friend of hers and I'd really love to see her, but..." she hesitated "I think I've got a bit of a throat virus starting up so I'd need to wait a couple of days. God I wouldn't want to add to her problems."

The receptionist smiled and tapped a few keys. "I'm sorry, she's been admitted with serious injuries, but I can't give out any further details."

"That's ok, I understand. I'll come back and see her in a couple of days. Thanks for your help."

As she left the building and headed for the subway there were threatening black storm clouds above being moodily lit from the west by the afternoon sun. Now she just had one more call to make on her way home.

9

August 2006

Up until a week before Christine received an unexpected letter from Geoff at her parents' house in Dallas, everything in her life had been going well. At work she had recently received excellent performance reviews and had now become eligible for promotion in October, and in her personal life she was enjoying the most promising relationship of the last few years. But then it all came to a crashing end when she discovered that her new boyfriend was seeing another woman in the evenings when he was supposed to be working extra hours on an important project. On the face of it their relationship had been fine, but then little signs started to appear, and eventually instinct told her that something was going on. So she decided to take action, and managed to surreptitiously catch him out by parking near his car one evening when 'another pile of crap had landed on his desk'. She didn't intervene directly, but managed to get a snap or two of him canoodling with another woman as they walked to his car. And then a few days later, at the end of a fantastic meal to celebrate their half year anniversary, she presented him with a couple of photographs at the same time as the waiter presented him with the bill. His face was a picture.

Geoff's impersonal printed letter didn't provide any new contact details, all it said was that he would be at Jodi's Diner in Austin every Saturday and Sunday morning at 8:30am for the next month and he'd really like to see her if she wanted to stop by. Christine was highly curious as to the purpose of the letter. When they were together Geoff had often talked about leaving America to go and live somewhere 'more interesting' overseas, so perhaps he wanted to meet up to say a final farewell before moving on. Or perhaps he had finally gotten his act together, finished university, and she was being invited to his graduation.

Perhaps she should stop speculating and just go and find out.

Even though their relationship had ended unpleasantly and there had been no contact since, Christine harboured no real ill feelings towards Geoff. He had always seemed like one of the good guys, with his only real downside being occasional silly fits of temper or inexplicable moodiness. So she decided to drive down and meet him, the clinching factor being that the air conditioning in her apartment had broken down, giving her several sleepless nights in eighty degree overnight temperatures. She even called one of her old girlfriends from college who still worked down there and arranged a night out on the Saturday. The last thing she wanted was for Geoff to think she'd made a special trip.

While they were together Christine and Geoff used to dine at Jodi's most weekends, so it was like stepping back in time as she walked through the door and saw him at his favourite table tucking into his usual; a short stack of pancakes with maple syrup and pecan butter, with an egg sunny side up and a few rashers of bacon. The largest mug of coffee that the house provided and a copy of the Sunday papers spread across the table finished the picture.

Christine had given no indication that she was coming down, or even that she had received the letter, so Geoff almost choked on his coffee when she approached his table with a smile.

"Christine!" he spluttered, standing up and moving to greet her with a hug, "I can't believe you showed up. This is fantastic!"

She sat down before he had a chance to embrace her. "Hey Geoff, it's good to see you. I was coming down this weekend anyway to meet an old college friend, so I thought I'd stop by."

Geoff sat back down too, slightly crestfallen. "Do you want me to order you some breakfast?"

She forced a smile. "Sure. My usual, if you can remember it."

"I remember it."

He ordered promptly and they sat in a brief uncomfortable silence. Christine was already feeling ill at ease, her stomach felt tight, and she was sure her voice sounded nervous and fluttery.

"So," he said after a while, because the powers of speech had all but left him.

"So," she replied, swallowing hard. "It's been a couple of years. How are you? You haven't changed a bit."

This wasn't exactly true, his hair had thinned noticeably from the unruly unkempt mop she remembered, and he now kept it cut quite short. He actually looked smarter, his clothes looked ironed, but his face carried a perturbed look.

He laughed politely "I'm fine, Chris, fine. My hair is starting a mass exodus, as you can probably tell, but other than that I'm good."

Are you married? Have you got kids? What are you doing now?" she asked.

"No I'm not married and no I haven't got any kids," he replied, "and I know it's going to sound ridiculous but I haven't really had the time…"

"You've had *five* years Geoff!"

He looked down. "I know, but I haven't just been sitting here. I've travelled around the US quite a bit; I lived in Santa Fe, then Las Vegas for nearly a year, then I moved up to the mid west and lived in Chicago. I went to Europe for a few months, and I've been to Australia and the Far East. I've had a couple of relationships dotted in amongst that, but … I don't know … somehow the last five years has gone by so fast. It's scary really."

Christine's breakfast arrived. "How are you anyway? You look fantastic."

"I'm ok too." She shrugged off his compliment, suddenly wondering how best to describe her last five years. "I've been working hard. I've managed to finagle my way up to chief medical reporter at a major Dallas newspaper, and I've just found out I'm eligible for promotion in October. No husband, no kids though … thank God…"

Geoff raised his eyebrows slightly, trying unsuccessfully to read her expression, and they chatted about nothing in particular while they ate.

After a few minutes Geoff signalled for some more coffee, feeling the initial tension between them was easing. "This is a great breakfast, huh? Do you still eat out a lot?"

"No, I don't," Christine replied flatly, "I have a kitchen and a dining table that I tend to use most days. So," she continued, before Geoff had a chance to reply, "is there a reason behind this surprise invite?"

"A reason?" He looked surprised. "Does there have to be a reason?"

She could tell that there was one. It was written all over his face. The waitress arrived and topped up his coffee for the fifth time. Geoff was a very good customer here, but sometimes it did seem as if he was testing the management's definition of 'unlimited refills'.

"You want some more coffee?" he asked, but Christine indicated that she didn't. He shooed the waitress away.

"A reason, a reason … well now, let me think." He stared at her.

Christine took a long drink of coffee and stared as he began to fidget uncomfortably. She hoped and hoped … *and hoped* that he wasn't going to disappoint her and suggest them getting back together again. But at the same time she struggled to think what else it could be.

Eventually he sighed. "Look, enough already, I want us to get properly back in touch. There, I said it, and I apologize if it was all so obvious."

Her expression barely altered.

"I've missed you like crazy every day for five years! I missed our road trips, I missed our breakfasts here, and I missed our weekends out doing stuff. We were *always* doing stuff together. Remember I used to say you've only got so many days on this earth, so don't waste a single one of them. Well I've wasted years' worth and I don't want to do it anymore. You know what I'd really like is for us to get back together. Just as friends maybe, so we can do stuff again, and travel, and get a house and…"

He hesitated, almost getting carried away and suggesting that he wanted them to start a family.

Christine's expression still hadn't changed, but at length she spoke. "Geoff, a few minutes ago you told me that the last five years have flown by really fast. You've lived all over the place. You've visited far flung and exotic countries. And you've *even* had a couple of relationships 'dotted in' amongst it all…"

Geoff was immediately floored. "Yeah, but … it wasn't…"

"It sounded like you'd had a really full calendar Geoff, but now you're telling me different. Which is it?"

"Chris, no, it wasn't like that."

"*Well what was it like?*" She demanded.

Geoff was practically writhing. "Yeah, I've been on vacation a few times. Yeah, I've had a few relationships. Yeah, I've lived a few different places. But I've missed you and I've been lonely. All of that time I've been lonely. That's why I kept moving. I went to Santa Fe, I got a job, I got an apartment, but I didn't make a friend in three months. So I moved, and I moved again, and I moved again. I need you, I need to see that smile, your eyes. You know how much I love your eyes…"

Christine deliberately looked away. "Come on Geoff, that's enough I think."

There was a brief silence, and Geoff's face screwed up in what looked like anger as he sensed things slipping away from him.

"Look," he said eventually, "I *know* I didn't give you enough attention when we were together. I *did* let things slide. I was lazy. I didn't care enough about things … about you … and I just assumed that you were always going to be ok with that."

"I can't think of many women who would be ok with that, Geoff."

"But I'm different now, *really* I am."

Christine shuddered. From the moment she sat down she could see this coming. *Why did she even come here?* Personality wise, the Geoff she was looking at now was not that different from the Geoff of five years ago, but she had moved on from the essentially student style life that they had shared, and so far there was no compelling evidence that he had done the same.

"You know what?" She said after a few moments. "I think I need to go now. This was a bad idea."

He stared anxiously at her as she rummaged in her bag, desperate to delay her departure.

"Are you happy, Chris?" he asked as she checked her face in a small makeup mirror.

She looked up, visibly surprised. "Am I happy … no I'm not; it's the middle of summer, I have no A/C, it was 86 degrees in my apartment last night and I think I slept two hours max."

He shook his head. "No, no, I mean are you happy with the way your life's turned out so far? You look great, it sounds like you've got a good job, and an apartment, but what about other stuff?"

"Other stuff?" Christine narrowed her eyes and scrutinized him carefully. "And why, after five years, would that be any of your business?"

Geoff looked up at the ceiling. "Oh, come on Chris, I'm getting a real sense that we're never going to see each other again after this, but we were friends once."

He took a long drink of coffee. "I don't know, you just seem … unhappy."

Again Christine stared hard at the person she had once been deeply in love with. Her life had been going well, but currently she wasn't happy with quite a few things. Her head swam momentarily. Why should she give Geoff the satisfaction of hearing her problems?

"Ok, Geoff, why not?" she said eventually, "yes, I am unhappy, I've just finished with a guy I'd been going out with for six months. He was really great, really charming, and I thought I could trust him. I even thought he might be 'the one'. But you know what, he was a *bastard!* You know when you get an inkling that something isn't quite right; when something doesn't quite hang together? Well, eventually I reached that point and took some action. I watched him at his office walking across the parking lot with another woman when he was supposed to be working late. And then I confronted him in a restaurant a few days later. To start with the son of a bitch tried to deny it. He tried to say there was nothing going on, and that they were just friends, blah, blah, blah… But later at his apartment he folded right in front of me. So I tore him to shreds. I think he might have even begged for forgiveness at one point…"

She sighed. "So no Geoff, right at *this* moment I'm not particularly happy."

Geoff avoided her eyes. "Shit, that's too bad. You don't deserve that."

There was silence for a while. The majority of the customers were now winding up their meals and the place was starting to empty.

"You know what?" Geoff said distractedly. "I've never been in that position. I've never had anyone, male or female, in such a place where I could verbally rip them apart like that; make them squirm … make them *beg!* It must be quite something to feel that power over another person."

Now their eyes locked together.

"And you know something else?" he continued. "I don't think I could do that to a person I cared for. Because you never forget when people treat you like that, whatever you've done to them. You always hold a special resentment for them in the back of your mind."

Christine looked suddenly uncomfortable. "You'd better tell me where you're heading with this, Geoff."

"Oh nowhere, nowhere really," he replied. "Except I'd like the chance to be in that position, to emotionally tear someone apart until they've got nothing left to argue with."

Christine shrugged. "It's easy, just get emotionally close to someone, wait for the inevitable moment when they piss you off, and then let it all happen. Yeah, that reminds me, you were never real hot on letting go of your emotions were you? Did stuff happen to you when you were a kid or something?"

This comment hit him in the chest with a thud and he looked down at the table. In all the time they were together he had never quite managed to tell her about the shooting and all that followed. Somehow the time had never been right.

"Well, I grew up in rural Texas; I'm bound to have suffered a bit," he muttered.

"Can I get you guys anything else?" their waitress asked.

Geoff didn't even look at her. "No thanks, we're all done here."

The waitress looked to Christine. "Ma'am?"

"No, I'm fine thank you." She turned to Geoff. "I'll pay for breakfast today."

"Yeah, whatever." His mind had started to whir away on a ridiculous idea as he finally realized the futility of this meeting.

The bill arrived promptly. Christine checked it and pulled ten dollars from her purse. "Have you got a couple of bucks for a tip?" she asked.

"Geoff, hello," she waved her hand in front of his face.

"You know what?" he said suddenly, "I need to become more like you. I need to be able to take my anger out on people the way you can," he paused. "But it's something I *really* don't know how to do. Not yet anyway," he smiled. "So it would have to be done on a stranger."

"*What!*" Christine was incredulous.

"Taking your anger out on inanimate objects is pointless," he continued. "It has to be done to a person, but in a non violent way of course. And you do it so well, Chris. From what you've just said, you sound like a Grand Master. So, if things in my life go bad for some reason, what can I do? Answer ... I find a stranger, I go out with her for a while, I wait until I'm sure she has feelings for me, then, I pick a fight and I let it all happen. I verbally tear her to pieces and then I'm out of there. Setting the record straight I'm going to call it."

Christine shook her head in dismay.

"I think it would be good for me. And the person at the receiving end?" he shrugged dismissively, "ah, she'd get over it."

"Geoff, I don't know what..."

"Hell, I could even put an ad in the paper." He pulled some coins from his pocket and scattered them on the table. "I'm sure there's plenty of guys out there who'd pay to see their estranged wives put through the emotional wringer."

"Thank you ma'am." The waitress came and took the money.

"Don't you see, Chris? Folks hire private detectives to spy on their partners, women hire hookers to see if their husbands will cheat on them. I'm just suggesting yet another option at the milder end of the revenge spectrum."

He laughed loudly. "What an absolutely superb idea!"

"Ok Geoff, you're scaring me now. What you're saying is bizarre; no it's totally insane... you're expecting someone to pay you to do this?"

He smiled broadly. "Who knows? Isn't it just the craziest thing you ever heard? But it could work; I know it could. Maybe not here in Texas, but in New York or LA I reckon there would be plenty of people who'd be motivated enough to do something like that."

"Look, I really do need to go," she replied, "but to set the record straight right here and now, I think you've flipped, ok? Seriously flipped!"

"Hey..." He shrugged again. "I quite possibly have."

"And before I go I'm setting you a challenge," she said.

"Yes ma'am." He sat up straight, now beyond caring what she thought.

"Where would you choose to do this, LA or New York?"

"LA, I'll have LA," he replied eagerly, "definitely more crazy people per square mile than New York."

"Ok, you never did tell me what you do for a living, but at a convenient point I want you to quit your job, move to LA, and I want you to try your crazy idea out, and then when you're done I want you to call me and let me know how you feel about things, ok?"

"You know, I might just take you up on that," he replied coldly.

"And I'll bet you fifty bucks, right here, that no one, nowhere, would ever pay for something like that. It's off the chart stupid, Geoff."

She held out her hand. "Fifty bucks; are you up for it?"

"Yeah, why not?" he replied casually, "I'll risk fifty that there are folks out there who'll see where I'm coming from."

They shook hands firmly. "Now, let's swap cell phone numbers," she said, "but I don't want you to call me until you've completed the challenge and I owe you fifty dollars."

Geoff's head was spinning; he couldn't quite decide how they'd gone from having a civilized meal to this! They exchanged numbers and quickly checked they were correct by ringing each other.

Then Christine stood to leave "Are we on for this or not?"

Suddenly Geoff didn't know what to say. "Err maybe ... I guess."

"Ok then, now I do have to fly."

She walked to the desk and paid the bill, with Geoff following along meekly behind. At the door she hugged him, and he put his hands around her waist very gently.

"Hey, thanks for breakfast," he said, "the eggs were a bit too runny today but…"

She turned. "I'll speak to you later Geoff."

As they stepped outside and she walked away he shouted. "Hey, remember you can do this too! If life gets on top of you, if someone else messes you around, then find a total stranger and *set the record straight!*"

She carried on walking.

"*Let's see who completes the challenge first!*" he yelled as she turned a corner and disappeared from his life again.

As she drove back to her hotel Christine made a major decision, spurred on to a large extent by Geoff's weird ramblings and to a lesser degree by her recent failed relationship. She needed a change in her life. *She* needed a challenge! Work had been good recently, so why not update her CV and get the hell out of Texas, to a city where she was pretty sure Geoff wasn't going to be.

As soon as she got back to Dallas, Christine immediately started applying for jobs in the New York metropolitan area, and after only her third application managed to land a job with the New Jersey *Garden State Sentinel* after two exhaustive telephone interviews and a third face to face grilling at their Newark offices. Suddenly she was excited to bursting point to be getting out of her home state to live somewhere that had proper seasons; a place where the leaves changed colour spectacularly and snow fell at Christmas time. A place she could wear big warm coats! This would be a new start, so she cleared out her closets to the bare minimum, and she went through the cupboards and the loft space at her parents' house and threw away almost everything. It was going to be a wonderful feeling to start off in a new city with a blank sheet of paper, and so in late October 2006 she boarded a flight to New Jersey, leaving sunny Dallas with a temperature of nearly seventy degrees, and arrived a few hours later to a mixture of sleet and rain slanting down from a solid grey sky. She rented the best apartment she could afford in Manhattan, which actually wasn't much larger than an oversized broom cupboard … and hunkered down to see out the bitter cold north east winter. Attempts at a social life could wait until spring.

For Geoff, the meeting also acted as a form of catalyst ... and he felt a strange form of unspoken obligation to move to Los Angeles and put his suggestion into practice. His comments about verbally ripping people apart had been pointedly directed at Christine, who had expertly done this to him on many occasions. And he hoped she realized it.

This was such a bizarre time! If he chose to accept her challenge his life could totally change direction. Did Christine really think he was being serious?

But why not, he thought? He had no ties in Austin; no family, no real friends, and no formal job, so why not rise to the challenge Christine had set him?

For Geoff, the process of moving was a lot simpler. He didn't really have much of a past to get rid of ... it had all been jettisoned years before. To him it was just another place to live, and during his separation from Christine he had pared down his personal possessions to such an extent that everything would fit into a couple of family sized suitcases. And so, around six weeks after their meeting, he loaded up his car, posted the keys to his landlord, and relocated to the west coast by road, taking four days to make the trip.

10

As the hour approached midnight, Geoff and Hannah sat by the pool on the terrace in Benedict Canyon; Geoff wore only boxer shorts and Hannah was lying on a nearby lounger in an extremely expensive dress and currently fiddling with the tiny buckles on her high heels … her legs splayed in a distinctly unladylike fashion. Both were very drunk. It had been a long, hot and sultry day, and now it seemed as if the heat from the concrete basin of downtown Los Angeles was gently flowing upwards through the canyons like convection currents in a pan of boiling water.

Geoff called out to Hannah. "You know what, I can't believe all the things I had to do today, *and* I can't believe all the times you called me after you left this morning."

He smiled. "Even more so, I can't believe the sexual Olympiad that took place here this evening."

He screwed up his face in deep thought. "You know, I think I was even going to buy a new car today."

Hannah laughed hysterically, because that's what she did when she was drunk. It was one of the few things about her that annoyed Geoff intensely.

"A new car – *excellent,*" she squealed, "maybe then I wouldn't have to be chauffeured around everywhere in a Goddamn pickup truck."

"Hey, a pickup truck commands respect in this town. People let me out at intersections. I could be the pool guy, for God's sake."

Hannah laughed loudly again; the piercing sound echoing out into the stillness.

"Where's my phone, where's my damn phone?" He reached over to the table. "I'm going to count the number of voicemail messages you left me."

He began checking his messages. "Six times you called me in

the space of an hour. I've got six messages on here."

Hannah was now slurring her words ever so slightly. "Was it really that many? I thought I only called you four times. No, hang on."

Having sat up briefly she slumped back again and began counting on her fingers. Her voice was incredibly seductive when she wasn't cackling like a banshee.

"Well, err, oh who knows, I only wanted to see you again that's all. Hey, where were you by the way? I thought you said you'd always answer my calls."

"I'm sorry hun, I was busy."

Surprisingly she seemed happy with this.

"I'm going to delete the rest of these messages. I can only assume they all say the same thing."

He shrugged and waved his phone around. The message now playing was from Christine, and a tiny tearful voice could just about be heard, but Geoff was not listening.

"Are you getting this Geoff? Are you fucking getting all of this?" it shrieked.

He pressed the delete key.

"Let's go to bed," she yawned, "I was supposed to be driving back to my apartment, but I'm way too hammered, *and* I'm way too tired! Will you set the alarm real early though? I've got to be at the office just after eight."

"As long as we can fit in at least another hour of highly athletic sex before we turn in."

"An hour? God Geoff, where are you getting all your enthusiasm from?"

Geoff bundled her in the direction of the bedroom. "*And energy!*"

"It's ok," he laughed, "you can sleep through it if you want."

Hannah put up a mock fight at the bedroom door, putting her arms out and wedging herself in the frame, but Geoff quickly tickled her sides and she squealed and let go. They both fell on the bed laughing and giggling.

But it never happened. Hannah was semi comatose within less than a minute of Geoff's initial foreplay, and then his enthusiasm drained in an instant when an alarm beeped at him from his phone on the bedside table. He knew what it said; a single word. 'Mom'. He had set it early this morning to go off at midday and midnight every day from now on to remind him to do something; to think about making a decision at the very least. It was now midnight on Tuesday and he had received the letter on Saturday morning. He needed to decide what to do. His mother was ill, potentially very seriously ill – she might even be dying – and all he could do was procrastinate. The idea of an electronic reminder was good in principle, but obviously his phone would let him keep on pressing the reset button forever.

He lay back and stared at the ceiling. He had to finish with Hannah as requested and then he *had* to go and see his mother. He desperately needed to stand there in front of her, as a man, and hear what she had to say.

11

Wednesday

Geoff was reclining by the pool on a sun lounger, having recently returned from handing over his rent cheque for Benedict Canyon to a stuffy receptionist who strutted around the landlord's office like she still had the hangers in her clothes. His payment was nearly a week late, and it was not the first time this had happened. Unfortunately, no one in authority was available to see him so the receptionist took undue pleasure in informing Geoff that he was being placed on a register of delinquent payers, and that if he was even ten minutes late next month then the matter would have to be taken further. Geoff tried to summon up the enthusiasm to rant and rave, but really couldn't be bothered … instead meekly signing his name where indicated, thus accepting his newly acquired status as a delinquent. What he *needed* to do was start to properly manage his money; his income from trading had earned him a six figure sum in the last three months, so there was absolutely *no* excuse to be late with the rent!

It was now 5pm and he was expecting Hannah to arrive within the hour, and it was his intention to finish it today. He *really* didn't want to, but had come to terms with the fact that he must. Everything was in place; thankfully the money she had invested with him had already earned enough to return her initial payment, and reimburse Ken as requested. It was cooking away nicely in a risky far eastern trade, and by the time it came to cashing it in he might well have earned a little extra for himself too. Also he had uploaded the video onto his PC of Hannah sitting naked in her manager's chair and merely had to click a button to distribute it for all the world to see.

The only thing he hadn't settled on was what to actually say to her.

He had a cooler by his side containing several bottles of beer, but he was currently on his third vodka and pineapple juice cocktail. Think, *think*; hopefully something would come to him before the alcohol numbed his senses completely, and then Hannah would also be out of the door and on her way. And then it would be payday. Whatever happened, Hannah was just a pay cheque on legs ... very, *very* nice legs. Breathe deep he told himself, and again, and again. Let the oxygen get into the bloodstream; something would come to him soon.

He looked around as a little bird alighted at the far end of the patio and scouted around the paving stones for some minute nubbins of food. He didn't know what sort it was ... they all looked basically the same. He needed to switch off his feelings for Hannah and just do this.

Suddenly the buzzer from the main gate pierced the tranquillity, jolting him upright and sending the bird scattering into the bushes. He walked into the kitchen with a horrible sick feeling developing in his stomach, and from there he let Hannah in with the push of a button. She drove through the gates, narrowly missing them with both wing mirrors, and when she pulled up outside the house Geoff was waiting for her. She got out and ran to hug him.

"Han, there's something I need to talk to you about," he said abruptly.

"Geoff, what's happened? You seem to have changed since yesterday."

She quickly let go of him. "What's going on, what do you need to talk to me about? Are my investments safe?"

Geoff laughed dismissively. "*Money*, when something unknown goes wrong, why does everyone immediately think of money?"

He rubbed his forehead in mock frustration. "Sure, they're safe."

"They'd *better* be, Geoff ... that was over ten thousand dollars I invested with you."

"No, it's not that; something's come up since we last spoke, something I wasn't expecting..."

"Well what, for Christ's sake?"

Geoff was visibly flustered. "Err I didn't plan on this happening."

"You didn't plan on *what* happening?"

He stood in front of her looking and feeling like a naughty schoolchild. This wasn't right; it should be him reducing her to a quivering wreck not the other way around.

"Tell me what it is that's come up, and tell me *now*. I don't much like the sound of this."

"Ok, just give me a second here." He walked around for a few moments, as if trying to summon up the courage. What eventually came out didn't sound at all convincing.

"I guess I never told you that I'm actually married."

Hannah bridled immediately. "*What the…*" She lunged at him with clenched fists but he managed to grab her arms and they grappled for a few seconds.

"Let *go* of me you asshole or I'll *scream this fucking place to the ground!*"

"I'm separated, for God's sake," he gasped, "that's why I'm living on my own here!"

Hannah desisted, but there was pure anger in her eyes. "Well, are you getting divorced? Are you getting back together? *You'd better tell me what the fucking hell is happening!*" she yelled.

"Hannah, calm down, for God's sake, I have neighbours to think of."

"I couldn't give a *shit* about your Goddamn neighbours!" she yelled back, tears welling up in her eyes.

Geoff assumed a grave tone. "It's just that my wife's had an accident. I only heard this morning. And I offered to let her come and stay here for a while."

If Hannah was at all concerned by this news she didn't show it. "I couldn't give a shit about your neighbours, I couldn't give a shit about your fucking wife, and I couldn't give a shit about you!"

"Hannah, look it's…"

"Share certificates, JJ, I want to see them. Ten thousand dollars I've invested with you and your supposed company."

"The money's fine you can have it back within a month if you want. I just need to…"

Hannah walked to her car and quickly climbed in, slamming the door behind her. Her tone was threatening. "I want to see those share certificates before the end of the *fucking week!*"

She started the engine and revved it hard. "I don't like liars, Geoff, can't tolerate them. Goodbye for now and please pardon the cliché, but if my money isn't safe then you'll be hearing from my solicitor very, *very* soon!"

Her car screeched off, veering across the immaculate lawn and leaving deep tyre tracks as she yanked on the hand brake and spun in a circle, flinging clods of earth high into the air. When she reached the gate he saw her arm pressing the button and then waiting impatiently, revving the engine hard as the gates slowly swung open, before driving quickly out of sight. As he heard the engine sound disappearing off into the distance he shook his head in dismay. The deed was done, the challenge had been met. Hannah was out of the door, and she was as mad as hell. So why did he feel so utterly wretched?

"Are you happy Christine?" He asked, looking up at the sky. "I've won my fifty bucks, but it ain't even gonna come close to covering the costs of repairing my *fucking lawn!*"

12

Thursday

It was just after midday, and in her New York hospital room Christine had been asleep for most of the morning. Her condition was nowhere near as bad as feared when she was first admitted. An X-ray taken yesterday afternoon showed that she didn't have any major breakages, but there was a hairline fracture in her left forearm down near the wrist. Elsewhere she had lacerations and bruising, especially on the left side of her face, but thankfully all important bones were intact. She had suffered a moderate concussion that accounted for her temporary blurred vision, but the major piece of good news was that the spinal injury didn't appear to have caused any permanent damage and she had already managed to sit up and swing her legs off the edge of the bed. The unofficial prognosis was that complete rest, followed by some serious physiotherapy, should lead to complete recovery in a couple of weeks. All in all she was extremely lucky to have had a cushioned landing in amongst the garbage bags, two of which burst open on impact, leaving her smelling strongly of rotting meat and pasta sauce upon admission. As it happened, they were due to be removed the following morning in a special collection by a private contractor, so Christine was indeed fortunate. One day later and the fall might have led to permanent paralysis, or even death.

"Christine, honey, how are you doing … are you ok?" Nurse Thurmann peered around the door.

Christine opened her eyes a fraction and turned her head in the direction of the voice. She was extremely groggy from drug induced sleep.

"Yeah, I guess, under the circumstances and all that."

The nurse approached the side of the bed and briefly fussed around, tucking in a stray bed sheet.

"Listen sugar I've got someone called Tara in reception. You know, the one who bought those flowers the other day. She's saying she'd really like to see you."

"Oh my God, Tara. You know, I was so spaced out when I got those flowers I didn't know they were from her."

Christine squinted and screwed her face up in pain as she tried to shift position slightly. "But how does she know I'm here?"

The nurse shrugged. "No idea. I can tell her to go if you want ... tell her you're not up to a visit today."

Christine weighed this up for a while. "No, I'm kind of interested in what she has to say, but I don't want her to stay too long. Can you come back after ten minutes to check on me?"

"Sure thing, I'll just go and get her."

Louise disappeared for a few moments while Christine struggled to look at herself in a hand mirror she had managed to get hold of and now kept by the bedside. After a short while, Tara appeared nervously in the doorway.

"Hi Christine, how are you? Did you like the flowers I got for you?"

"Tara, oh my God, what a surprise ... I didn't expect to see you again. Yeah, I got the flowers they're over there by the window. They're gorgeous."

Tara smiled. "How are you feeling? I read about the accident in the paper and..."

"*This was in the papers*?" Christine was shocked. "Jesus Christ, which one?"

"Oh, one of the tabloids," Tara replied, "it wasn't a big story but someone obviously thought it was newsworthy."

Tears welled up in Christine's eyes. It was bad enough that she had been assaulted by someone who was potentially a Mafia hit man, but to now find out that it was all over the papers...

"Here, let me." Tara stepped forward and fetched a fresh tissue from her bag. She moved to dry Christine's tears but decided to hold back.

"You'd better do it," she said, "I don't want to touch … I mean I don't want to hurt you."

Christine stared into space for a few moments, wondering quite how her life had disappeared down such a hole.

"Look, Christine," Tara said eventually, "tell me to leave if you want, but it really upset me when I read the article. I don't know, you seemed like such a nice person when we met before and I just wanted to come and see you, that's all … to check you're ok."

Christine smiled. "Well thank you, that's nice to hear."

"Have your folks been to see you?"

"Not yet," she lied, "they'll have to fly in from Texas. They should be here in the next day or so."

"Is there anything I can do to help you before they arrive? Get you some fresh clothes or something. Maybe I could go and get you some new things to wear in here. You know, pajamas and stuff."

The offer touched Christine. "Ah, thank you, that's sweet; and I might just take you up on it, these hospital gowns just aren't me."

Tara's face brightened. "Yeah, whenever, just let me know."

There was a lull in the conversation, which was eventually broken by nurse Thurmann poking her head around the door.

"Is everything ok, sweetie?"

"Yeah, thank you I'm fine," Christine replied, "give me another few minutes, ok?"

Many questions had formed in Tara's head since reading the piece in the paper, the most important one being – was Don Borello another assignment; just like Paul? Had someone else read the ad in the paper and this was the end result? If so, it concerned her greatly, because now the police were involved, and just how would they view Christine's little business service? Did she declare her earnings … or keep proper accounts? Was what she was doing even *legal?* And if not, could Tara get into trouble if there was any sort of police or IRS investigation? Would she be considered to have solicited the services of some kooky type of prostitute? The very thought made her shudder.

And there was another burning question too, although hopefully that would resolve itself in the next few days.

"Christine, do you want to talk about any of this?" she asked gently, "I know that what's happened here is nothing to do with me, *at all*, but … well, I'm here if you need me, ok?"

There was another long pause, but the atmosphere wasn't uncomfortable.

Eventually Christine spoke. "You want to know how come I'm hooked up with some Mafia guy, don't you?"

"Hey," Tara held her hands up, "I don't want to pry, really I don't…"

"It's ok; I guess if I were you I'd want to know too."

Christine really couldn't tell if Tara's interest was genuine or not, but she did feel she needed to talk to someone. There was always Geoff, of course, but right now she didn't even know if he'd received her message.

"Could you come back tomorrow?" she asked softly, "I'm really struggling at the moment. I think someone's given me a double dose of sleeping pills."

Tara leaned forward and brushed a few strands of hair from Christine's face.

"Sure thing," she said as she walked to the door, "I'll see you tomorrow; you get some sleep now."

Christine lay back on her pillow, easing the bedclothes up under her chin, and as she closed her eyes her relationship with Paul came flooding back. She remembered when they first met. She remembered Tara telling her where he was likely to be at a particular time of day; and at the third time of trying, eventually she saw him.

She even remembered her opening line. "Hi, I don't usually talk to strangers, but I think I've been stood up."

And she remembered vividly the look of mild amazement on his face as she suggested that it was a shame to waste her outfit and makeup on someone who hadn't shown up, and that perhaps they could do something together for an hour or two … if he wasn't too busy.

But the main thing that came back to her was the completely surreal feeling of walking over to a total stranger at someone else's instruction and asking them out; knowing for sure that the whole thing would be a fake. A large part of her couldn't quite believe what she was doing, but in the days following the assault on her on New Year's Eve 2006, she remembered the words Geoff shouted to her as they parted for the last time outside Jodi's Diner.

"Hey, remember you can do this too! If life gets on top of you, if someone else messes you around, then find a total stranger and set the record straight!"

And she remembered how the idea taunted her. She was even woken by it at night with sweat on her brow and a racing heartbeat. And then eventually she caved in to her own anger. Her affair with Paul would be revenge for what happened to her on New Year's Eve; revenge on an innocent person, a total stranger; pure and simple.

Damn Geoff Dealer for putting such a twisted idea into her mind!

13

Around ten minutes after Tara had left the building a police officer appeared at the desk and acknowledged Louise Thurmann who was on the phone at the time. They knew each other well.

"Hey Lou," he said when she finished her call, "can I see Christine Hudson please?"

"Sure you can, anything for one of New York's finest." They both walked the short distance down the corridor to where Christine was awkwardly sipping her coffee.

"Hi Christine, sweetie, we got another one of those nasty police officers here to talk to you for a couple of seconds. Now make sure you're nice to him, because I want him to keep on coming back."

She then looked furtively from side to side. "Between you and me, if my husband is ever off the scene, I'm making a move on this guy."

The police officer stepped into the room. "Get out of here Lou … you're after anyone with a pair of handcuffs."

Louise walked out of the room, but stopped in the doorway.

"Hey, how did you know handcuffs were my thing? You've only got five minutes."

"That woman is unbelievable," he muttered under his breath. "Hi Christine, how are you doing today?"

She smiled weakly. "Me, I'm fine. I'm not so sure that my legs are going to work properly again, but hey … there are other ways to get around."

She leaned forward as far as she could and placed her hands on the twin peaks of her knees under the bed sheets.

The officer's voice oozed calm. "That's not my department, I'm afraid. What is my department is the guy who did this to you. Now we've…"

Christine interrupted. "Now you've caught him … would be a nice thing to hear."

"No ma'am, we haven't caught him yet."

"Jesus you still don't know where he is!"

The officer raised his hands in a placating fashion. "Hey, hey, it's ok, calm down. What we need to establish is…"

Christine was suddenly calm. "What exactly do you need to establish? I don't like the sound of this."

"We have to establish a bit more about your relationship with him, and if you know anything at all of his current whereabouts."

"*I didn't have any idea about him!*" she gasped, "and I *certainly* don't know where he is now – on another land mass probably. Or underneath one would be good."

The officer stared hard, analyzing her expression, but didn't say anything.

"Look someone mentioned him to me … said he was from the Mid West, just moved here, and basically that he was a really nice guy."

"Well who introduced you? It sounds like some sort of dating agency."

Christine laughed, but her awkwardness was difficult to conceal.

"No, it was nothing as formal as that. She … the person who introduced us … said she knew this guy who lived in her building; he hadn't been in the city for long and was looking around to make some friends; nothing sordid, nothing sleazy."

"And you could give me her name, this person who introduced you."

Christine's heart was pounding. "Sure … yes, uh-huh."

He noticed her skin tone suddenly drain by a shade or two.

"If I were to ask, that is."

She didn't respond.

"So you made friends with him. What, did you go knock on his door? What happened?"

Christine was getting slightly annoyed. "We went out as a group … me, her, him, and a couple of others."

"And you and him hit it off, right?"

"Yeah, basically, I was unattached at the time; he looked kind of handsome, well very handsome. So we started dating. Nothing wrong with that is there?"

"No ma'am. Now look, don't get nervous, this is just routine stuff."

She gasped. "Routine!"

"Yes, *just* routine."

"Forgive me for being a little spooked after some guy I've known for a couple of months suddenly flips out, throws me down a flight of metal stairs, leaves me for dead and then disappears."

"And you had no indication of any links to organized crime, any wrong doings, anything suspicious about him?"

Christine shook her head. "No Sir, I didn't."

"Ok, look, you know the next part, if you do think of any more details, anything at all, then give me a call. Here's my number."

He handed Christine a card from his wallet and she reached out for it, visibly in pain.

"Ok, I'll leave it on the side table here. Now, you get some rest and maybe I'll come see you again in a couple of days."

Christine couldn't avoid sounding sarcastic. "Sure thing officer, I know you'll stop at nothing until justice is done."

He got up and walked out of the room without looking back. Something didn't quite fit. In fact quite a few things didn't fit at all. From what little he knew about Don Borello he just wouldn't mix in this type of circle; he wouldn't be in this type of situation. And his wife and two kids living out in Temple Beach would certainly have something to say about his marital status. Christine was obviously screwing him and then pissed him off somehow, and without question he had a sufficiently volatile temperament to push even his own grandmother down a flight of stairs. Back in her room, Christine reached over and managed to pick up his card from the bedside cabinet, but it accidentally slipped from her fingers and fell to the floor before she got close enough to read it.

"Hey Lou, do me a favour will you?"

The officer walked past the nursing station where Louise was grabbing a quick drink of coffee from a plastic cup.

"Hey gorgeous, just tell me what you need, I'll bring it to your house and I'll be naked under my coat."

"You show up at my house and my wife would beat the crap out of both of us."

"Yeah right, just bring her to me, I'll show her who's the daddy."

He coughed.

"I'm sorry, a favour you wanted, shoot."

"Just keep an eye and an ear on who visits Christine."

"Oh come on, that poor girl, some bastard throws her down a flight of stairs and you think *she's* done something wrong."

The officer was keen not to shed any light on his suspicions.

"It's just routine Lou … anything to do with the mob … you know what I'm saying?"

Louise nodded discreetly. "Ok, will do."

As he disappeared off around the corner and out of view, Louise growled under her breath. "Goddamn it, I wish that fella would push me up a wall and bang me to kingdom come."

14

After Hannah had left, Geoff made a few pathetic attempts to disguise the deep tyre tracks on his ornamental lawn before retreating to the patio area, drinking the entire contents of his cooler, and falling asleep on the lounger beside the pool. It was 3am the following morning when he awoke feeling chilled, dehydrated, and extremely nauseous. He felt utterly depressed too, and not the slightest bit vindicated that he had seen through the challenge that Christine had set for him. Had he met Hannah under any other circumstances he would now be fantastically happy … and looking forward to what their future together might have in store. But now he felt empty … literally empty … like he had no innards, no heart or soul.

"You are an asshole Geoff Dealer for letting that girl go; a total, complete asshole!" he said to himself as he looked into the bedroom mirror before climbing into bed to grab some proper sleep before morning.

Now he was sitting at his PC abstractedly watching some other video clips of Hannah when suddenly his mobile phone rang and showed a withheld number. Surely her lawyers weren't coming for him already.

He decided to answer it. "Hello…"

From her horizontal position Christine responded with a very loud sigh.

"Hello, who's calling please?"

"Geoff, it's…"

Then Geoff's eyes widened in amazement as he realized who was calling. "*Christine!*"

"Geoff it's good to hear from you, I thought you'd vanished from the face of the earth."

"But hey…" He was momentarily flabbergasted, "oh my God it's great to hear from you too Chris. What's…"

"Don't you listen to your messages, Geoff? I left one saying I was seriously injured in hospital after being thrown down a flight of stairs and left for dead. Perhaps it's on your 'to-do' list, huh?" Her tone was heavy with sarcasm.

Geoff was taken aback. "What? When did you..."

Christine raised her voice and it broke up slightly on the phone. "*Geoff!*"

Flustered, Geoff struggled for words. "You sent me a message? When? I didn't hear it, I didn't get it! Christine, what's going on? Calm down, are you really hurt?"

"Do you mean am I really hurt as in seriously hurt, or really hurt as in I might be making it up?"

"Who did this?"

Geoff ducked the sarcasm. But Christine was now very calm. "Yes Geoff, I am hurt ... badly hurt ... and I am calm, I..."

"I'll fly over tonight," he interrupted without thinking, "I'll book it now, just you hold on there and I'll be over in a couple of hours."

"I *just* want to know," she persisted, "how you might possibly have not heard a message left on your cell phone."

"Chris, I..."

"Have you got the same cell phone?"

He hesitated. "Look, do we have to have an inquest about this *now*? What about you? What's *happened* to you?"

"Just *don't* ignore your messages, Geoff! *Jesus Christ!*"

"I ... I didn't ignore it, really I didn't. It must have just..."

He clenched his fist and took a deep breath. There had been no communication from Christine since they last met two years ago, so where was the justification for this verbal onslaught? Ok, so she'd had an accident ... that was terrible ... but, really, what was it to do with him? And why had he just offered to drop everything and fly over to probably go through the same thing face to face?

He took a quick series of breaths to calm himself. "Ok, ok, look where are you? Give me the address and I'll be there within the next twelve hours. You're in Dallas right? Which hosp..."

"I'm not in Dallas I'm in New York City..."

"*New York City*?" Geoff gasped. "When did you move there?"

"Look, do we have to have an inquest about this *now?*" She mimicked his tone exactly.

"No we don't, ok, I'm sorry, now where are you? Oh, hold on, let me get some paper first."

As Geoff hunted around for a piece of paper and a pen a new clip of Hannah started up on the screen, showing her stripping off beside the pool and shaking her breasts at the camera. This distracted him immensely.

"Ok, hold on a second..."

Hannah turned, slipped down her knickers from beneath her skirt and then bent over to show her behind to the camera.

"Geoff!"

"Yep, I'm right here, ok, give me the address."

"I'm in the Brindley hospital in downtown Manhattan."

"And where is that?"

"Down *fucking* town, Geoff! You know Manhattan, there's uptown, midtown, and downtown. Well I'm downtown and that's down near the bottom, ok?"

Geoff snapped in anger. "Ok, I'll find it, I just need to..."

"You just need to what?"

"Look, I'm hanging up now to book my ticket, so I can come over as soon as possible to see you."

Christine sounded sad. "It's a pity you never heard my message Geoff. I finally got my name in the papers."

She hung up, leaving Geoff with a look of confusion and concern on his face.

"*Fuck it, fuck it all!*" he spat angrily. "Hannah, you've got it coming, honey."

He quickly navigated to the video of her at the law office and posted it onto the internet, then moved to a draft email from one of his many accounts, where he had a message ready to send. 'I think you might be interested in this' it said simply, and included a link to the clip. He also included it in the message, just to be sure it wasn't missed. He then waited a few minutes to test that the video was available to be watched, before dispatching the message twice; once to the law firm's contact email address, and then to Ken Kamplann.

"Enjoy everyone." he said as he shut his PC down and headed

for the phone to get a seat on the next available flight heading east, temporarily forgetting the mental commitment he had made to go and see his mother. He knew the toll free number for the airline off by heart.

"Hi, I need a flight to New York City today from LAX … soon as you can … JFK if you can get it, but Newark's ok … err round trip please … can we make that open ended … excellent … business class … cool … yep, credit card."

He read out the number.

Within less than two hours Geoff was at LAX airport boarding an evening flight to New York. He had managed to get a cancellation to JFK, so quickly packed a bag, called a cab, high tailed it to the terminal and arrived just as boarding was announced. He was mentally drained from recent events. On the face of it, things with Hannah had worked out just right; but something inside him felt deeply hollow as he remembered his original idea. He hadn't torn her to shreds; anything but. And he plainly hadn't reduced her to a quivering wreck, begging for forgiveness. But at least Kenneth Kamplann would be happy.

As he took his seat he closed his eyes as an unruly mob of coach class passengers pushed and shoved their way on board a short distance behind him. There was, of course, another major issue going on in his life; his mother, and it was becoming more obvious to him over the last few days that he was reacting instinctively to events without thinking things through. Right now, in a hospital in Georgetown Texas, his mother was suffering from cancer. Her operation might have gone well and she could already be on the mend. But, equally, she could have deteriorated and be on a life support machine. She could even be dead. And here he was heading across the continent in a different direction to see Christine, who as far as he could tell had picked on him just because his name was stored on her phone. Momentarily his thought processes went into meltdown and he contemplated running for the doors and getting off the plane. He hadn't seen his mother since he was a child. He might not even recognize her. But she was still his mother; the only close family he had left, and that had to count for something.

As for Christine, he had no idea what had happened to her. She said she'd been thrown down some steps and left for dead. He shuddered in horror. Had someone tried to kill her? He tried to summon up some feelings about this person who had consumed so much of his emotions in the past, but right now he wasn't sure what he felt for her after all this time. If she told him that she loved him and wanted him back what would he do? He really didn't know. He put his hands to his head and groaned as these conflicting thoughts bounced around in his brain.

Subsequently a deep rumble interrupted his mental torment and he opened his eyes in alarm. For a moment he had entirely forgotten he was on board an aircraft. Outside the window the standard airport panorama began to move slowly past as the large jet commenced its take off run. He felt the fuselage creaking and flexing, as the tyres ever more quickly absorbed the regular bumps between the huge concrete slabs that formed the runway. Then the acceleration kicked in hard, and within only a few more seconds his view angled upwards dramatically as they lifted off and banked around sharply. Sunlight streamed temporarily into the cabin windows and then switched off abruptly as the wings levelled and the aircraft began a steady climb heading east. For the time being it would have to be Christine's emergency that came first.

15

Friday

It was now mid morning in a luxurious Manhattan hotel room, and over by the window Geoff was sleeping awkwardly on the couch, which was large but not large enough for a full sized adult to rest comfortably on. Currently he was curled up with one arm hanging down onto the floor, one leg bent fully at the knee, and the other one elevated awkwardly to clear the armrest. Nearby there was evidence of eating and drinking littered across the floor, with two small wine bottles and a number of empty miniatures from the mini bar lying alongside the remnants of a club sandwich ordered from room service when he arrived in the small hours.

Geoff felt quite at home in New York City, despite not knowing where the hospital was. He had visited several times during the last few years and he knew some of the sleazier districts quite well. He didn't particularly like the place, it smelled, the people were often rude and impolite, and the weather sucked compared to Texas and California, but there was a sense of edginess about the place that he found hard to resist.

Late last night, as the aircraft circled widely over Manhattan and Long Island waiting for permission to land, Geoff stared down at the glittering mass of lights beneath, knowing that behind one of them Christine was lying in a hospital bed with injuries unknown. As the last few passengers took their seats and everyone prepared for landing he relived their final breakup; the moment a five year relationship ended because of a piece of paper.

It was a receipt, in fact, that indicated he had been out for a meal with someone, when he had led Christine to believe he was listening to a seminar at the university business school. The recollection of the actual moment of discovery still made him squirm in horror, even after all these years. He had spilled some guacamole down the front of his jacket during the meal with Laura Quinn – a friend who he used to turn to when he struggled with his course work, and with whom he had occasionally shared some of his relationship troubles. She was a very pretty girl and Geoff had fancied her like mad, even during the early stages of his relationship with Christine, but there had never been anything between them. She had a long term boyfriend who lived in Seattle and who used to fly down to see her every month, but besides that Geoff had neither the ingenuity nor the enthusiasm to try and maintain two relationships at once.

A week later, when the jacket was worn again, the stain showed up clearly.

"Oh I remember," he had explained when Christine asked, "I wore it for the seminar and they had some chips and dips at the buffet section afterwards. I think it must have happened then."

"Hey you never said anything about a buffet." Christine had joked in reply, "Why didn't you bring me a doggy bag?"

And they both laughed.

"You ought to get that dry cleaned," Christine had said, "that's a nice jacket; it would be a shame to mark it permanently."

"Ah don't worry about it," he replied, "I'm sure it will come off in the wash."

"No, hang on, there was a coupon in the paper to get a garment dry cleaned and another one done for free," she persisted, "I tore it out of the paper last night. How about that? Hey, gimme the jacket and we'll take it along with that nice long coat I use for interviews."

"Ok," he said, "I'll take it off now and we'll go to the dry cleaners tomorrow instead, we don't want to be late for…"

"You know that's your trouble; you procrastinate. Let's do it now," she insisted, "you're always putting things off. We can go via the dry cleaner on the way to the movies. Now gimme that jacket."

She then playfully wrestled the jacket from him.

"I know you, you'll hand the Goddamn thing over and leave twenty bucks in the pocket, and assuming they find it they'll think it's a tip."

He relinquished the jacket, still laughing from their mock fight.

"See," she said, fumbling inside, "here's some paper, oh, it's only a receipt for..."

She stopped and looked at the miniature document, simultaneously noticing the colour draining from Geoff's face.

"It's a receipt for a meal for two at Brett's. When did we..."

Geoff shook his head but didn't speak.

She looked at the date and time. "This is for a week ago," she said, "at five thirty. Hold on a second." She quickly looked over at the calendar on the kitchen counter. "This was when you told me you were at that seminar."

Geoff then immediately panicked. He had bumped into Laura on campus and she had asked him if he wanted to meet up for a coffee or a sandwich or something. They hadn't spoken in a while. She had suggested the time. There had been a seminar at the business school, but he'd had no intention of going to it.

"I, err ... the seminar was cancelled. I..."

Up until that point there had still been a way out of this situation but Geoff wasn't quick enough to spot it. Saying the seminar was cancelled was not good, because Christine could have easily checked with the business school. He should have said he bumped into one of his, *male*, buddies and they went for a meal instead. And Geoff could have owed this particular buddy dinner from some fictitious time before.

"So, who did you go out for a meal with? *Who* did you buy dinner for?"

By then Geoff's mind had gone blank.

"Give me your phone, now!"

"What? Oh come on, I just went to get some..."

"*Phone! Now!*"

"Oh Chris, what do you need to see my phone for? There's nothing going on here."

"I know you, Geoff. Since you've had that new phone you always forget to clear out your sent messages."

"There's nothing on my phone, damn it!"

"Maybe not, but hand it over now so I can check."

Geoff meekly handed her his cell phone, knowing full well that Laura had sent him a message to check if they were ok for their date. He had immediately deleted it, but then sent her one back saying 'yes' they were ok, and this would still be in his sent messages folder.

Christine quickly flipped through the menus on his phone as Geoff stood and watched. He felt powerless. What was to come would be truly awful.

"Here, sent messages, look there's a whole bunch of them. Now let's go back a week. Ha!"

She turned to him. "There's a message here sent at 3:30pm saying, 'ok see you at five'. Now how about that? It seems to have been sent to a contact called 'UT Phil'."

Geoff sighed. "Yeah, Phil, I saw him earlier that day, we decided to skip the seminar and go eat. I owed him from the time before."

"Well why did you say you spilt food on your jacket at the buffet after the seminar?"

Geoff then looked down and muttered something under his breath.

But Christine smiled. "So you went out to eat with Phil, that's ok, and you owed him one, which explains the receipt, that's ok too."

Geoff managed a slight smile. "See, there's always an explanation for things…"

"And I would have believed you, Geoff, if you'd have said that up front. You met this Phil guy, decided to skip the seminar and went out to eat."

Geoff's stomach then turned upside down again.

"The trouble is now I'm going to have to call him to check. You don't mind that do you? Then we can put this whole little incident to bed and go to the movies. I really don't want to miss the start, do you?"

She smiled sarcastically.

"Ok, I'll call him." Geoff replied feebly.

"Sorry, no," she replied flatly. "Did your description of events actually occur in reality? I'll ask you one last time. If it did, fine. We'll go to the movies and perhaps even forget about when and where the stain on your jacket appeared. How does that sound?"

Geoff couldn't speak. He shook his head with his mouth hanging open, and then he died inside as she hit the button to call 'UT Phil'.

"Let's hear what Phil has to say then, shall we?" She said, switching the loudspeaker on.

Geoff's mind raced, willing Laura not to pick up the phone. Please, he thought, buy me some time. Please, the answering service, please... It rang and rang and rang.

"Actually, you speak to him." Christine walked over and thrust the phone into his hand.

"Hi Geoff." The bubbly voice of a female echoed around the room.

"Hi," Geoff replied, sounding like a man condemned.

"Ask if you can speak to Phil, then," Christine said. "That must be his girlfriend, right?"

"Is ... Phil there please?" Geoff asked quietly.

"Phil, who's Phil? Geoff, is that you? My boyfriend is called Dominic, remember? He's in Seattle all week..."

Then Christine smiled enigmatically and took the phone from Geoff, before hanging up the call and switching the phone off.

"If you take only one thing away from this," she finished, "let it be that perception is key. Up to a point, I don't even care what *actually* happened; my perception is that something did, and you tried to cover it up. And I'm afraid there ain't nothin' you can do to change that; not now, not ever."

Christine left one week later, although her decision was already made on the day the incident occurred. Things had been slowly stagnating between them for months and this was probably why. She was tired and needed a change, and so when Geoff came back home from an afternoon study period in the campus library a week later, there was a cab waiting outside the apartment with her stuff already loaded in it. The engine was running, as was the meter, so there was little time for explanation. She presented him with an envelope containing the keys and left with scarcely a word spoken, and with no forwarding address.

It was now just after 10:30am and an alarm clock was ringing noisily by the bed in Geoff's hotel room. It took a while for the noise to register, but eventually he heard it and groped around trying to switch it off. When his hand scattered the wine bottles with a noisy clatter he looked up in surprise, realized he wasn't on the bed, and groaned noisily. He slithered off the couch and crawled across to the bedside table to silence the clock.

After Christine left him, the sparkle seemed to go out of Geoff's life for quite some time. He felt no need to socialize with anyone. Phone calls from friends went unanswered. Things that he used to find funny now seemed flat and pointless, and the music that used to move and inspire him just made him feel like bursting into tears. The relatively healthy eating regime he and Christine had previously stuck to went by the wayside, as did any semblance of pride in the way either he or his living space looked. One thing he did maintain was the condition of his car, because whenever he had any free time at all he would load it up with a cooler and some food and head out along the empty roads of rural Texas. Somehow the freedom of driving in the beautiful countryside surrounding Austin with the windows down, with only the roar of the wind and the noise of the engine, just about helped him to keep his sanity. He did resolve to win Christine back though, even if it took him twenty years. He had let her down by meeting Laura behind her back and lying about it when he got caught. And he had let himself down in the process. He discovered a new form of loathing every time he looked in the mirror; quite different from what he had felt after killing Danny Stanley. He was determined to become a 'tragic' human being, and for a long while felt totally undeserving of most of the things that constituted a normal life. This was to be his self proclaimed wilderness period.

As he sat on the bed and yawned though, he tried his best to feel positive. Because after his gloomy recollections on the flight over he had made a major decision in the early hours, as he rattled into Manhattan on the A-Train subway. There would be no more 'setting the record straight'. Hannah was the first and the last, and he had lost an amazing girl and a fantastic potential opportunity for happiness in the process. There would be no more answering small ads from people plotting revenge on ex-lovers, no more relationships with an end point determined by someone else, and no more concocting lies and excuses. Once was enough. It had been a stupid and embarrassing idea, and one that he felt no need to share with anyone else. Hopefully Christine had dismissed it from her mind within minutes of him suggesting it.

And, significantly, there was something else. Any females he became close to from here on in would be told the truth about his unpleasant past. This wouldn't be easy, but it had happened, it was done ... he had killed someone, and there was absolutely no changing it. And from now on it wasn't going to stay hidden.

He even casually wondered if he should tell Christine.

He got up walked over to the window and smiled, determined to make the best of the day. The sun was shining, he was here in New York City, and nothing was going to go wrong. The only downside was Christine's unfortunate situation, but at least he was going to see her again and that had to be a good thing.

Also, he would go and see his mother immediately after this trip and try and make his peace with her. But first he would call the hospital; he would do it now.

He quickly obtained the number for the hospital in Georgetown, Texas and dialled before he had the chance to think too much about it.

"Hi, yes, I'm enquiring about Lizzie ... err, Elizabeth Dealer ... I believe she's a patient there."

"And who is calling please?" Came the reply in a smooth Texan drawl.

"I'm a distant cousin ... I heard about it in a letter. I was just wondering if..."

"I'm sorry, we only ever speak directly to immediate family Sir, you'll have to..."

Geoff sighed in agitation. "Ok, here's the thing; I'm her son, my name is Geoff Dealer, and I received a letter from her a few weeks back but I've only just opened it. I mean, I only went to my PO Box a few days ago and I found it there..."

"Ah, I see..."

"Is there any way at all," Geoff asked in a semi pleading tone, "that you can *not* actually tell her I've called. It's complicated, see, I live in California, but right now I'm in New York, and I *do* want to come and visit but I'm not sure when … and I don't want her to…" His voice tailed off.

"We know about the situation, Sir," the voice replied softly, "I understand why you don't want her to know you've called."

Geoff sighed and looked up at the ceiling. "Is she ok?" he asked.

"She's stable after the operation, but if I were you I'd try and come over if you can. She's not in any immediate danger, but … well … she's an old lady and you never know with this sort of thing."

"Ok, thank you, *thank you*" Geoff said, relieved. "I'll come over as soon as I can, I promise."

He hung up the phone and put his shoes on, wondering briefly whether he had already got up and dressed or whether this was how he slept, then disappeared into the bathroom to clean his teeth and take a pee. He returned shortly after, drying his hands on a large bath towel, picked up his jacket and left for the restaurant with a sense of urgency in his step.

16

It was now approaching midday and Tara reappeared at the hospital. This would be her second extended lunch break in the same week, but she promised to her line manager that she would make up the time after normal hours.

"Hi Christine, how are you feeling today?" she asked as she was shown in.

"Hi Tara, I'm fine ... I guess ... a little better than yesterday anyway."

Tara sat by the bed and held Christine's hand. "The offer is still on for me to go and get you some fresh stuff to wear if you want. It won't be designer stuff, but it won't be bargain basement either ... I'll aim for something in between."

Christine laughed. "No, I'm fine, really I'm fine. I don't plan on staying here long enough to need new stuff anyway. Thank you though; really, I mean it."

"That's ok, if you change your mind though, let me know." Tara sat back and fanned herself. "Gee, it's hot in here. How do you stand it?"

"I know," Christine joked, "I guess my health insurance doesn't stretch to a room with A/C."

"Have you had any visitors yet? Have your folks been?" Tara asked hopefully.

"Nope, no one else has been yet apart from you ... and the police, of course." Christine suddenly felt humiliated that her bed wasn't surrounded by devoted visitors.

There was a long pause and Christine analyzed Tara's expression as she fiddled with her phone.

"Sorry," she muttered abstractedly, "I guess I need to turn this off..." It was becoming increasingly obvious that they didn't know each other well enough for small talk, and suddenly Tara started to feel on edge.

"I hope you don't mind me asking this," she said eventually, "but Paul … what did you actually think of him, as a person? You know, if the situation had been different and all that."

Christine closed her eyes and groaned to herself. She really didn't need this. "You know what," she sighed, "this is kind of a weird situation, and I don't know if I…"

"I know, I'm sorry, and you don't have to say anything, really," Tara interrupted. "It's just that I liked him a lot, and what he did, well, it wasn't really that bad."

She looked away. "I guess I never told you the full story, and you probably don't even care, but I think I put a lot of blame on his shoulders for other things. Things that weren't really even his fault."

She bit her lip in frustration. "Ah, this is stupid, I shouldn't even be here."

"I liked him," Christine replied eventually, "I liked him a lot. I guess if I'd have met him under different circumstances I might have asked him out. He didn't seem the sort who would do the asking."

Tara sighed and her face brightened. "Thanks Christine," she said quietly, "I'm glad you liked him too, that makes me feel good in a strange way."

"You know what?" Christine said, sensing Tara's awkwardness, "I do need to talk all this through with someone, but unfortunately you're not the person."

"Oh that's ok, really it is." Tara shrugged nonchalantly, "I just thought that maybe you…"

"But I will put you in the picture about one thing," Christine continued, "I met a guy when I was in college. We were together for five years. I loved him to bits. But there was something going on in his head somewhere; some trouble. Part of him seemed completely closed off. I actually gave up trying to find out what it was. Eventually we split up, and I heard nothing for another five years until I got a letter from him at my folks' house. He suggested we should meet up again and at the time I couldn't think of a good reason not to. I actually thought it would be nice to catch up. I thought he'd have a family and be all settled down, but he wasn't…"

"Ah." Tara nodded. "Couldn't let go, huh?"

"And he started going on about us getting back together again. It spooked me a bit, to be honest. So I decided to leave, and his parting shot was this crazy idea about getting revenge on strangers; about setting the record straight. I thought he'd flipped and I didn't give it the time of day until something happened to me here in New York over Christmas 2006…"

She stopped abruptly and stared into space for a while.

"All I will say is something changed in me after that 'thing' happened, and since then the idea of revenge has seemed more and more attractive. So yes, if you were thinking of asking, Don Borello was down to someone answering my ad in the paper. But no, it wasn't my idea. And right now, given my current situation, I wish I'd never even damn well *heard* of it! So if you wouldn't mind, I think I need some rest," she grinned sarcastically, "but please stop by again if you're in the area."

"I, err … sure." Tara stood abruptly and walked towards the door. "I'll see you again, Christine. I guess. And I'm sorry for what's happened to you; really, I mean it."

But as she disappeared from sight and closed the door Christine reached for the buzzer in despair.

Thankfully the nurse arrived quickly. "Nurse, please see if you can find Tara; she only left a second ago. Please hurry."

A few moments later Tara reappeared in the doorway and Christine sighed mournfully.

"Tara, please forgive me." She looked up to the ceiling. "You don't deserve to be spoken to like that. None of this is your fault, so *please* stop by again if you can. I'd hate to lose my only visitor."

She reached out her hand and Tara stepped forward to squeeze it gently.

"That's ok," she smiled, "you've been through a lot. I'll call and see you again soon."

Christine nodded in relief.

Tara turned and walked out once again, with a vague smile playing on her lips.

17

"Excuse me, I'm here to see Christine..."

"There'll be a staff nurse along in a second, Sir." A porter replied tersely.

Paul Herrycke quickly cast his gaze in all directions, but at present no one else was in sight. The orderly vanished before he could pursue his enquiry any further, but not long after a nurse appeared at his shoulder, making him jump.

"Can I help you?" It was Louise Thurmann.

"Hi, yes, excuse me, nurse..." he squinted to read her name badge, "nurse Thurmann, can you tell me if I can see Christine Hudson please?"

"And you are?"

"Paul, my name's Paul."

"And are you family?" Louise was mindful of her recent conversation with the NYPD.

"I'm a friend of hers." His voice softened. "I'm sorry, I used to know Christine really well and I've flown in to see her. I've come a long way and I'm still kind of jet lagged."

"I'll just go and check, Sir. She's only allowed a single visitor at a time, and we're restricting it to ten minutes per person at the moment due to her condition, so just hang in there for a few more minutes."

At this point Tara emerged from around a corner, stopping dead in her tracks when she saw Paul a short distance ahead of her. As he looked up his face froze in amazement, and she allowed her smile to widen very slightly, because this had worked out better than she could possibly have hoped.

After notifying Paul's mother on her way home on Monday afternoon, she guessed correctly that if he was going to come over from London he would probably do it sometime this week. And here he was.

"*Tara … what the hell are you doing here?*" he gasped.

And now, although she hadn't exactly planned on what to do next, she felt a sense of wicked satisfaction that she had reeled him in from halfway around the world.

Louise Thurmann noticed his sudden blank stare and looked anxiously back and forth between the two of them.

"I, err, hi Paul. It's nice to see you again."

"Is Christine ok for another visitor?" Louise asked.

"Err, yes ma'am, I'd say she is," Tara replied confidently.

"What are you doing here?" Paul asked again, as his time zone fuddled brain eventually registered that Tara and Christine shouldn't even know each other, and that unless Tara had somehow pried into his private life after their friendship fizzled out, there was no reason at all for them to be acquainted. His mental circuits went into overdrive until Tara broke his train of thought.

"I notified your mom when I found out about the accident." Her eyes widened. "I hope that was ok."

"*You did what?*" Paul blinked hard. "But how do you…"

"I called round on my way home on Monday; she's really nice, your mom … she made me a cup of coffee and told me all about your new life in London."

Paul's head was spinning. "*You* went to my parents' house?" He held his hands up to try and stem the flow of information.

"Tara, what are you doing here?" He asked his original question for the third time.

"Well, it's kind of hard to explain and I'm afraid that I really have to go now," she replied casually, just about managing to stifle a grin of self-satisfaction.

"You make the best of your time now," she added, as she turned to walk away.

"Hey, wait a second," Paul called after her, "how come you even *knew* about me and Christine? I mean…"

She raised her eyebrows enigmatically.

Suddenly Paul became very focused and moved in close to Tara's face. "Look you're going to have to explain this to me, because at the moment it makes absolutely *no* sense!"

By now Tara had also regained her composure. "Yeah, well,

you'd better go in now, I guess you've come a long way."

"Oh, I'm going in alright … but I want to know why you're here?"

"Paul, look, there is a reason, but now's not the time … really it isn't."

"Well for sure you'd better *make some fucking time then!*" he snapped back.

"Look," she whispered awkwardly, "it wasn't my intention to run into you here."

"How do you know Christine, why did you tell my mom, and why are you here? Three questions which are *not* difficult. Unless of course you don't have any answers."

She backed off. "Look, can we talk about this somewhere else?"

Paul was incredulous. "Look at you … you're anxious, you're nervous! I can see it in your face. *What's going on Tara?*" He stared at her angrily. "Because I'm getting a really strong feeling that you were expecting me."

Tara waited an age; her gaze wandered everywhere but she wouldn't make eye contact.

"*Tell me what's going on, damn it!*"

She seemed to be wrestling with her conscience as he stared intently at her. Eventually she relented. "Paul, look, I do know Christine."

Despite this now being obvious Paul was still shocked. "What? *How*?"

Tara attempted to be reassuring but failed. "Oh, just a friend of a friend, hold on, actually a friend of a friend of a friend. Isn't it true that any two people are never more than six levels of separation apart? Well that's…"

Paul was unimpressed by this banter. "I don't believe you." He said flatly.

"You don't? Why?"

"*How did you know I had anything to do with her*?" he shouted, ignoring her question.

"Paul, for God's sake, this is all in the past! I mean, isn't it? Look, go in and see her and we'll talk later. Where are you staying? I'll call you."

Paul narrowed his eyes suspiciously. "I'm at the Welford Hotel on Broadway; room 713. I suspect that when I get back I'll be in for the rest of the day."

He scrutinized her face as she quickly scribbled the number on a scrap of paper from her bag and then he turned to walk towards Christine's room.

"Catch you later," she said casually.

When he reached the door to Christine's room, he stopped, closed his eyes, and breathed deeply. The meeting with Tara had seriously rattled him. What was he going to do? How should he act? Tara and Christine knew each other and something, somewhere, felt deeply suspicious. Tara didn't seem surprised … or at least not surprised enough. She had just met someone from her past, seemingly out of the blue, and she had scarcely batted an eyelid. Paul felt suddenly nauseous; something was wrong, and he questioned his whole reason for being here, for deceiving his girlfriend in London by telling her this was a last minute business trip. His stomach turned over and his mouth went dry; the door to Christine's room was right in front of him. After what seemed like an age spent mentally composing himself, he tapped gingerly on the door and stepped in, but stopped just inside the doorway because she obviously hadn't heard him. He stared briefly at one of the loves of his life hunched up under the blankets and didn't quite know what to do.

Inside, Christine had been trying to reach over to her bedside cabinet for her glass of water but couldn't quite reach. She turned back awkwardly when she heard a phone in the corridor and saw Paul inside the room.

"*Paul!*" she gasped. "*Oh my God, what are you doing here?*"

After a few seconds had elapsed he spoke, somewhat falteringly, and for the moment dismissing the appearance of Tara. "Christine … hi, my mom called me when she read about the accident and I just had to come and see you."

Christine shook her head slowly in amazement but didn't reply.

"I've come over from London. I got in last night."

"Paul, it's so incredible to see you, but why did come all the way over here?"

"How *are* you?" Paul's eyes had yet to stray from Christine's, and suddenly he felt an overwhelming urge to pick her up, take her away from here and look after her.

"Me? I'm fine … never better."

"God, what bastard did this to you?"

Christine shrugged. "Oh just some guy; I really know how to pick 'em, don't I?"

Paul appeared to be in a dream-like state. "I can't believe it. I'm just so sorry this has happened to you," he mumbled, "I keep thinking, you know … if we hadn't argued the way we did; if I'd listened to you a bit more, If I hadn't been so stupid…"

Christine was suddenly dismissive; his devoted stare was starting to make her feel a little on edge.

"Yeah, well, that's relationships for you. Maybe I should stop setting my expectations so damn high, then I wouldn't get disappointed quite so often."

There was a long pause as Paul struggled over what to say next. "So how have you been, well apart from this, of course? Are you still working for the *Garden State Sentinel*? Do you still live in Manhattan?"

It very rapidly became apparent to him that the end of their relationship had closed off so many possible topics of conversation. When they were a couple they *never* struggled for something to talk about.

"Yes, I'm still with the *Sentinel*, and yes I still live here in the city, and … apart from my current situation … everything's been fine. Life's been ok."

She sighed and then winced in discomfort; the events of the day were draining her rapidly.

"Look, I can see you're tired," he said, realizing the need to go away for a while and think of something sensible to say, "but can I see you again?"

"Oh Paul, I don't know. I mean where is this going? We're history aren't we … as of quite some time ago?"

"I don't know where it's going," he replied, sounding increasingly frustrated, "probably nowhere … but I'm in town over the weekend. Please can I see you again? I've…" He stopped. The fact that he had come a long way was irrelevant.

"*Oh, I don't know,*" she replied, irritated, "what do you want from me?"

"I don't want anything!" Paul decided to change tack. He wasn't going to get anywhere by questioning her or being obnoxious. "I can get you some stuff if you need it. Or I could just come and keep you company, if you want; tell you all about life in London. Anything you want me to do, just ask, ok?" His eyes widened, "anything at all."

She studied his face carefully. Apart from Don Borello, Paul was one of the last people she expected to see, but the more she thought about it, the more she remembered what a nice guy he had been when they were together. It was her that constantly threw obstructions in the way, because she had to. And in the latter days she had instigated a non-stop series of bitter arguments, eventually pushing him almost to the point of violence.

"Alright, yes," she said eventually, "come back tomorrow, or the day after, maybe. Now I really do need to call the nurse."

"Ok," he said quietly.

Christine turned away and reached for the buzzer at her bedside, and as she did so Paul walked out of the door. As he wandered absent-mindedly out onto the street he put his hands to his head in despair. A few days ago he was living in London, with Helen, doing his job, going about his business, and all thoughts of Christine and New York were a million miles back in the far distance. But then Tara, for reasons as yet unknown, threw this hand grenade into his life from another continent and turned things completely upside down.

Why had she done this? How did she know Christine?

And, significantly, why had he felt such an urgent need come over here? What was the likely endgame? His thought processes were in free fall; he couldn't fathom his own logic, and the mountain of explanations he had left behind in England scared him half to death.

"Hi sweetie, it's been like Grand Central Station in here today," nurse Thurmann said as she popped back into Christine's room to answer the call.

"Can you make sure that if Tara shows up again, to say that I can't be visited until Monday at the earliest? Say that my parents are coming, or I've caught a bug and need to be in isolation; anything."

"Is there anything wrong?" Louise asked, concerned. "Has she upset you at all?"

"No, everything's fine. I need to say a few things to her, but I need it to be on equal terms. At the very least I need to be up and out of bed, but hopefully I'll be out of here."

"Sure, no problem, I understand. I'll notify the folks on the front desk." Louise smiled. "Between you and me there's something about Tara that I don't much like anyway." She winked and left.

18

Approximately thirty minutes later Geoff Dealer walked towards the waiting area outside Christine's hospital room, his stomach crunched into a knot of nervous energy. When he woke this morning he felt fine. When he ate breakfast in the restaurant he felt fine. And when he hopped the downtown subway and walked the short distance to the hospital in the beautiful sun he felt fine too. The feeling of unpleasantness had started as he approached the main doors and walked purposefully through the lobby, and within a matter of minutes it had rendered him on the verge of throwing up. He was here, at a hospital, to see Christine – the only person in his adult life that he felt he had truly made a connection with – and he had no idea at all how to approach it.

What if she was seriously injured, or maimed in some way? He winced and took a deep breath. Play it cool, he needed to play it cool; definitely cool. Whatever she looked like, however she seemed, she was still Christine, and he was here to help. He was *here* to help!

Only to help.

"I'm here to help," he mumbled under his breath.

"Pardon me, Sir." Louise Thurmann was still on duty and she greeted him with a beaming smile.

He attempted to beam back. "Hi, I've come to see Christine Hudson."

"And you are?"

"My name's Geoff Dealer, ma'am. Me and Christine go back a long, long way."

Louise headed off towards Christine's room. "I'll be right back."

Geoff leaned against a nearby wall and straightened himself up against it. He pushed his pelvic bone and his shoulder blades back against the unforgiving surface, closed his eyes and tried to invoke one of the relaxation exercises he had taught himself. Breathe slowly, from the diaphragm, and visualize a tree. Zoom in slowly, look at the branches, then the leaves; focus on the details. Calm, stay calm; focus on the tree. For a brief moment his anxiety receded, but then, without warning, the memory of the shooting started again in his head. He saw his mom and Danny through the gap in the door, he saw what he thought was a fight, and then … suddenly … the noise and confusion and violence of it all. He saw his mom's face contort in horror as the bullet struck. He saw her naked body spattered with tiny droplets of blood. He saw, and heard, Danny Stanley drop to the ground as if the bones in his legs had shattered. And he saw himself, a diminutive figure brandishing a massive shotgun, advancing into the room, ignoring the frantic pleas and screams, standing over Danny, bringing the barrel into line and pulling the trigger again. The blood, there was so much blood after the second shot! He would never have believed so much could come from one person. And then his dad was there. Geoff remembered hiding with the gun, but his dad found him. He took the gun with such force that Geoff was hurled across the floor and hurt his head on the side of a cupboard. And then there were police, an ambulance, sirens, confusion…

"Ok, you can see her, but only for a few minutes." The nurse's voice shocked Geoff out of his silent torment.

"Oh!" he gasped loudly, "oh yeah, yeah, ok; *damn!*" He felt as if he'd just been wrenched awake from a nightmare, with that real sense of fear and disconnectedness from his surroundings. His heart was pounding and he could feel the adrenaline shock in his chest.

"Say, are you ok? You look like you're about to hyperventilate."

Geoff blinked hard and shook his head. "Yeah, it's ok, I'm fine, just having a bit of a panic thing. No big deal." He took a deep breath and closed his eyes.

"Do you need anything? Some air, a glass of water, a chair maybe?"

"No, I'm good, just let me see Christine please."

"Sure thing, just as long as you're not going to croak on me right before I go off duty; I'd have all sorts of papers to fill out."

He managed a half hearted laugh as he followed Louise Thurmann into Christine's room.

"Geoff, oh my God," she cried out, "at last you've got here, I've been lying here for days!"

"Chris, baby! Oh Jesus, how did this happen? Who did this to you? I'll fucking *kill* the son of a bitch who did this to you!"

He reached forward to try and touch her but she put her hands up to stop him.

"I left you a message on Tuesday, or it might even have been Monday. I can't believe you never got back to me."

He shook his head in dismay. "God, Chris, I'm sorry. Someone had been calling me earlier in the week, err..." he hesitated, "a business colleague. He left me a ton of messages, and then I ... *shit* ... I deleted the messages is what I'm saying. I thought they were all from him. Come on I've hardly heard from you in ages."

But Christine was angry. "*I know that, damn it!* But we could at least have a proper listen to our voicemail, couldn't we? We could at least notice who they are from before we delete them!"

"I know, I know, normally I do, but..."

Geoff was silenced for a moment and just about stopped himself from asking why she didn't have any new friends to turn to. He was fuming but didn't want to further inflame the situation.

"Have your folks been up to see you?" he asked, trying to rescue his position.

"No they haven't; they don't even know yet," she replied, looking away.

"Oh my God, Chris let me call them; they need to come up to help you out, to help you get well! Give me the number, I'll do it."

She stared at him. "I haven't told them and I don't intend to."

"What? *Why?* Jesus, Chris you need some support here."

Christine tried to adjust her position and yelped out in pain. "I haven't told them because I'm embarrassed. I'm ashamed at what they'll think."

"*Well, what can they think?*" he spluttered. "You're seriously injured and they need to be here."

For a while there was an uncomfortable silence, until Christine looked him in the eye and sighed out loud. "I was *setting the record straight,* Geoff. I put an ad in the paper ... just like you said you were going to."

"You did what?" Another surge of adrenaline coursed through his chest and welled up into his throat, almost choking him.

"Yeah, how about that?" she continued, "Somehow you still manage to rule my life, even from three thousand miles away."

Geoff was dumbstruck. He shook his head and looked down at the floor.

"So no, I'm not going to tell my mom and dad, because I couldn't look them in the face and lie about how this happened."

"You know who this guy is then?" he asked hopefully. "I hope you've had him arrested."

"Yeah, well there's a problem with that; he's disappeared."

"*What?*"

"Yep, he just vanished into thin air."

"Holy shit, Chris." Geoff looked exasperated. "Are the police looking for him?"

"You betcha." Christine decided not to mention the Mafia connection for the time being.

She put her hands over her eyes, blanking out the harsh light, but leaving luminous green imprints on the insides of her eyelids.

"Damn it, Chris!" Geoff paced over to the window and stared out at the busy street below; the noise of the people and the traffic softened gently by the double glazed windows. Christine wouldn't be in this predicament if it weren't for him and his ridiculous idea. This was all *his* doing! Inside he was seething with anger, but right at that moment he couldn't decide who he was most angry with. Why had she done this? What must have gone wrong in her life to make her even consider it?

Christine shifted position slightly and grimaced as she placed the load on her left elbow.

"You know, you're such a big fella, you're one hell of a guy! I hope this lifestyle choice gives you a nice, warm fuzzy feeling when you climb into bed every night."

"Look, Chris, we've got to talk about this," he said, "Why *did you do it?* Why did you listen to me? I wasn't being serious. I was pissed off and I should never have said those things."

"Yeah, we do need to talk about it, but not now. I feel wasted; I've had too many visitors today."

"Well, who else has been here, for God's sake?"

"Oh, no one important; just two sets of consultants and a detective from the NYPD," she said quickly, deciding now was not the time to mention Tara and Paul.

Geoff avoided her gaze and stared around the room.

"Come back tomorrow evening," she said, "I'm having some scans done during the day and I might have to have an operation to set the fracture in my left wrist. They're saying the bones aren't knitting together properly."

"Oh my God Chris, this is awful," he said earnestly, "I can't believe someone has done this to you." But now it was her turn to avoid his gaze.

"Ok," he whispered, "you rest and get well and I'll come back tomorrow."

He moved over to kiss her, but she made a big effort of turning away, groaning in discomfort as she did so. He managed a peck on the side of her forehead before walking through the door.

Outside, he stepped off the pavement in a daze and a cab almost ran him over. Luckily it was for hire so he jumped in and asked for the South Street Seaport. He needed to stare at some water to calm himself down. As the cab jostled its way through the downtown traffic, Geoff closed his eyes, took a deep breath, and struggled to decide how he felt about all this. He certainly felt deeply shocked that *somehow*, through a few ill chosen words, he had managed to put someone through a terrible ordeal that would never otherwise have happened. But he didn't actually know what he felt for Christine herself, lying there, pale and washed out, bruised and battered, looking almost androgynous in her white shapeless gown, with her hair scraped back. He decided that he had never formally fallen out of love with her, but … but, he couldn't feel anything for her in the state she was in, which was a truly awful thing to realize.

Suddenly the image of Danny Stanley came back to him again, lying there on the floor, staring up with that crazy expression as blood gushed from his neck. Geoff shuddered in horror at the recollection as the cab dropped him off. He had seen two or three people at or very near the moment of death, and for some weird reason Christine had a similar, haunted look on her face.

"Jesus!" he thought as he walked to the rail at the water's edge and stared over at the Brooklyn Bridge. How and why had she ended up like this? He breathed in the fresh cool air from the East River and wondered, semi seriously, if he should go back at all.

19

"Hi, can I speak to Tara?"

"Who is this please?"

"It's Paul, Paul Herrycke. I used to see Tara on the train ride into work."

It was 10pm and Paul was back in his hotel room after having just returned from the restaurant where he had gorged on a massive four star luxury hamburger with all the trimmings. It felt like such a treat to eat a proper hamburger again. Not quite as good as from his favourite diner in Hoboken but far, *far* better than any of the lame attempts he had experienced on the far side of the Atlantic in London.

There was no message on his room phone to indicate that Tara had called, so he quickly browsed the numbers on his phone and, amazingly, her parents' number was still there. So he called and Tara's mother had picked up the phone almost immediately.

"Oh, that Paul, hi, where did you ever disappear to?"

"Err, well, it's a bit of a long…"

"I'll shout her. Hold on."

Tara's mom shouted loudly up the stairs, from where the muffled sound of music could be heard. Within a few seconds, Tara appeared on the line, followed by a loud bang of static as her mother put the phone down.

"Did you see her then?" Tara asked.

"Yes I did."

"And did you tell her how you found out?"

"I told her my mom had read it in the paper." Paul's voice was a flat monotone.

"Well, that's good then," she replied flippantly.

"So how come you know her? Come on, you've had a couple of hours to think of a story, so I hope it's a good one."

Tara sighed loudly. "Well, you know what? I really can't think how best to put it. You want to know what I was doing at the hospital, and how I know Christine, but it's complicated. It's a definite can of worms."

Paul was blasé. "Hit me with it."

After an extremely long pause Tara spoke. Her voice was calm but unsteady. "It was a set up; the whole thing with Christine was a set up."

"A set up, how?"

"Like I said, the whole thing."

"What? I don't know what you're saying. Do you mean at the hospital today?"

"No, no, the whole thing from day one was a set up; from start to finish. I introduced you two; well I pointed her in your direction and she did the rest."

Paul was dumbstruck; he reached over to the phone to hang up but stopped just in time. He remained calm.

"Why would you do that?"

Tara didn't answer.

"And, equally, why would she?"

Still she didn't respond.

"Well, if that's your explanation, then it doesn't really…"

"Revenge," she interrupted, "revenge and to earn money, in that order."

Paul's state of calm quickly evaporated. "Revenge on whom? *Revenge on me?* You introduced Christine to me as an act of revenge! Tara, I … I"

"Yes Paul, revenge." Tara was now serene, "It's as simple as that. It's a very basic human instinct and I have a huge capacity for it."

"But revenge on me; *why, for God's sake?* What did I do to you? Did I ever hurt you? I mean, we weren't even properly together as far as I was concerned. I don't understand. How do I qualify for revenge?"

"You misled me."

"Misled you? How? When?"

"And you hurt me emotionally."

"But…" he replied, now visibly agitated.

"I was very vulnerable when we first met; well actually when we first spoke. I'd been going through a real bad time with my boyfriend. He was a bastard. He promised me all sorts of stuff and then systematically went back on every single word of it."

"He sounds like a real asshole. So where do I come in?"

"I thought you were going to be different."

He gazed at the ceiling. "Well, I was, wasn't I? I don't remember promising you a single damn thing."

Tara didn't rise to this. "Those times I used to see you, on the train into the city every day. I was really beginning to fall for you."

"Oh God," he muttered quietly, "but you didn't even know me."

"From a distance obviously; I mean I'd never even spoken to you, but haven't you ever fallen for someone you've seen walking down the street?"

"A couple of times a week usually."

"Well that's the difference between the sexes. Men are sexual predators, women don't think that way. Well I don't."

Paul couldn't resist sarcasm. "Oh, I hope this isn't going to turn into a sociology lecture."

"And after the first couple of times I saw you I decided for myself that you were a decent person. I saw you give up your seat on the train, let women and old people on and off first; oh I don't know, all kinds of little gestures that led me to believe you were a good person."

"I *am* a good person."

"And then it went on and on, for several weeks. I felt sure you were going to come and talk to me. By this time we had exchanged a couple of glances. I even remember you letting me get up out of my seat when everyone one else was pushing to get off."

"I remember that."

"But you never spoke to me! I felt let down; you could have spoken to me. Couldn't you tell from the look on my face?"

"You could have talked to me."

There was a lengthy pause. "That's not the way it works."

"Oh right, right. Huh, boy do I feel stupid now," he replied caustically.

"And please don't be sarcastic. Why are men always, *always* sarcastic?"

"I'm only sarcastic when someone gives me cause to be."

"Forgive me," she said eventually, "I'm the kind of person with an unending amount of faith in human nature. I always think the best of people. I always give them the benefit of the doubt."

"Ok, ok, but we did talk eventually, didn't we? And didn't I tell you what a shy person I am? I think I did. You know, if we hadn't met on the reverse commute that day, with a whole train carriage to ourselves, I would probably never have talked to you at all. It's stupid, it's a definite character flaw, but shy people like me get to miss out on all sorts of things."

"Oh *stop it*, you're killing me!"

"Anyway, hold on a minute, you said I misled you and I hurt you. How precisely did I do that?" But as Paul asked this question something clicked. Suddenly a grain of sense appeared like a beacon in his confused mind.

"You disappeared from the face of the fucking earth, remember?" Tara shouted hysterically.

"Oh, *right.*" He sighed loudly, putting his free hand to his forehead. "Suddenly the mists are clearing. You want to know what happened there? When I disappeared? I'll tell you. Remember that…"

"Look, it doesn't matter now," she interrupted.

"*Oh, I think it does!* I went to a conference in Las Vegas," he continued, "it was called 'Managing Software Requirements in Enterprise Computing'. Riveting, huh? You'd be amazed at how boring IT can be. I got there, rented a car, drove to the hotel, left the car outside for five minutes, no, *two* minutes, and the Goddamn car was stolen! Right under the stupid jackass valet parking guy's nose! And I'd even left my jacket in there 'cos it was so damn hot. I lost my laptop, my luggage, my phone. So I couldn't call you because…"

"Because you were a jerk off who left his car unlocked and full of valuables?"

Paul just about managed to ignore this. "Because I'd lost your number and, believe it or not, I couldn't actually remember where you lived, because I'd only been there once and that was in the dark! And guess what the final straw was? Within two days of coming back to New York I was transferred to another office out of state for three months. Now how about that? So yes, I did disappear. *Sorry!* But that's the nature of my job. I had no way, *at all*, of getting in touch with you. It was impossible!"

There was a pause while both gathered their thoughts, but their states of mind were very different. For a brief moment Paul felt as if he had Tara on the ropes.

"So," he continued brightly, "you mentioned revenge as your motive, although entirely misplaced revenge as it turns out. What about hers?"

"Look Paul," she sighed ruefully, "I don't know what…"

"What about hers?" He pressed her again.

Tara suddenly felt like throwing up, but she just about managed to stay composed. "Like I said, earning money."

"She earns money from going out with me? But how?"

Then the penny started to drop. "Whoah, hold on. Are you saying that you paid her?"

"That's about the size of it. She ran an ad in the paper. 'Set the record straight', it said. So I called her. And yes, I paid her to go out with you."

Paul was aghast. "For God's sake, how much?"

"Now that, I'm not about to divulge."

"Well give me a clue; fifty dollars an hour, one hundred dollars a date?"

"Nope, it didn't work like that."

"*Well, how did it work?* Was she seeing other guys when she was seeing me? Jesus, we were sleeping together! I want to know what kind of deranged psycho you are to do something like that."

"No, she wasn't sleeping around when she was with you."

"Well, that's good to know! Excuse me."

He dropped the phone, walked over to the mini bar, pulled out a handful of bottles, opened them all and drank them quickly.

He returned to the phone moments later. "Pardon me; I needed a drink."

"Hey, don't mind me."

"It must have cost you a Goddamn fortune then. To buy a girl for, how long was it?"

Finally Tara regained her composure. "You mean you don't remember how long you went out with her for? That's terrible Paul. She'd be devastated."

Paul shook his head. "Jesus, this just keeps getting more surreal. You have to tell me how much this whole thing cost you?"

"I'm not saying?"

"A grand, five grand, *ten grand*?"

"More than five, less than ten," she replied vaguely.

"But how come you had that amount of cash kicking around to spare?"

"Oh, it wasn't spare. I had it earmarked as a deposit on a house. I mean honestly, living with the folks at my age."

"But, but why..."

"Believe it or not, I won on the State Lotto a few years ago. I won a tad over a hundred grand. Not the jackpot, by any means, and certainly not enough to retire on."

Paul was now bewildered. "Jesus Christ, you could have done so much with that amount! You know five minutes ago I could have..."

He sighed; this conversation was draining him. The line went quiet for a while.

"Hey, it's only money," she replied eventually, "and you know what they say; you can't take it with you."

"And was it worth it?" Paul asked quietly.

"Oh yes," she replied with an expression like stone, and hung up, leaving him staring into space. He sat rooted to the spot for a short while; his face contorted, trying to digest what he'd just heard. Then he called her back and Tara and her mom answer simultaneously.

"Hello, who is..."

Tara interrupted rudely. "Mom, it's for me, get off the line."

Her mother put the phone down heavily, sending a loud clatter up through the earpiece.

"Just tell me this; Christine, now in hospital?"

Tara appeared disinterested. "Like I said before, just earning a living."

"So this was just another assignment for her?"

"Yep, looks like she overcooked it this time though. I think it's very important to know just how far you can push people. She shouldn't be in this line of work if..."

Now Paul hung the phone up, and then took it off the hook. He walked across the room with his fists clenched and then smashed them as hard as he could onto the surface of the bed, over and over until his arms ached and there was a cloud of dust in the air. His first thought was to run downstairs, get in a cab, go over to New Jersey, find Tara's house and then ... and then ... and then what?

He drank the small bottle of champagne from his mini bar in a couple of gulps and then called room service and asked for his supplies to be restocked. He felt stupid, utterly stupid. He felt taken for a ride, he felt foolish. He felt 'flawed' as a person. The last several months of his life had turned completely on the breakup of his relationship with Christine. He had taken a perpendicular career move when he relocated to London. Things were going well before, he was in his stride; he had received a discretionary bonus of a thousand dollars for innovation on the project his team were working on. He could well have been promoted. And then Christine fluttered into his life. Ok, things remained on the straight and narrow to start with, but she was disruptive, she demanded too much. She was sky high maintenance! And as things at home started to drift, so did his performance at work. Looking back, it was all so clear. At the time he just wrote it off as 'pressure', but no, it was Christine. She had slowly but surely dragged him down.

Part of him suddenly was of the opinion that she thoroughly deserved her current position. Jesus, the whole direction of his life had changed because one vengeful vindictive woman had decided it. He didn't know who to blame the most; Tara for setting it up, or Christine for offering such a *service* in the first place. Whichever, or whoever, they both deserved many years of unpleasantness in their lives for this. He pulled off his clothes and disappeared into the bathroom to take a shower.

A few miles west in New Jersey, Tara stood and punched the air victoriously. "*And we have strike number two against Paul Herrycke!*"

She picked up the phone and spoke into the disconnected

receiver. “Sorry doll, maybe you didn’t *really* deserve all this, but…”

And then she put the phone down. “Nope, can’t think of a ‘but’.”

She walked across to her bedroom window and stared out at the dimly lit street and the well tended gardens below.

“My work here is almost done,” she said, her breath misting the glass. “Now I just need one more visit to Christine to assess the damage.”

20

Saturday

It was just after 9am and Paul was asleep in his hotel room, dead to the world. After last night's phone call he'd had a brief, angry shower, and then he'd paced around dripping wet trying to see his relationship with Christine from a different perspective other than his own; trying to see it in the context of a business arrangement. He created little scenarios. He imagined Christine calling Tara from a payphone to give her a weekly briefing. He imagined monthly expense forms being written out, then scrutinized and approved by Tara. Also, he imagined her outlining the parameters of the relationship. You can go this far but not that far, you can do this but under no circumstances do that. But it all seemed so real. He just couldn't imagine Christine switching off from the emotions that she showed when they were together. It certainly felt like she loved him as much as he loved her. Perhaps for the duration of the whole thing it was real. Either that or she was a fantastically good actress. Oh God, would Tara have requested a detailed account of all aspects of their relationship? He shuddered. At this stage in his analysis he became temporarily very angry, especially when he considered if Tara would want Christine to rate him sexually. An athlete in bed he most certainly was not; in fact some of their biggest fights were about lack of satisfaction in that department. Christine had threatened to leave on several such occasions. Now it became clear why she didn't! Paul suddenly wanted to physically destroy something, such was his anger, but he managed to calm himself and stuck his head out of the window for a lungful of traffic fumes.

As he stared vertically down five stories to a fabric awning and a concrete pavement he decided that something *had* to be done about this. The need for revenge consumed him, and he felt he could quite easily watch the two of them drown in dirty water. But no, he had to try to think rationally, and Christine was the person who had inflicted the most grief and disruption in his life, irrespective of the fact that she was only 'acting under orders'. But was he capable of taking revenge on her in a hospital bed? What were his options? Physical revenge? Should he threaten her with violence? Should he go to her apartment, kick the door in and break a few things? No; absolutely out of the question. Well, what about emotional revenge? Should he storm in there tomorrow shouting the odds, calling her an expensive prostitute, or even a cheap whore; surely the names didn't matter that much. Should he threaten her with some sort of legal proceedings? A law suit perhaps, for emotional stress and the misrepresentation of a relationship? There must be something in the statutes that he could litigate against. And what about the subsequent disruption of his life! It should be possible to sue her into oblivion over that.

But personal confrontations were never his strong point. She would probably dismantle him in the resulting argument, even under the influence of sedatives. What could he do? He went to bed at that point, and lay there for a while with the window cracked open letting the sounds of the New York City night filter into his thought processes. He heard car horns, the occasional siren, voices raised in alcohol fuelled arguments. He half expected to hear the chatter of small arms fire. He drifted off to sleep for a while, but was awoken by a group of people outside in the corridor, noisily trying to keep quiet. And then an idea came to him, an easy way to get back at Christine. He would think about getting revenge on Tara another time. He smiled at the simplicity of his plan and then fell into a few brief hours of sound, peaceful, sleep.

The phone rang, waking him with a start, and for a few seconds he experienced total disorientation as to where he was and why.

"Err, hello?"

"Afternoon, or I guess it's still morning for you."

Paul sat up immediately and peered across the room at his reflection in the mirror. He rubbed his face with his free hand.

"Helen, hi, sorry, it's nine and I'm still fast asleep. I was wide awake four hours ago though! So, what are you doing?"

"Oh, not much, I was supposed to be going over to the West End today to do some shopping with Laura and Kaye, but I decided to stay home so I could call you. I'm sorry if I woke you."

"No, no problem, I needed waking; pity you didn't do it earlier actually. They stop serving breakfast at nine, I think."

"What's going on? Is the job thing going ok? I didn't hear from you at all yesterday."

Paul sounded somewhat hesitant. "Err, yeah, it's going fine, no problems. I've got to go in later on today; some clients are in from the West Coast who..."

"You're going in on a Saturday?"

"Well they brought me over here, so they're damn sure going to make the best use of my time. A couple of the guys are going out to the Jersey shore this afternoon, but I guess it wouldn't look too good back in London if I reappeared with a tan."

"When are you coming back?"

"Don't know just yet; it shouldn't be any later than early next week."

He blinked and shook his head at his convoluted sentence.

"Shouldn't be or won't be?" she asked carefully.

"Shouldn't be..."

The conversation stalled. "Have you been eating ok?" he asked, "I know you; it'll be microwave meals on a plate every night if I'm not there on kitchen duty."

"I'm eating just fine," she replied, mimicking an American accent. "I'm slowly getting through all the frozen stuff, so we're going to have to do a major assault on the supermarket when you get back."

Paul felt himself start to sweat as he struggled for something to say. Bizarrely, he somehow felt alienated from the person he had lived with for the last several months.

"Hey, I'm really *missing* you." she said suddenly.

"And I'm missing you too!" he replied earnestly. "I love y..."

"And I'd really love to be there with you," she continued, "I still can't believe you've gone on a business trip to New York and left me here."

"I know, I know, I'm a bastard and I hate myself." He laughed. "You know how many times I've said I'll bring you over here. And I will; this whole thing was done at such short notice, there was no way I could get you in on it."

"It's fine, I understand," she replied, although in the several months they had been together Paul had never given any inkling of being involved with his company's overseas offices. Something, somewhere, didn't feel quite right, but there was no point in questioning it until he came back.

"Ok then, I'd better go. I'll speak to you soon. And why don't you go out with your girlfriends and hit the stores. It'll..."

He stopped before saying it would make her feel better.

"You know, I think I will, because, yes, it *will* make me feel better. I'll give my credit card a hammering. Why not, eh? Perhaps you can buy a few nice things for me? I like it when I buy stuff and you say you'll pay for it instead."

"Why not indeed?" He frowned. "Ok, I'll speak to you soon. I've got to go and get something to eat now, and be at the office by 10. I love you, and I'll speak to you later, and I'll be back to London as soon as I can."

"Yeah Paul, I love you too, and you take care over there. Bye."

"Hey, this is my home town, but yes I will take care, bye."

As he hung up the phone he groaned loudly and flung himself full length on the bed. Last night he only felt pure anger, but this morning the much more sober realization was starting to dawn that the last several months of his life had been completely artificial. They had been *created* by two fucking crazy women, one of whom was hell bent on some sort of revenge, although for the life of him he couldn't see that the punishment fitted his supposed crime. He felt totally overwhelmed, and as he tried to assess the twists and turns and intricacies of it all, his senses started to shimmer and he could feel the red mist rising. How could talking to a stranger on a train have led to *this*? And what about Helen; a beautiful, innocent, English girl who was almost certainly wondering what the hell was going on? He shuddered as a wave of guilt combined with the other emotions he was feeling.

He needed to get away on his own for a few days, preferably

somewhere remote, to try and clear his head. He couldn't go straight back to London feeling like this, and he hoped and prayed that Helen would understand. Maybe he would try and explain it all when he returned. Right now though, he needed to go and see Christine. There were things that needed to be said.

21

Just over an hour later Paul appeared in the reception area near Christine's room. Since talking to Helen he had been to the restaurant for a full American breakfast of pancakes with maple syrup and pecan butter – oh how he had missed that – plus eggs over, bacon strips, sausage patties and two medium sized vats of industrial strength coffee, and since returning to his room had sat with a copy of the papers, scrutinizing the nationwide baseball news in great detail. He was a keen baseball fan but keeping up with things from London always proved difficult.

He had deliberately tried not to think about the specifics of what was to come. He had the general outline of his story, his stomach was full and his head was clear. He planned to just breeze on in there and let the situation develop with the one certainty being that, barring something amazing happening, he planned never to see her again after today.

He approached the duty nurse at the desk. "Hi, can I see Christine Hudson please? I was here yesterday; she is expecting me, I think."

"Sure, I'll…"

"And is it ok if I leave these somewhere safe out here please?" he added, gesturing towards the two items of luggage he was carrying.

"Sure thing," the nurse continued, "you can leave them behind the desk with me. I'll just go and check with her."

She stopped. "Sorry, who are you by the way?"

"Paul, my name's Paul. I was here yesterday."

She scuttled off in the direction of Christine's room and peered around the door, standing for a few seconds nodding her head as if in animated discussion. Then she returned smiling.

"Go straight in," she said.

Paul nodded a silent 'thank you' and walked over and into the room.

"Hi Christine, how are you feeling today?" he said brightly.

She smiled. "Hi Paul, getting better every day, and how are you?"

"Yeah, I'm good." Paul walked over to the bedside, his stomach churning at what he was about to do. It had never been in his nature to do anything unpleasant to anyone in a calculating fashion, but today that was set to change.

"So what have the doctors said?" he asked, by means of small talk. "What actually are your injuries?"

"Well thankfully they're not nearly as bad as they thought when I first came in," she replied. "To begin with I couldn't feel my legs and they thought I might be paralyzed, and I also had blurred vision from the concussion, but that's kind of eased off now. I'm actually feeling reasonably ok. I've got out of bed a couple of times and walked a few steps. They've told me to be careful, but I should be properly up and about and hobbling around in a couple of days. I'm going to need some help though, because of this." She raised her arm in its plaster cast. "Getting the screw cap off a coffee jar is going to be difficult for a couple of weeks yet."

"Well, I think you're amazing," Paul said earnestly, "going through all this crap and keeping a smile on your face…" He hesitated as the saliva dried up in his throat.

"May I?" he asked, pointing towards a glass of water on the bedside table.

"Sure, go ahead."

Paul took a cautious sip and put the glass down. "Look Christine, I have a suggestion to make; and it might sound absurd, but I just want you to hear me out ok?"

She shrugged. "Sure, go ahead."

"You know what, I really flipped out when we split up; I genuinely lost it," he said, "I felt that I had to get out of New York, immediately, and I just went to my boss and said, I need to get out of here, are there any opportunities going out of state, or even overseas."

Christine raised her eyebrows; she had no idea of the depth of his feelings towards her.

"And they were really cool about the whole thing," he continued. "They put me up for a post in London within a matter of days. And it's been fantastic over there. I think it really did me good to move to a different country for a while; somewhere where they only have one season, and where there's nothing but Charles Dickens on the TV."

Christine laughed slightly at this.

"But, and here is what I came here to say to you, I'm a New Yorker. Ok, I grew up in New Jersey but who cares, I'm a New Yorker for all practical purposes and I need to come back. My contract is up in the next couple of weeks so I'm planning to come home anyway. I do have a girlfriend in London but…"

She looked harshly at him.

"But she's not the one for me," he hesitated. "I met her shortly after I moved over there but she's suffocating me. She questions every move I make, every time I'm not where I'm supposed to be, every…"

"Does she know you're here?"

"In New York, yes."

"In this room?"

He looked away. "No she doesn't."

"She's right not to trust you then?"

"Look, I haven't thought it through completely, I'll grant you that. But what is certain is that I'm coming back to the New York office. I'll get an apartment, and what I'm saying to you is I'll look after you for a while; you can come and stay with me 'til you get better. Nobody needs to know where you are, so that way you won't have to worry about anyone coming to call. I'll get you well again; I'll cook for you and do your laundry. And there are no strings, well except that perhaps we could be friends again in the future. But I won't hold you to that."

He gazed at Christine, but he couldn't read her expression.

"I go to the gym now, I work out. I lift weights. I could protect you."

She smiled. "That's very nice and I appreciate the offer, really I do. Even if it is the craziest thing I've ever heard."

"Well, I'm glad you think it's nice," he replied, "I seem to do 'nice' really well."

Christine exhaled deeply. "Look, I'm really tired right now, and I think I'm due another shot of painkillers pretty soon. But, well, don't leave town just yet, ok?"

Paul's face widened into a grin. "Do you mean it?"

"I don't know; it depends if you mean it."

"Mean what?"

"That stuff about keeping me safe." She smiled at him. "I haven't heard anything like that in a long time and it's not as if I'm exactly surrounded by people who care about me."

"Trust me; I'm a nice guy." He smiled back.

"But what about your girlfriend?"

"Oh, don't worry about her."

"I'm the same gender as her. I feel I should worry."

Paul stood up and reversed towards the door. "I'll go then, and leave you to think about it. If a better offer comes up, then fine, or if you recover really quickly, that's even better. But if you need a hand for a couple of weeks, or a couple of days even, then let me know, and when I come back I'll take care of you."

He took a business card from his pocket. "Sorry about the card," he said, "that's not even my correct job description anymore. But it's got my latest cell number on if you need to get in touch with me."

Christine smiled broadly; this felt like the nicest any one had been towards her in years.

"Come back next week," she said, "and I'll let you know what I've decided to do."

"Ok, that's good enough for me." He smiled and turned to leave, slowing in the doorway, wondering if he should kiss her goodbye to complete the picture. He decided against it.

"I guess I'll see you next week then," he said.

She smiled. "Yeah, I think you just might."

"Except that you won't," he mumbled as he walked to the nursing station to pick up his bags. As he turned a corner he discreetly punched the air in triumph; his face, though, betrayed some amount of confusion. He had never done anything like this before. But then again, no one had ever put him in such a situation before. And somewhere, deep down in the pit of his stomach, this actually felt good.

The intense heat of the afternoon sun warmed the top of his head as he emerged through the doors. "*Taxi!*" he yelled, as soon as he saw one, and then called out 'Penn Station' through the bulletproof shield as the cab pulled away. And from Penn Station in New York he boarded a New Jersey Transit train bound for Penn Station in Newark. And from there he boarded a bus to take him to Newark International airport.

Once his flight had been booked and he had checked in he went to a payphone, punched in his credit card number and dialled. The decision had been made; the lies would continue for now, but still Paul was not far from gibbering with nerves when Helen answered.

"Hi Helen, it's me."

"Oh my God Paul, I was worried! I called your room a few hours ago because I forgot to tell you about something that came in the mail and they said you'd checked out. What's going on? Are you coming back?"

"Err no, not quite. I'm at the airport. I'm flying over to the Chicago office," he hesitated, "probably only for today and tomorrow. It's an important meeting with a customer."

"*What?*" Suddenly Helen became very suspicious. She didn't know the full details of his work but he had always boasted of staying 'as far away from the customers possible'.

"Paul, come on, is this for real? It's just that you never…"

A loud announcement on the public address system drowned out the last part of this.

"Sure it's for real! Look, I've got to board soon, but I'll call you when I get there and I promise I'll be back in a few days; three days tops, ok?"

Helen sighed in defeat. "Yeah, do whatever you need to do."

"I love you and I'll speak to you soon."

"I love you too; have a safe trip *now*!"

Paul noted the hint of sarcasm as he hung up the phone; he also realized that the hole he had created for himself was deepening by the day.

Within the hour he was climbing into the clear sunny sky, heading due west. Beneath him somewhere in the sprawling mass of the New Jersey suburbs was his parents' house, and not far away in an adjacent township was the house where Tara lived. As he looked down at the random scattering of suburban streets, shops, and parkland he acknowledged the fact that Tara had seized yet another opportunity to wreak havoc in his life by reporting Christine's accident to his mother, suspecting quite rightly that she wouldn't be able to resist telling him, and he would then come running like a well trained dog. He shuddered as the seat belt lights blinked off. At least where he was heading he would have a little time to try and think this whole situation through.

22

"Hey Geena, what's the deal? Has senior staff nurse Thurmann got the day off today? I thought she worked here permanently."

"She's flown off with her daughter to Fort Lauderdale for the weekend. They've gone to soak up some Florida sun."

The police officer was incredulous. "But it's been *ninety degrees* outside! I don't know about you, but I've pretty much got all the sun I can handle."

"Tell me about it; in this weather give me a darkened room plus some serious A/C. So, what can I do for you today, officer?"

"It's Christine Hudson; can I see her for a minute?"

"Sure thing. She's still in the same room, but let me just go and check on her first."

Geena walked to Christine's room and poked her head in for a few moments.

"Go right in," she said on her return, and the officer walked over, tapped the door gently and disappeared inside.

"Hi Christine," he said softly, "and how are you doing today? You're sitting up; that's got to be good hasn't it?"

"Yes Sir, everything's just ducky," she replied confidently, although the sight of a police detective at her bedside still sent a needle of fear shooting down her spine.

"I have some news for you," he continued, "but it ain't the best news I'm afraid."

"Why, what's happened, what's going on?" Christine's expression froze.

"Well, we still haven't tracked Borello down, but there have been some developments…"

He hesitated; a mutilated body had been found in the boot of a car around the back of the premises used by Don Borello and his company in Alveston, New Jersey, so the hunt for him had intensified. His alleged assault on Christine was now an also-ran by comparison, but nevertheless she was still the last person known to have spoken to him.

"Developments, what do you mean by that?"

"Don't worry ma'am," he laughed, "it's nothing too serious; there was a minor traffic accident on the Turnpike yesterday and the car was registered to Borello, but he drove off leaving the other guy stranded. It was a dark grey Lincoln Sedan with New York plates. Now when you were out with him on Saturday night, did he use his car? I know its minor league stuff, but we're clutching at straws here trying to find him. Do you remember what model of car it was?"

Christine didn't, there were far too many other things on her mind at the time. She shook her head. "I don't remember, no, he had a driver. I never noticed the car, but it was a dark colour and it had four doors. I didn't check the plates, I'm afraid." She shrugged. "Sorry, I tend not to notice regular cars. If he were in a Porsche, maybe I would have."

The officer turned to leave. "That's ok Christine, we'll catch him in the next couple of days, I can feel it, and he'll go to trial this time; if not for the assault on you then the IRS have got a pile of warrants waiting for him."

"Well, will I have to give evidence or something?" she asked, suddenly panicking. "Right now I'd be too scared even to be in the same room as him."

"Neeaah, don't you worry about it, these guys aren't the bogey men everyone makes them out to be. They're just two bit criminals, and just as vulnerable to prosecution as everyone else. I think you've been watching too many gangster movies."

"Yeah, I guess." Christine laughed unconvincingly.

"Now you get some rest and I'll catch up with you later."

And then he was gone, leaving Christine not reassured at all. This was *completely* new territory to her. She had never had any dealings with the police before, in any capacity, so to now be embroiled in an investigation involving assault and organized crime was too frightening for words.

Geoff Dealer arrived in the waiting area just before the police officer came out from Christine's room. He was almost an hour later than planned after ignoring the alarm call he had programmed into the phone in his room, and when he eventually woke up he bolted from the building, hurling himself in front of a speeding cab to get over to the hospital.

"Hey, excuse me," he gasped to the first nurse he saw, "excuse me, nurse, can I see Christine Hudson? I mean is she ok today?"

"And you are?" Geena asked politely.

"I'm Geoff Dealer, I flew in from LA yesterday … you weren't on duty then."

At this point the police officer appeared. "Geoff Dealer you say?"

Geoff was suspicious. "Who's asking?"

"My name's Officer Wallace, I'm with the NYPD."

He produced a badge and as he did so Geoff went pale.

"And you are?"

"Like I said, Geoff Dealer, I'm Christine's, well I'm her…"

"Her what?"

Geoff laughed. "Well, I never made it to be her husband. We kinda split up a while ago and now we live on different coasts. But we keep in touch; I flew in yesterday to see her."

"Well that's nice, my ex wife would run me over with her car if she got the chance! I take it you don't know anything about anything?"

"All I know is that some guy tried to kill her and I was concerned enough when I heard that I've come to visit. I'm just here to see how she's doing."

"And how did you find out? Do you get the New York papers every day?"

"She called me, left a message with my answering service."

The police officer nodded approvingly towards the nurse, who was still in attendance.

"Well, that is mighty civilized. Did you guys have any kids together?"

"Nope, can't stand the little fuckers." Geoff turned to the nurse. "Pardon me ma'am."

"Well, I have to go; it was nice speaking to you, Geoff." Officer Wallace stifled a laugh as he walked off.

"Yeah, likewise, officer."

"Yes you can go see her for a while," Geena continued, "but let me just check if she needs anything first."

Geena went into Christine's room and emerged a short time later. "Come on in."

"Hey Chris, what the hell's going on?" he joked. "Some cop outside has just questioned me. Am I wanted in three states or something?"

Christine blinked hard. "Not funny Geoff. None of this is funny, *at all!*"

Geoff put his hands up apologetically. "Chris, hey I'm sorry, I was just a little spooked to be interrogated in the corridor. So, let's start again; how are you doing this evening?"

Geoff moved over to kiss her, but again she leaned away. "I'm sorry baby; you know I still can't believe this! I still can't believe that my best girl for all these years has been…"

"And don't call me your best girl, for God's sake. I'm not now and I don't think I ever was."

Geoff sighed heavily and turned away as the prospect of a positive outcome from this visit rapidly shrank to nothing. Since finding out the reason for Christine's hospitalization, his thought processes had fluctuated wildly between two extremes. A lot of the time had been spent wondering how quickly he could get out of this situation and get back to LA. What if she was stuck here for weeks? Should he stay? And if so, how long could he afford a nice hotel in Manhattan? How long would it be before he'd end up renting a room in some squalid bedsit in Brooklyn, being offered crack cocaine in the hallway, and not daring to leave during the hours of darkness? But each time his thoughts strayed in this direction, he forced himself to stop and think about the person involved. This was Christine, the gorgeous girl he'd fallen in love with all those years ago; the girl who wouldn't be in this position if she hadn't listened to his stupid idea.

At length he mumbled into life. "*Chris, why did you do it?* Why did you feel you had to 'set the record straight'?" he quoted theatrically, "I didn't mean those things I said the last time we met. Something strange was going on in my head…" His voice tailed off and his head hung down.

"So why did you say them then?" she replied very precisely. "Something must have prompted you to say those things. You were very, *very* specific."

He sighed again and walked over to the window.

"Ah, c'mon Geoff, open up for a change; let's have a little honesty here, huh? I'll tell you why I did it if you tell me why you said it. And believe me, I have an *extremely* good reason."

He mumbled something under his breath.

"I'm sorry, but you'll have to speak to me; like I am actually in the room."

He turned to face her and their stares were locked together for what seemed like an age.

Outside in the reception area Tara turned up and asked to see Christine. She had a bottle of wine in her hand and was on her way to meet Becky at Gerhard's flat for what promised to be another alcohol-fuelled, sweaty sexual encounter. When the three of them first got together nearly a month ago, the whole thing felt totally liberating; a real adrenaline rush. But now a large part of her wanted out; she felt she was being drawn into a web of pornography, which Gerhard was probably filming and distributing to his deviant friends. Maybe she would make tonight's meeting the last.

"Hi, yes, can I see Christine please?" she asked the receptionist.

"Sure, just wait one second." A few keys were tapped. "No, I'm sorry, she's not allowed visitors right now. She's caught a stomach bug and is being kept in isolation for a few days."

"Oh." Tara was visibly disappointed. "Oh no, that's too bad. Does it say when she will be well again?"

The receptionist raised an eyebrow at the stupidity of this question. "It says she will be in isolation over the weekend at least."

"Oh right," Tara replied distractedly.

"You can check again on Monday if you like."

Tara sighed. "Ok, thank you ma'am." Even though she and Christine had so obviously run out of things to say to each other, she desperately needed to find out if Paul had gone back since their recent phone call; since finding out about the arrangement. She turned and walked out despondently. Things would have to wait until next week now, although she wasn't sure how long her curiosity could hold out.

"Come on Geoff," Christine persisted, "I'm waiting."

But he had no answer that could stand any level of scrutiny. His mind was racing, desperately searching for a way forward in this conversation that wouldn't leave him looking utterly foolish. But he couldn't see one. He was trapped; just like so many times before.

"Ok then," Christine continued, "it's obvious you weren't of sound mind when you said those things. So let's move on. Did you accept the challenge I set you? Do you remember *that* part at least?"

Geoff seethed and quickly decided to dissociate himself from his idea.

"No I didn't," he muttered.

"Oh, you didn't? You didn't accept the challenge to see through your own idea?"

"No, I didn't, for Christ's sake. It was a stupid idea, a ridiculous idea. I never gave it another thought to be honest."

Christine stared hard until Geoff looked down submissively.

"Well, congratulations," she said flatly, "for the first time since I've known you, you've actually made me feel stupid. So make the most of it, ok, because it's never going to happen again."

Geoff shrugged; he didn't know what to say.

"You know I actually thought you were going off on a mission, to put an ad in the papers, to get revenge on total strangers and get paid for it. That's what you suggested, wasn't it?"

Geoff shook his head in dismay. "C'mon Chris, can't we leave this?"

"No we *can't* damn well leave it," she spat angrily, "I'll tell you what happened to me then, shall I?"

"Look, can't we just..."

"I moved up here a few months after we last met; not because of what you said, but because I needed to get out of Texas. I was stagnating; I'd never been anywhere other than Dallas and Austin. So you did me a huge favour in that respect. But the first Christmas something horrible happened. I went to our office Christmas party and I met this guy. He was really charming, really good looking; he said he was an IT contractor working on redesigning the company website, but he wasn't, and in fact no one knows who he was. Anyway, we spent most of the evening together and then he invited me to another party on New Year's Eve, at some new club on the upper west side. He said it was exclusive, that it was hidden away in some warehouse. And, hey, guess what; I believed him."

Geoff was starting to look increasingly agitated. "Chris, please don't tell me that..."

"It was pretty near my apartment, so I walked over there, and I went in," she continued, her voice starting to falter, "and he was there to welcome me. But something was wrong. There was nobody else there, and straight away he started to make suggestions; vulgar suggestions. And then when I said I wanted to go, he grabbed at me; he shoved me against a counter, but I grappled with him and somehow I managed to break free. And I ran for the door. But I'd lost my bearings and actually ran deeper into the building. And then he was chasing me, down corridors, through empty rooms, laughing hysterically like it was some big game. But I felt like I was running for my life! Soon I was gasping for breath, but I kept going until he caught my shoulder and I ran into a doorframe. I went down, and the bastard was standing over me, exhausted and coughing his guts up. I actually thought he was going to have a heart attack, but he kicked out at me on the ground. The son of a bitch caught me right in the stomach and then in the chest. God knows what damage he might have caused..."

Her voice cracked as Geoff winced in horror.

"But you know what?" she continued, "I must have been fitter than him because I managed to haul myself up and I ran and I ran until I burst through a door and out onto the street. I don't think he even followed me because I was lying in the gutter for ages trying to get my breath. And no one came past, can you believe that? Out of the millions of people crammed into Manhattan on New Year's Eve, not one of them came by."

"What did you do? Jesus Christ, did you call the police?" Geoff asked urgently.

"I did, yes, but it was New Year's Eve, for God's sake, and all I could say was that some guy assaulted me, but I didn't know who he was or where he was. And when I told them I wasn't in any immediate danger they all but hung up on me."

"Oh Jesus, Chris, I can't believe this! So they didn't find him then?"

"No they didn't. And when I went back to work and asked questions, nobody knew who I was talking about. He was a total stranger, who had somehow gotten into our Christmas party, and out of everyone in the room, he chose me!"

"Oh my God, Chris, oh my God!" Geoff paced around in circles.

"Yeah Geoff, how about that? Your 'best girl' escaped from the clutches of a madman in a deserted building."

But Geoff couldn't speak. He felt like there were hands around his throat, squashing his windpipe.

"I'm telling you, I couldn't sleep properly for weeks after that." She stared him straight in the eye. "And you know what I kept thinking? You know what words kept coming to me when I woke up terrified in the night?"

Geoff shook his head, even though could sense what was coming.

"I remembered what you said outside Jodi's Diner the last time we met. You said if life gets on top of you, if someone else messes you around, then find a total stranger and set the record straight."

"Oh no, Jesus, *Jesus!*" Geoff wrung his hands in despair.

"And here I am," she smiled sarcastically, "just escaped from someone else who tried to kill me. Boy oh boy, I must be doing something wrong."

Geoff muttered incoherently.

"But I did do it though. I carried out your idea. Are you proud of me Geoff? Huh?"

Tears had formed in Geoff's eyes by this point. "God Chris, I want you back! I want to look after you, and try and make up for all the crap you've been through. I can't believe all the stuff that's happened to you, which wouldn't have happened if it wasn't for me. *Fucking hell!*"

He smashed his fist against the wall and hung his head in desperation.

But Christine was very calm, and at that moment she saw a tiny opportunity for revenge. "Geoff, I want you to get out of here for a while, because smashing the place down isn't going to solve anything. Give me an hour. I need to think about a couple of things and I need the nurse to help me get to the bathroom."

He turned back to her, desperately trying to stifle the tears. "I'm sorry Chris, really I am."

She smiled softly. "An hour Geoff, ok?"

"Ok, I'll be back in an hour," he mumbled. "I'm sorry Chris, for all of this."

As he walked out, Christine smiled to herself as she climbed out of bed and walked slowly into her en suite bathroom, placed some toilet paper on the seat and sat down to pee. She had already decided she was checking herself out on Monday, whether or not Paul came back, so here was a golden opportunity for Geoff to receive a token payback for the way he had somehow managed to steer her life off a cliff without even having to think about it. But she would have to approach this carefully. What she was planning to say to him mustn't sound like too much of an about turn.

23

"Excuse me Sir."

Geoff looked up a few minutes later and realized he had stopped in a doorway and there was an elderly gentleman trying to get past.

"Hey sorry fella, I'm daydreaming." He stepped to one side as the man hobbled past, relying heavily on a walking stick.

"I'd say cheer up, it might never happen," the man said, "but you'd probably ram this walking stick up my ass."

Geoff was taken aback, but then the old man laughed, swapped the stick between his hands and reached out. Geoff laughed too and shook the old man's hand.

"You have a good one, Sir." Geoff said.

"You too, Son."

They walked off in opposite directions and suddenly Geoff was flooded with a warm sensation in the pit of his stomach. He turned back to see the old guy hobbling off around a corner and thought for a moment, trying hard to remember the last time he was called son.

As he wandered the streets of Lower Manhattan, he desperately tried to take stock of what had just happened, and more importantly his pathetic outburst that he wanted her back. Yes, he did feel some strange unidentified obligation to look after Christine until she was well again, but did he really want her back?

In his estimation, she had treated him like dirt since he had dropped everything and flown over to see her, so now, deep in his heart, he really wasn't sure what he wanted to do. And also he didn't really *feel* it could ever be possible to make up for all of this. It had quickly become apparent when they were together that Christine just wasn't the sort of person you made up to. God knows, he had tried enough times; but it seemed like she was the one who arbitrarily applied some unwritten rules to decide when things were alright again. He could be making up for this for the rest of his life. And, of course, it would be used as a stick to beat him with at any point stretching far into the future. There was no way this would ever be expunged from his record.

He sighed and gazed up at the night sky.

How could one person have the ability to so comprehensively turn his emotions on their head, over and over, with a few simple words? In a strange way he admired Christine immensely for the way she could crush him with a simple statement of unhappiness, how she could cause his blood to run cold with dread at the prospect of upsetting her. There were so many times during their relationship that she had deserved similar treatment, but he just didn't have it in him; and he doubted he ever would.

Also, as he walked he cast his mind back to their last meeting in Austin. "*You can do this too.*" He had shouted. "*Find a total stranger and set the record straight!*"

He stopped still in an empty side street and closed his eyes tight, acknowledging a sudden burning need to confront what he had done to Hannah and why.

"You ok, Sir?" A voice bellowed a few moments later as a New York City police car drew alongside a solitary figure staring into space.

Geoff jumped in surprise. "Me? Yes officer, I'm fine, just doing a quick lifestyle assessment."

"I suggest you move along, Sir," the police officer replied abruptly, "this block ain't the safest to be walking along any time of the day."

As the car pulled away, Geoff decided he would tell Christine about Hannah. He had to get it off his chest somehow.

An hour passed quickly and soon he was back in the hospital again, but as he was shown to Christine's room there was a different nurse in there and he overheard a snippet of their conversation. 'Tara was here earlier,' the nurse said, 'I know you told Lou that you wanted to be informed if she showed up again.'

"Oh, excuse me." The nurse apologized as she came face to face with Geoff in the doorway.

"Pardon me, ma'am." He stepped back deferentially to let the nurse leave.

As he entered the room he chose not to ask who Tara was, but somehow Christine was different. Her mood had changed.

"Geoff, I was pretty angry earlier on," she said straight away, "but I think I'm entitled."

Geoff shrugged helplessly and shook his head.

"And yes," she continued, "I'm feeling pretty sorry for myself at the moment, but wouldn't you in my position?"

"Err, I guess."

"But you know what?" She looked him straight in the eye and her expression softened.

"None of what has happened to me is *really* your fault."

She let this statement hang in the air for a while.

"It's like you saying to me, 'If you want the best adrenaline rush ever, try skydiving', and then I try skydiving, something goes wrong, and I end up as an imprint in the grass. Or maybe you say to me, 'If you want the best seafood go to such and such a restaurant', and I go there to eat, get food poisoning, and end up hospitalized for a month. Were either of those your fault?"

Geoff shook his head vaguely to indicate that they weren't.

"I'm an independent person Geoff, and yes some bad things have happened to me, but it's not right for me to blame someone else. Not *really* it isn't."

Again, Geoff couldn't think of anything constructive to say.

"We had fun me and you, didn't we?" she said, suddenly smiling.

"Err, yeah we did," he replied cautiously.

"You remember how every weekend we used to get up early and go for breakfast at Jodi's or Brett's, and then go out and spend the whole weekend travelling around in that crappy old car of yours?"

"Sure I remember, Chris."

"Monument Valley was my favourite of all; when we got up at 5am and drove out to see the sunrise. That was just awesome; with that thunderstorm off in the distance."

"Yeah it was," he sighed, now intensely curious.

"And the time we drove up to Zabriskie Point in Death Valley and the car overheated." She laughed. "We had to abandon it in the middle of the road."

Geoff laughed too, more out of nervousness than anything else.

"What's on your mind Chris?" he asked.

She looked away, embarrassed. "Oh, I don't know. I don't know how you're fixed. You've flown all the way here from..." She stopped. "I don't even know where you've come from."

"LA, I'm living in LA at the moment."

"Oh, but."

"Yeah, I moved there not long after we last met. I think the change of scenery did me good."

"And do you like it over there?"

"No, but it has an ocean, which makes up for a lot of things. Look, Chris..." he paused for several moments, gathering his thoughts. "You know what I said earlier, about not giving my idea another thought."

"Yes Geoff, I absolutely do."

"Well it isn't true." He looked down at the floor. "I did put an ad in the papers, and within a week I got my first call. I met a fantastic girl called Hannah. I only just finished with her, in fact. My client was very pleased; she had embezzled some money from his company and I got it back for him, and then to complete the job I've done something that'll almost certainly get her fired. So yes, I did it too. I did what I said I was going to do."

He looked her straight in the eye. "And do you know what? I feel like a piece of crap because of it. At least you had a reason for wanting to get equal."

"And you didn't, I take it?" she replied.

"I was lost, Chris," he said simply. "I felt there was nothing for me in Austin any more so I went to LA, but I was alone, and I was pissed off. I felt I'd wasted a chance to try and get you back. So I started going to the ocean, for hours at a time, sitting on the beach thinking about stuff. And then one day something just went *ping* in my head. And I just thought why not? I'd try and get back at someone. Just to see if it would make me feel better."

There was a long pause before Christine spoke. "Well, well Geoff, I'm almost impressed. In all the time I knew you, you were always full of big ideas, but not one of them ever came to fruition. You could have done so much when you finished your education but it seemed like something, somewhere in your head, was holding you back. You were drifting, and that's one of the reasons I couldn't stay with you."

Geoff cast a quick glance at the clock and saw it was nearly the end of visiting hours. Could this be his moment to tell her about Danny Stanley?

"But this is a real turning point," she continued, "it's a shame about poor Hannah of course, but finally you've delivered on something."

She smiled enigmatically and Geoff managed a nervous laugh. He really couldn't tell where this was heading.

Christine closed her eyes and took a long, quiet, deep breath. "Look Geoff, you were always one of the good guys," she said eventually. "I'd only been out with one guy seriously before you, and a couple since, and you know what? They were all assholes in one way or another. I mean, I know we had our problems and differences, but I felt we were good together."

Now Geoff's stomach was churning. "We *were* good together."

"We had fun; and fun is *so* important."

"What are you trying to say, Chris?" he asked; his mouth was now dry.

Christine looked visibly uncomfortable and sighed loudly. "I don't exactly know what I'm trying to say. We were good together, and, perhaps we could be good again."

"*What?*" Geoff gasped in amazement.

"And I'm not just saying this because I'm incapacitated at the moment, I really do think that. Oh, I don't know?"

She looked down as Geoff scrutinized every aspect of her body language. Was he really hearing this correctly? This was what he had always wanted, since the day she first disappeared out of his life in the back of a cab, and then the second time five years later at Jodi's Diner. But after all that had happened in the last few days, any suggestion of it coming from her seemed utterly absurd.

"Think about it Geoff, please think about it. That's all I'm asking. Please, *please*, think about it."

"Jesus, Chris, yes, of course I'll think about it."

"And can you come back on Monday afternoon? I'm having some more tests and some physio tomorrow, so I'll be whacked."

Geoff reeled through his mental timetable in an instant. He needed to get to Texas to see his mother, but it could wait another day or so surely.

"Yeah Chris, I'll come back," he murmured.

"I need some fun in my life again, Geoff," she said earnestly, "and that's one thing you always gave me."

Geoff left the hospital for the second time, probably more confused than he'd ever been in the whole of his adult life. Yesterday Christine had taken him apart for not listening to a voicemail, earlier today she had all but blamed him for her assault, and now she was hinting that they should get back together again. This was all too much to take in at once. Relocating to the other side of the country would certainly solve the problem of Hannah trying to find him again, and his work as a trader could carry on from anywhere. But there were bound to be a boat load of other problems to consider. He needed to think.

"Times Square," he yelled as he hailed a cab and jumped in.

The taxi spluttered and lurched forward, its engine sounding desperately in need of a retune, and in the back Geoff's head lolled from side to side as the bodywork undulated in response to the rise and fall of the Manhattan streets. There wasn't much traffic around and they seemed to be travelling much too fast. Geoff felt slightly nauseous as the slack suspension singularly failed to cope with the road surface. He wondered vaguely if he would make it to his destination. Then suddenly the ride was over.

"Times Square," the cab driver called out.

Geoff paid him and clambered out, heading straight for a topless bar that he'd seen while out walking last night. He pushed past a hefty doorman into the gloom and was immediately hit by a wall of rock music.

"Hi, my name is Cindy; can me and my friend come over and talk to you?"

A woman in a sheer lace kimono and a shiny silver thong immediately descended on Geoff. Underneath her garment the outline of her breasts was visible, even in this dim light, but she looked haggard and care worn and she had to yell in his ear to be heard.

"Sure, where's your friend?" he yelled back.

She pointed in the direction of a clutch of similarly attired women standing by the bar.

"Oh, she'll be right over. Are you gonna buy us both a drink?"

Geoff knew what was coming. "Yeah, why not; you want a beer?"

The woman looked as if she'd just been offered dirty dishwater.

"*No*, we only drink champagne cocktails."

"Uh-huh, and how much might those be?"

"Forty five dollars."

"I sure hope that's for both of you!"

"No Sir, that's forty five dollars each."

Geoff shook his head, although not entirely in amazement.

"Hey, it's only money, line 'em up. Can I have a beer though?"

The woman peeled off and headed for the bar.

"And can I have the second friend on the right please?" he shouted.

"Sure thing, you just sit yourself down sugar, and we'll be right back."

"Ok, but I sure hope you're gonna get naked after finishing your drink."

This time the woman hadn't heard him. He sat down at one of the many vacant tables and put his head in his hands. Nearby on a small stage a tired looking woman sporting a tiny fur covered G-string gyrated around a shiny metal pole, looking intensely bored with the situation. She was obviously young; she had a fantastic figure, nothing sagging anywhere, but her face looked almost middle aged. She wasn't even moving in time with the music, but the sparse few patrons didn't seem unduly concerned.

Much later, Christine heard the sound of a text message being received on her phone. She reached over to her bag and read it.

"What is going on? Have things been finished up as requested? Can't get in touch with him at all now. Need an answer soon."

She sighed and sunk her head into the pillow, wondering if her client, Anna, was similarly in the dark about who she was dealing with. It would be stupid to ask now, but did Anna really know about Don Borello? If she did then maybe this was part of some internal family struggle. Christine shuddered as her mind raced, exploring all sorts of crazy scenarios. Not surprisingly she didn't know much about the organized crime scene, but from the tabloid headlines she knew these people were not to be trifled with. For the moment she couldn't think of a suitable reply to the text so she switched the phone off and turned over. Currently sleep was impossible.

24

Sunday

Paul was standing alone at a scenic outlook in the Badlands National Park where he had parked his rental car, and was staring out at the massive panoramic sky and the miles and miles of strangely pockmarked flatland stretching out in front of him. This part of South Dakota was a place he'd wanted to visit since he was a kid. There was so much American history here, and so much wild and desolate beauty, which right now was what he really needed. As he gazed out over the huge expanse of land stretching ahead of him he felt lost, insignificant, just a tiny speck on the ground. It was a clear morning with little wind, and even though it was still early in the day the temperature was climbing rapidly. He had been here for over half an hour, totally absorbed in absolute solitude. A single car had passed by, but didn't stop. Perhaps its occupant couldn't deal with a crowd of one either.

He was still contemplating how to approach the immediate future. On the issue of how to deal with Christine, his conscience was now much clearer. She was expecting him to return to the hospital tomorrow to find out if she had accepted his offer of refuge; a place to get away from the memories of her accident and recover in peace. He wondered casually if she would have said yes. He wondered if she was excitedly waiting for him to turn up, and then he wondered how she would feel when she received the message from the front desk saying he couldn't make it. Not today. Not ever. He still couldn't quite believe what he was going to do. Oh well. People are cruel to each other on a daily basis, and this would perhaps go some way to repaying all the times she had treated him like dirt, even if she was being paid to do it.

He hadn't spoken to Helen since yesterday morning, so she

certainly wouldn't be aware of his current location, and he was now starting to wonder how to get out of the hole he had dug for himself by taking this random trip away from his supposed business in New York. His flight back to London was tomorrow evening and he was torn. Should he leave it until he returned to try and explain in person? Or should he call tonight from his motel room and attempt to explain his actions over the phone? Both options would be dire, but face to face had a better chance of eventual success. Whichever way he did it, he had decided to come clean and tell her about Christine and his need to go and visit her following her accident. But the information he had learned since then he would almost certainly keep to himself.

After a few moments, another car pulled up and a young woman got out. Paul sighed; his peace and quiet was about to be disturbed. She walked forward to the barrier that he was leaning against, obviously excited and eager to engage in conversation. Paul looked away back to the two cars, which were parked nose to nose, and noticed his was now almost blocked in against a concrete post. A man was still sitting in the driver's seat of the other car with the engine running. The woman took several deep breaths, inhaling and exhaling loudly. Paul pretended not to notice, but already he was wondering. Maybe she and her partner were sex-mad swingers, or maybe serial killers, attempting to lure their next victim to a grisly and untimely death.

"Oh wow, just look at the size of that sky. I mean just look at it. It's awesome!"

Paul looked round, surprised by her English accent. "That's kind of what I am doing."

She was still in a visible state of wonderment. "It's just incredible. I'm not used to being somewhere this open, this massive."

She whirled around, ooh-ing and ah-ing. Paul realized he was expected to partake in this conversation, but did so reluctantly.

"Yeah, it's a big old sky alright."

She gesticulated, indicating largeness Paul guessed. "In England, I'm from England by the way, everything feels so claustrophobic. Everyone is packed in so close to each other. The whole south east of the country is virtually shoulder to shoulder. This is just so wonderful and the air is so clean. I hate London, it's just so grimy."

Paul considered whether to take this any further.

"Tell me about it. I've been living there for the last year."

The girl was amazed. "*Really!* You live in London; whereabouts?"

"Docklands."

She sneered slightly. "Nice if you can afford it. I live in Hackney."

"Yeah, I know Hackney. I ended up there a couple of times."

"When you took a wrong turn, I bet."

"Actually, yeah, both times."

"Wow, that's amazing! So how come you live in London? You don't sound like an East Ender."

Paul attempted drama. "I escaped there from a dangerous woman."

"Shit! And why are you here now?"

"Same reason. Different woman."

"Oh no!" By this time the occupant of the car had switched the engine off and was strolling over. "This guy's on the run from a dangerous woman." she yelled to him, laughing, and Paul started to become restless.

"I'm Leo by the way, Leonora actually," the woman said, "and this is Bruce. He's American."

"And I'm Paul. Hey great, now we all know each other we can swap addresses and stay at each other's houses. That's what polite and friendly Americans do; right Bruce?"

Bruce didn't miss a beat. "Sure thing, I got spare rooms."

Leo looked back and forth between them.

"Hey look," Paul said, turning to walk back towards his car, "it was nice meeting you both, but I really do have to shoot."

"Yeah, it was nice meeting you too," Leo shouted after him.

But then Paul turned around and walked part way back to them. "Actually, no, I need to run something past you guys. Is that ok?"

Leo and Bruce both shrugged indifferently, but didn't actually say no.

"I wouldn't normally do this, but I want your opinion on a little scenario. Ok, here goes. Guy meets girl … guy falls in love with girl … girl is a pain in the ass for all sorts of reasons, but guy still loves her … girl causes guy all sorts of grief and hassle … girl eventually dumps guy after massive fight … guy leaves town … actually leaves country and continent … guy falls in love with new girl on new continent … some time later guy finds out that original girl is in hospital after being assaulted by new guy … original guy comes back to visit … original guy then finds out that he was set up by another girl he knew from before … and that pain in the ass girl was being paid by the girl from before to go out with him … as she was being paid to go out with new guy who assaulted her. Question, what does the guy do? You got all that?"

"And this guy is you, right?" Leo asked.

"The original guy, that is," Bruce chipped in.

Paul rolled his eyes. "Yeah, it's me. Who else is it going to be?"

"Well, I wouldn't have anything to do with this girl, or the girl that set you up, and I'd go back to my new girl," Leo said immediately.

Bruce nodded sagely. "Yep, uh-huh, me too."

"Unless, of course," Leo qualified, "you're in trouble with the new girl for visiting the old girl."

"Which you almost certainly will be," Bruce added.

Paul reached forward and shook both their hands enthusiastically. "Good answers, both of you. And now I really do have to go."

He walked straight to his car without turning back, started it up, and carefully manoeuvred past the other one. He drove off, watching Leo and Bruce disappearing in his rear view mirror as he went.

25

Much later that day Paul was pacing up and down in his shabby motel room near the airport in Rapid City, South Dakota, desperately contemplating what to do. It was now 11pm in London and Helen would probably be getting ready to go to bed, but he felt an almost unbearable need to speak to her; to come clean, well partly, about what had been going on. His flight back to New York was tomorrow morning, connecting with an overnight flight to London, getting him back home on Tuesday morning. But he couldn't wait until then; in fact he couldn't wait another second. He picked up the phone and dialled.

In London, Helen was just leaving a trendy city bar after spending the last few noisy hours in the company of a rowdy gang of her work colleagues. Mark from the customer liaison team had been all over her like a rash, using the excessively loud music as a pretext for pushing up unnecessarily close to her, breathing all over her, and shouting in her ear. It was all predictable stuff; what he'd done before working here, how he'd spent last summer travelling in Thailand and Vietnam, and how he was 'fast tracking' his career and heading for an almost certain promotion at the next round of pay reviews. Somehow Helen managed to feel simultaneously old and out of her depth with this bunch of drunken twenty somethings, but she loved the attention that Mark gave her, and couldn't deny that she had flirted shamelessly with him by surreptitiously undoing an extra button on her blouse and leaning forward more than was strictly necessary. Also, she had stayed until nearly closing time, which was much longer than she had thought would be tolerable.

The gang were all still inside, scrabbling for last orders and contemplating heading for a club, but outside the streets were relatively quiet as Helen walked the short distance to the tube station. She felt good. It was very rare that she went out with Paul on a Sunday night, it was warm, she had a pleasant alcohol buzz, and the almost certain knowledge that Mark would be there for the taking should the need arise. She had scarcely thought about Paul for the last twenty four hours.

The phone rang and rang until the answering machine kicked in and Paul hung up in despair. The last thing he wanted to do was leave a message. He wondered what was going on. Perhaps she was already in bed and had switched the phone ringer off. Perhaps she was in the loo or in the shower. One thing was certain, the phone in their apartment was always ringing, usually with one of Helen's girlfriends at the other end of the line moaning about the latest crisis in her life, and it rarely went unanswered. Paul ambled over to the window and flung back the standard issue heavy duty curtains. Outside, it had clouded over and the atmosphere had become oppressive; they were probably in for one of those spectacular mid-western lightning storms.

He went back to the phone after a few more minutes and dialled again. Surely if she had been in the middle of something it would be done with by now. He thought to himself for a moment. Helen never showered late; she said it woke her up too much. So she wouldn't have been in the shower. No, this time she would answer if she was in. And where could she possibly be if she wasn't? The phone rang and rang until again the answering machine triggered into action.

"Fuck it, where is she?" he hissed out loud.

Then he started to worry. Perhaps she was ill and couldn't get to the phone, perhaps she'd had an accident and had been rushed to hospital; his mind instantly imploded in a meltdown of possible nightmare scenarios. He dialled her mobile phone, and despite himself still winced in anticipation at how much it would cost if she answered. He hoped and hoped that she would.

Helen's phone started to ring in her handbag, and by chance, at that moment she happened to reach inside to look for her travel card, before stepping onto the escalator. She saw the display glowing in the gloom, extricated the phone and saw that the number was withheld. This was strange; a withheld number at this time of night, but something told her to answer it.

"Hello?" The quality of the connection was terrible.

Paul let out a massive sigh. "Helen! Oh thank God, it's great to hear your voice."

"Paul?" she responded cautiously.

"Yeah, it's me, shit this is a bad line. I've been calling the apartment, but you didn't answer."

"That's because I'm not there," she replied calmly.

"Oh well, that's ok I guess."

He wanted to ask where she was, but didn't feel in a position to.

"Err, will you be there soon? I really need to talk to you, to explain what's been going on."

She was currently standing at the entrance to the subway station and stood back as a crowd of revellers barged past.

"Yeah, an explanation would be really good. I'd like that. Call me in twenty minutes. I've got a train to catch."

"Ok, I'll be…"

She hung up and descended into the subway station for the short train ride home. She felt simultaneously angry and relieved, but also quite pleased at the way she'd handled the situation.

Back in his room, Paul put the phone down and sat nervously tapping his feet. She had disarmed him with her cold response and he felt the impulse of the moment draining away. Whatever he needed to say should have been said there and then. He switched the TV on as a distraction and flipped through the small number of channels until he found an old sitcom episode to watch. Also, he noted the time.

Eighteen minutes later Paul guessed that if she had been waiting to catch a train from the city out to their apartment then she should be there by now. For some reason he checked his reflection in the mirror before phoning. Helen had not long returned and was currently drinking a latté that she'd purchased from a late night sandwich bar. This time she answered straight away.

"Hello?"

"Helen, hi there." His voice sounded strained to her.

"So, how's it going?" she asked calmly, "How's your customer doing?"

Again Paul was wrong footed. Given the situation he was expecting instant fireworks.

"Helen, look, there's been something going on here. I've been having a bit of a personal crisis, but I want to tell you about it, and I want to come back; back home."

Helen was sitting at the table in the kitchen with the coiled phone lead stretched out like a tightrope from a nearby work surface. There was a pile of today's washing up in the sink, and a stack of discarded mail and newspapers by her elbow. She was tired, slightly drunk, and not in the mood for a telephone argument, but the coffee was working miracles at sluicing the blood around her veins. She felt as if she hadn't slept properly for days, and she felt angry that Paul was putting her through this; whatever it was.

"Go on then, tell me about your crisis. I could do with a bit of drama to relieve the boredom of living here on my own."

"Helen, look, I'm sorry for…"

"Where are you, by the way?" she interrupted.

"Rapid City, South Dakota. I was…"

"*Where?* I've never even heard of it! Does your company have offices there, by any chance?"

"No, no they don't, I've just come out here to clear my head a bit. There's a fantastic national park nearby called The Badlands. It's like a lunar landscape and it's…"

"Sounds great," she interrupted again. "So this isn't work then?"

"No, this part's not; it's … I just came here because…"

"Is this to do with your crisis?"

Paul squirmed. "Well, no, that kind of happened at the weekend. I just thought I'd…"

"Right, this isn't work, and it isn't your crisis. So what is it? Sightseeing?" She felt her anger rising.

The line fell silent for a moment.

"Look," Paul said eventually, "I've got something to explain here and I *really* didn't want to do it over the phone, but it needs to be said, and you need some time to think about it. So I'm going to tell you, and then I'm going to hang up the phone, then I'm flying back tomorrow night, so I'll be in London first thing Tuesday morning."

"Tuesday! So you're *still* not coming back yet?"

"I'm flying back to New York tomorrow morning, I can't get back from here any sooner than that; and then I'm taking the red eye back to London and I hope…" His voice cracked momentarily, "I hope you're going to be there."

Suddenly Helen was incredulous. "Of course I'm going to be here. Unless you're throwing me out, that is!"

"No, no … I just…"

He pulled and stretched the skin on his forehead in frustration, but Helen was calm again.

"How much of a misery your life is made when you do get back will, of course, depend on this crisis of yours, so you'd better tell me about it. But summarize please, because it's late and I'm tired and I've had a few drinks and I really need to go to bed."

Paul seethed internally. He knew that the misery part of this statement wasn't an idle threat.

"Ok," he stated placidly, "you remember when we first met, I'd only been in London a few weeks, and you asked me why I was over here; well there."

Helen didn't answer, she had decided to let him have his say and contemplate what to do about it another time. Now his unusual behaviour prior to the trip made more sense, but there was no point in prolonging this and losing out on valuable sleep.

He continued. "Well, I said I was over here on a project transfer, which was true, but the reason was that I felt I had to get out of New York. And the reason I had to get out of New York was because I'd been in a relationship that had just ended. And it left me devastated."

He paused; tact was needed now. He didn't want to betray just how strongly he'd still felt for Christine, right up until the point when he found out the truth about their relationship.

"Devastated? Ok," Helen chipped in.

"So I left town. I decided to get out of New York and make a fresh start. And it was working," he emphasized.

"It *is* working! I've been really happy since I met you and I think we're really great together, but, well you know how it is when you've been really in love with someone and you lose them. You always keep a little place for them in your heart, for a while at least."

"You might keep a place for them, but that should be where it *stops!*" she snapped angrily. "You went back to see her, right? Is that it?"

Paul was struggling. "I did, yes, but only when I found out that she had been seriously injured in an accident. It made the New York papers. She was assaulted and thrown down a flight of metal steps and left for dead outside the back of a restaurant. I just couldn't *not* go and see her. I felt I had to!"

"Ok, ok, stop for a minute, we've got a couple of issues here." Helen was now up and pacing around the room, stretching the telephone cord to its limits.

"First off, you went on a trip that you said was work related, so you lied about that. And it sounded like Simon was in on the deal too, because he was trying to cover for you, I could tell. I called him twice! And you went to see an ex-girlfriend while you are seeing me, while we are living together, sleeping together! *Fucking hell!*"

"I know, but it was only to see her, to see how she was..."

"And how was she?" she shouted.

"Not too good actually, she's..."

"And," she continued. "I presume you paid for this yourself, flying out to New York at short notice, staying in hotels. Did you get a cheap fare? Did you go standby?"

"Yeah, I did get a cheap fare," he lied.

"And what did you say when you saw her? 'Hi, how are you? Sorry about your accident, here's a bunch of grapes. Hope you get better soon.' How many times did you see her?"

"Twice, only twice."

"Ok, you saw her twice, so why then did you go off to some park in the middle of nowhere to clear your head? Did you want to get back with her? Did you feel sorry for her and want to look after her? Why didn't you just come home? You'd still be in deep shit, but there's something else going on here. You must have found out something. You must have been trying to decide what to do."

Paul felt physically battered. "No, I just felt that..."

"Ok, enough now, I need to go to bed. We've got the auditors in tomorrow and I need to be awake for when they give me the third degree on our new quality assurance strategy."

Paul tried in vain to change the subject. "God, don't you just hate QA? We had that whole thing a couple of months back."

"Goodnight Paul, thanks for phoning. What time do you get in on Tuesday?"

"About 7:30am, I think."

"Well don't expect me to be there to welcome you home, you total fucking *arsehole!*"

"Oh Helen, please don't let's..."

"But I will be waiting for you when you get back here. Oh, and by the way, there's a week's worth of laundry to do, I haven't vacuumed at all and I'll probably leave you a huge mountain of washing up, starting from now. Bye, safe journey home."

She hung up, leaving Paul staring into the receiver. He calmly put the phone down and lay on the bed, pulling the quilt cover over himself in a vain attempt to shut out the world.

26

Monday

Christine was sitting in a chair by the window in her hospital room, feeling the periodic breeze across her face as a fan swept back and forth in a predetermined arc. She sighed deeply as she gazed down at her restricted view of the street corner below and watched everyone racing about their daily lives; it would be a while before she could run to catch a subway or jaywalk her way through the traffic.

She was dressed and ready to face the outside world; she was even wearing a little makeup, because today she was leaving, irrespective of who showed up, and irrespective of the fear and dread of being alone in her apartment. The evening of the accident was now fading rapidly from her memory. Everything from what she was wearing, to what they ate at the restaurant, to what the final words were that caused her to be pushed down the stairs and left for dead in amongst a pile of stinking garbage bags. In fact, she couldn't properly remember now whether she was pushed or if she just fell. One thing that hadn't faded though was the terrifying thought that the person who did this to her was still a free man, and that she would probably not sleep a wink alone in her apartment when every footstep in the hall outside could be a potential mob assassin.

Louise Thurmann had just started her shift and came into the room.

"Hey, Chrissie girl," she beamed, "you is looking real sassy today."

"Why thank you, that's real nice of you to say. Did you have a nice time in Florida?"

"Awesome honey, just awesome! So the forms are on my desk, you're heading on out then?"

"I am, yes," she replied with a cautious smile. "Hopefully someone is going to be swooping in today to come and look after me for a while."

She hadn't given any further thought at all to the practicalities of Paul's offer. As far as she understood the situation, he still worked in London, was in a relationship, and didn't have an apartment here at the moment. The assumption was that he would somehow have taken care of all this in the last few days.

"Listen, I've got my rounds to do, but I'll be within shouting distance for the rest of the day. You be sure and let me know your plans, hun."

"Will do, ma'am."

The nurse left the room and walked off down the corridor.

Uptown, Tara had just eaten a bagel at her desk while ordering a massive bouquet of flowers to take to Christine later today.

"She's gonna love 'em, she's gonna just *love* 'em," she said out loud, and then stood up. "Hey, any of you guys need coffee from the machine?"

Several of her colleagues called out numbers corresponding to the drinks they required. She remembered the first couple of items and then had to grab a pen and paper and start writing them down.

In Rapid City South Dakota, Paul was preparing to check out from his cheap motel room. His flight to New York via Minneapolis was at midday. He had slept terribly last night; his mind constantly churning over the decisions he had made over the last few days, and the inescapable fact that none of them seemed to have been the right ones. He even got up at 3am and went out for a drive in his rental car, stopping off at an all night diner for an undercooked hamburger and some excessively greasy French fries. The coffee was excellent, mind, although it only served to heighten his wide-awake state. Today he felt wrecked. Calling Helen last night was definitely not the right thing to have done, and he imagined her going through every inch of the apartment looking for evidence of an affair. He would probably return to find the place trashed and have to pay the company for the damage, before getting sacked for taking an extra two days' leave without proper approval. It hadn't even occurred to him until last night that he was now missing from work without notifying his line management. He probably needed to make that phone call sooner rather than later. A quick burst of mental arithmetic told him it was the middle of the afternoon in London. He would call them before he checked out. But first, another important phone call was required. He dialled the hospital where Christine was staying, and took a long deep breath before someone picked up.

"Hi, I need to leave an important message for Christine Hudson. I'm supposed to be visiting her today, but I can't make it. Hold on, can you actually take this down and tell her the exact words please. Yeah, I'll hold for a second. Ok, this is a message from Paul Herrycke. Tell her I can't make it today. In fact I can't make it at all. Not ever. Yeah that's the message, can you read it back to me? Ok, that's fine, and can you make sure she gets it this morning? Thank you very much. Bye."

Christine had been doing a lot of thinking about her situation over the last few days, but it didn't take long to come to the obvious conclusion that none of the options available to her were without significant downsides. So the decision she had made was a strategic one based on her immediate needs alone, and she would rethink and update her plan on a daily basis.

She still had family back in Dallas, but would rather pee her pants struggling to get to the toilet than go back home to hang out with mom and dad and her delinquent, unemployable brother. Therefore she must stay here. But for now she would need some practical help and ideally some protection in case Don Borello came to call. She took some level of comfort from the fact that her apartment building was secure and had a 24 hour doorman, but ideally she would like a burly NYPD detective standing guard on her landing.

So that left Geoff, the person who stood in this room a few days ago with a straight face and suggested, very sweetly, that he would give up everything to look after her until she was fully recovered. And it left Paul, who did the same a few days before that. In

Geoff's case, she couldn't decide how much of this offer was motivated by guilt, and how much was based on genuine sympathy for her predicament. And with Paul she had a slight problem with the credibility of his offer full stop.

Of Geoff and Paul, obviously she knew Geoff much better, and she remembered clearly when he nursed her through a bout of glandular fever when they lived together. She was flat out for nearly three weeks and Geoff fetched and carried and waited and attended to her every whim without question or complaint. But he was also a slob, and during this period he let the rest of the apartment turn quietly into a total mess. When she was well again, it took her a week to secretly clean things back up to her standards, using energy that would have been much better spent in contributing to her recovery. If he was a slob then, he was sure to be one now, and she would have to watch his every move, making sure he put the milk away, wiped the splashes of piss from the toilet seat, washed his hands before and after handling raw meat, and took his dirty shoes off at the door.

She knew less of Paul's domestic habits, but one thing for sure was that he was always fastidious and clean. The plates and knives and forks in his apartment were always sparkling, he always made a point of washing up straight after a meal, and he always put the laundry away as soon as it was dry. And he ironed too!

So her decision was made based on the flimsiest of evidence. She would take up Paul's offer and she would give it a week in the first instance. Perhaps having the opportunity to recover in peace would also allow her the chance to properly clear her mind. Decisions needed to be made. She mustn't waste time. She needed to get over this and move on.

But Paul had to let her.

As she contemplated the immediate future with a slight sense of optimism, a nurse came to her door and tapped gently.

"Hi." Christine smiled at her.

"Hi, is it Christine? Well, that's what it says on the door."

"Yeah, I'm Christine."

The nurse looked edgy. "I've got a telephone message for you from the front desk, from someone called Paul. It says…"

Christine's heart missed a beat. Why a message? Why wasn't he here?

"Yeah, what does it say?" she asked nervously.

"Err, maybe you want to read it, ma'am."

The nurse advanced and she grabbed the slip of paper from her hand and read it.

"Oh, that's ok," she sighed, "I know what that's about. Thank you. Phew, I was worried for a minute then."

She wanted to cry, but managed to maintain her composure. "Thank you nurse. Do you know if all the paperwork has been signed for me to be discharged this morning?"

The nurse backed away. "I'm sorry, I don't. Your main staff nurse should be able to help you though."

"Ok, that's fine, no problem."

The nurse disappeared and Christine quickly buzzed for attention.

"Hi Chrissie." Louise appeared within a matter of moments.

"Louise, can I get a porter to come and help me down into the lobby? Oh and I'll need to call a cab."

Louise frowned. "Oh, isn't Sir Galahad riding into town then?"

"Err, yeah he is, but," she hesitated, "but he can't make it this morning, so he's coming to my apartment later."

"Ok then. Well, wherever you end up, I hope you have a great time and get well soon."

She scurried over and hugged Christine carefully around her neck,

"You take care, sweetie," she mumbled, with her face pressed against Christine's skin, and Christine could feel the words vibrating in her throat.

Thirty minutes later she was outside.

"Mm, oh my God, fresh air." she marvelled to the porter, who was pushing her wheelchair. "You know you can have ten windows open, but it's no substitute for actually being outside. I'm amazed at how good it smells."

"Yes ma'am, it's a beautiful day today," the porter replied casually.

She struggled into the waiting cab, wincing in pain as she tried to swing her legs in.

The porter looked concerned. "Do you need some help, ma'am?"

She lifted her weight off the seat and adjusted her position slightly. "No, I'm ok; just one more shove."

He moved forward to help but didn't know where to put his hands.

"I'm ok, honestly," she stressed.

Eventually she was in, the door closed, and the destination shouted out. The cab then lurched off into the Manhattan traffic and Christine sat pensively in the back, staring at the walls of concrete and glass and not bothering to strain her neck to look up and find the sky. She was determined not to let this affect her, and she breathed slowly and deeply, forcing a smile towards the pair of eyes that she could see in the rear view mirror. She tried to convince herself how ridiculous it would be to accept the offer of help from anyone without there being an ulterior motive; especially from a person who's life she'd done her best to ruin for a short period. Suddenly she became angry and her head started to hurt as the stress levels rose in her body. How could she have fallen for this? Just how *stupid* was she? Breathe deep, she told herself, breathe deep; and another, and another. She was going back to her apartment alone, and she would just have to deal with things one day at a time. From a practical standpoint, she would need some groceries. Perhaps she could ask Mr Lieberman across the corridor? And she needed to contact her employers. They were notified of the accident a few days after it happened, by the hospital authorities, but they would need to know that she'd now been discharged. Perhaps she could do a little bit of work from home, just to get back into the swing of things. Despite this unforeseen start, everything was going to work out fine.

Momentarily she thought about Geoff, who would be showing up at the hospital sometime this afternoon.

27

Just after lunch, Tara left her office and hailed a cab to take her to the hospital, via the florist to pick up the bouquet she had ordered. After waiting patiently all weekend, she was now desperate to find out what had happened in the aftermath of her phone call with Paul. Maybe he'd been too embarrassed to go back at all and had slunk off back to England, in which case today's visit would be a waste of time. But if his anger on the phone last week had been anything to go by, he would have returned as mad as hell and ready for a massive fight.

So maybe both of them hated her now? If that was the case then so be it, but if she had made Paul's life just a little bit more difficult in the process, then these last few days had been well worth it. Whatever the outcome between Christine and Paul, she was not going to be coming here again. Initially she had thought that some sort of friendship with Christine was possible, but after two brief visits and the forced conversations that went with them this idea was quickly shelved. Hopefully the flowers would cheer Christine up, but Tara was well aware that this meeting could go either way.

Could she rest after today and leave this all behind her? Maybe.

"Excuse me. I've come to see Christine Hudson, she was in isolation over the weekend; I hope she's better now."

The receptionist tapped a few keys. "She's been discharged this morning, ma'am."

"*What?*" Tara gasped. "Well, where did she go? Did she leave a message for me at all?"

"We're not really at liberty to discuss our patients' personal business. Who are you please, and I'll check if there's any messages?"

"My name is Tara."

"Are you related to her?"

"No, but I visited her a lot. I saw her last week and," Tara became flustered, "I bought the flowers for her as a surprise."

"No ma'am, there are no messages. Now is there..."

"Well, did she say where she was going?"

"Once again, we can't discuss patients' personal business. I can tell you that she's been discharged, but that's all."

"Did she go with her parents, do you know?"

The receptionist remained calm. "Ma'am, I don't think you're hearing me."

"No, thank *you* ma'am, I'm hearing you just *fine!* You've been an absolute library of information." She squinted at the receptionist's badge. "Thank you miss Kerry, I'll write to HR and absolutely insist you get promoted for your total devotion to customer service!"

Tara pushed past a group of people and headed for the door.

At this precise moment, Geoff was walking across the plaza area outside, and passed within a few feet of Tara as she stormed out. He had spent most of yesterday in his room with the curtains drawn, either sleeping or watching old movies on cable TV, desperately trying to divert his thoughts away from what could be about to happen. And now as he walked the final steps to her bedside, the potential opportunity of realizing his dream of getting back together with Christine seemed a little hollow. His life was different from when they last met five years ago; the west coast had changed him as a person. He felt he had opportunities now, and that stepping back in time might not be the right thing to do. Part of him had wanted to flee to the airport and go home, but somehow he was drawn here, like he was being led with an invisible rope. And he could feel his sense of self importance dwindling. It was as if whatever Christine suggested, he would feel somehow obliged to go along with; whatever the problems it would undoubtedly cause.

Geoff walked in through the main doors of the hospital and up to the desk. The same receptionist was still on duty.

"Hi, I'm here to see Christine Hudson. I've been before, she's in..."

The receptionist turned to a colleague. "Well, isn't she a popular lady today?"

"She is popular, yeah," Geoff replied flippantly, "she gets lots of visitors and I'm one of them. Am I ok to go up?"

"She used to get lots of visitors, before she discharged herself."

Geoff shook his head in disbelief. "What, you mean she's not here anymore?"

"No Sir, she was discharged this morning."

"When this morning?"

"Very recently this morning, I think." The receptionist was starting to become annoyed.

"Well where did she go?"

"I'm afraid I'm not at liberty to…"

Suddenly he felt almost serene. "Pardon me ma'am, you're telling me you can't disclose where she's gone?"

"No Sir, only to immediate family."

"But I am her immediate family." He stopped and took a deep breath. "I guess I was her immediate family. Well no, I came pretty damn close though. So there's no way?"

"I'm sorry, no."

Geoff scratched his head and looked around. "Ok, you have a great day now."

He turned on his heels and sloped out, but with a strange sense of relief beginning to percolate through his veins.

28

It was now almost 3pm on the same afternoon and Geoff was wandering aimlessly through Washington Square Park looking for somewhere to sit down, but all the benches he had passed so far were occupied by happy, babbling, individuals. The events of the last few hours had left him feeling totally disconnected from his surroundings, like he was plodding around in a diving suit; the hustle and bustle, the voices, the car horns, were somehow softened. He felt a sense of loss too, despite the curious wave of relief he had experienced at the hospital. Christine had disappeared from his life, for the *third* time, and he really wanted to know what had happened. Perhaps she had transferred to another hospital, perhaps she had gone back to Dallas to be with her folks; or perhaps she just needed some time on her own and she would call him soon. One thing was for sure he couldn't imagine she would have done this with any deception in mind. He needed to sit down, alone, but the possibility of a vacant bench seemed remote. He got out his phone as he walked and scrolled through the numbers. First he found Christine's apartment; which he didn't actually know the location of. The phone rang and rang, and eventually he left a message.

"Hi Chris, this is Geoff. I came back today and you'd gone. Can you call me please to let me know you're safe?"

Next he rang her mobile phone and left the same message.

In her apartment, Christine had now been back a few hours, but she was struggling. After checking her refrigerator, she had hobbled to Mr. Lieberman's door just across the landing, but there was no one home. Hopefully he was just out for the afternoon, because she had no milk or any fresh food that could be safely eaten. She was desperate for a cup of coffee, but even if she could stand to drink it black she only had enough in the bottom of the jar for one weak cup. She had failed to open a can of tuna because of the plaster cast on her arm, and had already spilt half a carton of apple juice down the sink and on the floor as she tried to break the seal on the screw top. This wasn't going to be easy, and she stifled a sob as she listened to Geoff's message.

But she wasn't going to call him back, even if Mr. Lieberman had left town and malnutrition threatened. Enough already! As difficult as her life was going to be for a while, she couldn't face racking up any form of emotional debt to Geoff Dealer. This really had to be it.

And as for Paul; well she really needed to try and forget that he ever existed. If he *had* come back today her plan had only been to use him for a few days, a week tops, to fetch and carry and help her get back on her feet. But it was obvious from the wording of his message that this was never going to happen. He too had taken revenge in his own small way, it was just a shame that he had picked the easy target and not gone for Tara's throat instead.

Christine decided that out of the four individuals in this distorted little square of deception, Tara had clearly suffered the least, and for this she reserved for her a massive amount of contempt. Looking back now, it was clear that Tara had interfered in this matter from the start, and that Paul's involvement was down to her alone. But there was no point trying to dish out appropriate amounts of blame to all of those involved. Practicalities must come first, so she decided to write a note and hobble across the landing again and pin it to Mr. Lieberman's door. There were two other apartments on her floor, but one was quite possibly vacant, and the other was only occupied at weekends. So if her next door neighbour didn't return in the next few hours, she would have to plead with the doorman instead.

Geoff wandered on aimlessly after leaving his messages. Then he saw some people get up, leaving a bench with a single occupant. He homed in quickly and asked the obligatory question.

"Do you mind if I sit here?"

Tara seemed disinterested. "Sure."

He hesitated. "So, you do mind then?"

"No, go ahead."

"Oh, ok, 'cos when I just asked if you minded you said 'sure'."

"Huh?"

"As in 'sure' I mind you sitting there, so don't do it."

"Oh, just sit down already."

"Don't know if I want to now."

Tara looked up at him. "Whatever."

Geoff smiled. "I'm joking."

He sat down and there was silence for a few moments.

"You know, I'm one of those..." Tara immediately sighed at the intrusion, but Geoff appeared not to notice. "...naturally un-talkative, or is it non-talkative, people. I'll sit in the barber's chair thinking, don't talk to me just cut my hair. You know, I think you should be able to specify up front whether you want to be talked to or not. It would save a lot of awkwardness. I'm not a miserable person, but I don't want to tell you what I do or where I'm going on vacation; or whether I'm going out tonight."

"Uh-huh." Tara responded because she felt obliged to.

Geoff paused for a while and looked up at the sky, while Tara shuffled, changed her seating position, and discreetly checked her watch.

"I'm sorry, I don't mean to bother you, but I've just been stood up. And I'll tell you what; I'm pissed off."

Tara suddenly showed a flicker of interest. "That's funny, I've been stood up today as well. Well, not really, not in the normal sense. But I've just been to see someone who I thought was expecting me and they weren't there."

"Well, doesn't weirdness just abound in this city; your story is very similar to mine."

Tara smiled. "How about that?"

"Do you want to talk about it?"

"No, do you?"

Geoff managed to resist the obvious question; was the person Christine Hudson?

"Was the person who stood you up male or female?" he asked casually.

"Why should that matter? And anyway, I don't have to answer your questions."

"You sure don't."

They sat in silence for a few moments watching people pass by.

"Do you want to go somewhere for some coffee, so we can talk about something else?" he asked vaguely.

Tara wrinkled her nose. "Hmm, I don't know." She looked cautiously around her. "The air feels funny today. I think it could be a bad idea."

Geoff turned to her. "You know what? I feel the same; it's a strange day today, but I can't quite decide why."

"Why suggest it then?"

"I'm suggesting it because I've found that a person with whom I have a considerable history has, well, disappeared." He sighed. "I know neither of us wants to talk about this, but I could use a real strong cup of coffee and there's a diner on the next block that came through for me last time I was here. Do you want to come?"

Tara backtracked. "Hmm, maybe."

"Come on, I might be really interesting to talk to."

"I'm supposed to be back at work very soon. I'm on my lunch break."

Geoff checked his watch. "What? It's nearly 3 o'clock, for God's sake."

"Well, I guess it's already run over a tad."

"Come then. Just for coffee, and maybe some cheesecake. This place does killer cheesecake."

"Clogs your arteries in an instant, does it?"

Geoff stood up. "I need coffee. If you don't want to come, speak now, we'll say our goodbyes, it's been nice meeting you, by the way, and then we'll go off in our separate directions."

Tara got up as well. "Ok, I'm coming, but not for cheesecake. My hips inflate like tractor tyres when I eat cheesecake!"

They began walking.

"That accent of yours doesn't sound like east or west coast."

Geoff nodded. "You're right, I've been trying to modify it to a mixture of Ivy League law school and network news reader, but I'm originally from Texas; from Austin in fact."

Tara scrutinized him. "Austin huh? I had a girlfriend in high school who went there to study Chemistry. She never came back."

"Well that doesn't surprise me, Austin's a beautiful place," he stated proudly. "And UT is just *the* best university in the land."

"So why'd you leave?"

"Now that *is* a long story, which would take a full meal including starter, dessert, and coffee and mints to tell, but it does involve the person who stood me up today."

Tara spoke with mock sympathy. "And that's too painful for right now, huh?"

"It's gonna be tough for a while, but I think I'll pull through."

They reached the diner, walked in and sat down in an empty booth. A waitress came by straightaway and Geoff ordered two coffees and a piece of cheesecake. Then they sat in a not unpleasant silence for a few moments until the coffee was served. Geoff heaped in sugar and some cream and took a sip.

He sighed with pleasure as the caffeine hit the spot. "Oh man, that tastes good! It's almost worth a round trip ticket from loo-loo land for such an experience."

"Loo-loo land?"

"Los Angeles, I flew in last Friday, or was it Thursday?"

Tara ignored this and tried her coffee. "Hmm, it's pretty good, but there's a place on the next block that does it better."

Geoff sipped again. "You know what, we haven't introduced ourselves. I'm Geoff."

Something told her to be cautious. "I'm … err, Lillian," she replied.

Geoff extended his hand and she reached over and shook it tentatively.

"Well, I'm pleased to meet you Lillian, that's a pretty name; it sounds like some old English Victorian grandma's name."

"It's my great grandmother's name, and she was from England," she lied. "That's perceptive of you. Do you like English Literature? I mean have you read the Brontë's?"

"No, but I read the sequel; *The Brontë's 2: This Time It's Personal*."

Tara laughed loudly. "You're so full of crap; you haven't read them have you? I bet you read science fiction instead."

"Nope, can't stand science fiction. Yeah I did read *Wuthering Heights*, and some of *Pride and Prejudice*, which…" he held his hand up as Tara moved to speak, "…was written by Jane Austen, I do know that. But I gave up on it. I thought it was too chatty; just a bunch of women yakking."

Tara was astonished. "*Just a bunch of women yakking!* That's your considered opinion of one of the great works of literature?" She shook her head in disbelief but didn't pursue the topic.

"So, what do you do?" Geoff asked. "What should you be doing now, assuming you still have a job?"

"What do I do? What do I do? I'll tell you what I'd like to do. I'd like to get into films."

"Yeah, and I'd like to be the lead guitarist in a major rock band," he replied. "I tried to learn the guitar when I was a teenager. Gave up, couldn't be bothered to grow my fingernails."

"Well, I've been in one short film when I was back in college," she stated proudly, "and I've been in two commercials since, both for one of the local cable stations. I have tapes to prove it."

Geoff was impressed. "Well you've already got your foot on the ladder then."

"Yeah right, I'm registered with an acting agency in Manhattan; they haven't gotten me any work in two years."

"Do you live in the city?"

"Err, no; can't afford the rent."

"Brooklyn, Queens?"

"No, I live in suburban New Jersey, just off the Erie Lackawanna."

"You have your own apartment?"

"You ask a lot of questions."

Geoff paused as his portion of cheesecake arrived. He took a large forkful, then, with his mouth still full, he continued, "You want some? I can get an extra fork and you can have some from the other end."

"No thanks, tractor tyres, remember?"

"Come over to LA with me," he said suddenly, surprising himself. "Bring your tapes and see if you can make it in Hollywood."

Tara gasped. "*What are you, nuts?* I hardly know you! No, wait a second; I don't know you at all."

Geoff's mind worked quickly. "Look, I've got two places out there right now. I've got a..." he hesitated. He needed to return the keys to his Benedict Canyon residence by the end of the month; which was now just over a week away. But he had already planned to lease a more expensive, but slightly less opulent house on Mulholland Drive. He would have to get on the phone and try to speed this along.

"You've got two places?" she interrupted. "What do you *do?* Are you a drug dealer or something?"

He frowned. "No, nothing as exciting as that."

"So what do you do?"

"I trade."

"You trade?" she asked. "Trade what?"

"Currency, foreign exchange. I work from home."

She nodded dismissively. "I know a couple of guys who trade down on Wall Street. Stocks, bonds, equities, derivatives; it doesn't make a whole lot of sense to me. It seems like they make a fantastic living out of nothing. You'll have to explain to me how it works someday."

"I can do that. It's a piece of cake really."

He took another bite of his dessert. Half of it had disappeared already.

"So," she continued, "you've got two places."

"Yeah, I've got a nice little apartment in West Hollywood, just off Santa Monica Boulevard. And then, then there's another one, a house nearby."

He faltered momentarily. "You can have the keys to the apartment, stay for a while; knock on a few doors and see what comes up. You can even pay some token rent if it'd make you feel better."

"Are you *serious?*"

"Of course! We can travel over there separately, or together, whatever you choose; and we can see as little, or as much, of each other as you want. You never know, if you've got audition tapes you might be able to get your foot in the door long enough to say hello."

Tara couldn't quite believe this. As she'd stated earlier, today felt strange. She was well into the second hour of her late lunch break, but for some inexplicable reason she didn't really care. Her boss had now returned to the office after a week long conference visit, and an absence like this would definitely be noticed. She already had three missed calls and two messages on her phone. She had some proofs to get out by tomorrow, and at this rate she would be pulling an all nighter to get them finished. She had argued with Gerhard as well, over something incredibly stupid and sex related; it was unlikely he would call again before he went home to Germany at the end of the month. And now a total stranger was presenting her with an absurd proposal to leave home and fly across country with him to try and break into the movies.

"God, I don't know what to say. It's the craziest thing I ever heard!"

Geoff could only shrug in agreement.

"But what about my job?"

"You never told me what it was, so how can I say whether or not you should give it up?"

Tara sighed. "Oh it's boring, real boring; I'm behind a desk with, to use your term, a bunch of women yakking. It doesn't matter what I do; I answer the phone, I type on the computer, I print documents, I surf the Internet..."

"That bad, huh?"

"Yep, that bad and then some."

They sat in silence for a while.

"What do you say then?" Geoff said eventually, "Why not come back with me to LA for, let's say, a month. See if you can make it big. You'll get a job over there, no problem. I mean, you could always wait tables; isn't that what struggling actresses are supposed to do?"

"Stereotypically, yes."

"So..."

"Oh, I don't know. I need to think about it. I mean for God's sake I know it's still America but it's a long way from home."

"Don't think about it. Just do it!"

"And are there any strings attached? Come on, there have to be some."

"None that I can think of right now."

Tara was curious. "There's something I don't get here."

"Shoot."

"Why are you suggesting this? You've only just met me; you haven't got the faintest idea who I am."

Geoff breathed deeply. "Didn't you say earlier, it's a weird day? Well I agree. Something's definitely blowing in the wind."

"And?"

"And I don't know; sometimes something just clicks. True, I hardly know you; also true, I don't make a habit of inviting strangers to stay at my apartment. Maybe if you say yes it will turn out to be a huge mistake. The outcome of my life could hinge on whether you say yes or not."

"Oh great, so no pressure then!"

"It's true though isn't it, every decision you make, at every point in the day, could affect the direction your life takes. You step out of your apartment, you walk to the subway, and everything's fine. Or perhaps you step out of your apartment, you think you've left the TV on, so you go back to check. But you haven't, so you walk to the subway again and get hit by a car on the corner and killed. Ten minutes earlier and everything would have been just like a normal day. But the original normal day never existed. On this normal day you ended up dead."

He stopped briefly to let the weight of these words sink in, but then an argument erupted three tables away, providing a welcome diversion from the awkward silence that had descended. A young couple were now on their feet shouting at each other and gesturing angrily. Then the young woman stormed off, leaving the man behind, scrabbling to gather up a laptop and a small pile of books. When he had done this he threw some money at a waitress and disappeared.

"So, will you come with me?" Geoff asked, wondering to himself why on earth he was doing this.

"I don't know." She sighed heavily. "I have family here; it's complicated."

"Hey, I'm not pressuring you," he said, "if you've got commitments in this area then that's fine. I'm not suggesting you relocate permanently; if you don't like it you can be home in a few hours."

"Where's your family?" she asked, "Are they still in Texas?"

Geoff scratched his head. "Yeah, they are but, well, nobody speaks to each other very much these days."

He hesitated. "My dad's dead. He died a while ago. And my mom's in hospital at the moment."

"Oh, I'm sorry, I didn't mean to pry."

"Actually, I'm going to Austin to see her soon, hopefully this week."

Tara drained her coffee cup and quickly glanced at her watch.

"So, I'll be gone for a couple of days and that's good because it'll give you some time to think it through; to ponder your potentially momentous decision. And it'll give you time to tell your folks if you decide to come. Do they live round here, by the way?"

"Yeah, they live not too far from me," she lied again. "I see them every couple of days."

"Well that's good; it's good to keep in touch with your family. It's important."

He finished his coffee. "Shall we exchange numbers then, and you can call me later when you get home. Who knows, you might get back to your apartment and remember you're getting married next month or something."

Tara laughed. "Yeah right!"

Geoff tore a serviette in half and they scribbled down their numbers.

"And if that's the case, then at least I've had an enjoyable afternoon. Ma'am."

Geoff called the waitress who came over promptly; he paid the bill, then they got up and left. As they stepped outside Tara turned to him.

"You are a nice guy, aren't you? I mean, you're not a serial killer or anything; not that you'd tell me if you were."

"I am a nice guy. I just hope you are a nice girl."

"Ah, I knew there'd be a catch."

Geoff laughed. "It's been a strange day. One of the strangest days I've had in a long while."

"I'll speak to you soon." She said smiling, and promptly turned and walked off.

Geoff watched her closely, as he contemplated what had just

happened. Could it possibly be that in one fell swoop he had just bypassed the introductory drinks, the candlelit dinners, the movies, and all the 'what do you like, what do I like?' questions and managed to coerce a woman into living with him? There was definitely something about her. She wasn't normally the type he would go for; with her plain, slightly boyish features. But she had something; she had an air of confidence. And a great walk. He watched her until she disappeared around a corner and out of sight. She didn't look back.

29

Geoff returned to his hotel room, turned the air conditioning up high, and decided to sit tight for the rest of the day. Outside in the city the temperature was nudging ninety degrees, but it felt like a hundred as acres and acres of concrete and glass relentlessly reflected and amplified the heat, making it feel like the whole of New York City was sitting under a giant magnifying glass. He was quite sanguine about the fact that he had just invited a total stranger to come back to Los Angeles with him, and though he was not expecting her to actually say yes, he felt a strong need to have someone thinking he had done them a good turn for a change. So, whatever happened over the next few days, weeks or months, he was looking forward to it. And who knows, if she did come over, she could make it big. She might become a star, and if that happened she would always have him to thank.

But there was something niggling him, and as he laid outstretched on the bed with the curtains pulled tightly shut, he wondered if he should do something about it.

For years now he had been vaguely planning to tell someone about the day he shot and killed Danny Stanley. He almost told Christine one night many years ago as they were lying on the beach in Carmel, staring up at an intense tapestry of stars, with the cold waters of the Pacific Ocean lapping at their bare feet. They were in the middle of one of their biggest road trips; two fantastic weeks of driving around the South Western desert states and up as far north as San Francisco. And if his memory served him correctly, it was one of the highlights of their relationship; they were very, very much in love, and he'd felt that the bond between them was unbreakable. He remembered being torn apart wondering how she would react. He wondered why he should even take such a risk by telling her at all? He came so close that he even started the first sentence, but a wave crashed noisily onto the beach and Christine didn't hear him properly. She turned and asked him what he was about to say, but in that split second he realized he couldn't do it. And that moment never cropped up again.

So he decided he would tell Lillian, even if it meant that she put the phone down and he never heard from her again. In this particular case, where so little time and emotion had been invested, what did he have to lose? He needed to come to terms with his past, he needed to be open about it, and he desperately needed to move forward. So any new relationships from now on would not be kept in that horrible state of limbo. He reached over to the bedside table and checked that he still had her number on the torn up piece of serviette. He had, so he lay back for a moment, composing himself.

Approximately seven hours later, his phone rang and woke him from a really deep sleep. The noise shocked him to the core, and he hauled himself upright in a daze, stretching and rubbing his bleary eyes, his heart pounding.

"Hi, this is Geoff speaking." His voice was almost a whisper; he must have been sleeping with his mouth open, because his throat was totally parched.

"Geoff, its Lillian. I'm sorry, I guess I woke you up. Are you ok to talk for a minute?"

"Yeah, hold on, I need a drink though."

He reached over for a plastic bottle of mineral water and swigged thirstily from it.

"Oh man, was I crashed out. Damn it, I must have been asleep since this afternoon. What time is it?"

"Ten pm, I'm sorry if I disturbed you."

"No, no it's fine, I need to eat anyway. What's going on?"

The line went quiet for a moment.

"I've got a bit of a confession to make," she said, "I lied about something earlier on."

Geoff was still half asleep. "Err, well you didn't tell me very much, so how bad can it be?"

Tara hesitated. "It's my name, I lied about my name."

"Your name?"

"Yeah," she replied sheepishly, "my name's not Lillian," she coughed, "my name is Tara."

Geoff felt all of his nerve endings twang simultaneously. The last time he'd visited Christine someone had mentioned a Tara. Of course there was bound to be more than one Tara in New York City, but suddenly he was very much awake.

"Tara!"

"Yes, Tara, what's wrong? Do you prefer Lillian?"

"Tara, oh my God. And you say you were stood up today."

"Yeah, but…"

"Can I ask how? I mean, was it on a date or were you visiting someone?"

At the other end of the line, Tara was puzzled. "Why do you ask?"

"Were you supposed to be visiting Christine Hudson in hospital and when you got there she'd already left?"

"What?" Tara was incredulous. "Yes I was, but, well, who are you then?"

"I was supposed to be visiting her as well. I'm her, well I don't know what I am now. We lived together many years ago, and we're still good friends, I guess. Jesus, I can't believe this."

Tara's heart started to pound as well. "Me neither, but…"

"Can I meet up with you tonight?" he interrupted, "Like, right now."

"Err, well; I don't know." She sounded flustered. "Where? I mean it's a bit late isn't it?"

"I'll get a cab, I'll come over." There was a sense of urgency in Geoff's voice. "I'll meet you somewhere near your apartment, a diner perhaps? This is so weird, but, well the thing is, I was going to call you, because I have a bit of a confession to make too. But it's important; too important to do over the phone. Please say you'll meet me."

"Uh, ok."

"Ok, I'm coming over, where are you?"

"Not far from Maplewood train station, in Essex County."

"I'll get a cab and I'll be there in about thirty minutes," he paused, "will it take me that long?"

"I'd give it forty five, even at this time of night. I tell you what, I'll meet you by the train station at eleven, but don't make me wait, or else people will think I'm a hooker."

"Ok, I'm out of the door. I'll see you shortly."

He hung up before she had a chance to reply, put on a jacket and a pair of shoes, checked he had his wallet and his phone and ran from the room.

Fifty minutes later, the cab containing Geoff and an extremely reluctant driver threaded its way cautiously along the quiet suburban streets, heading for the railway station in Maplewood. Tara saw a taxi approaching from inside the doorway of a nearby bar and as it passed she saw Geoff in the back with his nose pressed to the glass, so she ran out to flag them down.

The cab pulled up and Geoff managed to convince the driver to wait, have a cup of coffee or a beer somewhere and take a break for half an hour before taking him back to Manhattan. This cost him dearly, but after a brief period of haggling the deal was done.

"Hi," Geoff said finally when they met at the door, "I hope this isn't too much of an inconvenience for you."

Tara shrugged. "Neah, don't worry about it. I only live a few minutes away."

He reached out to shake her hand. "It's Tara then. Pleased to meet you; I'm still Geoff, by the way."

They shook hands politely. "C'mon, let's go in," Tara said.

He followed her and they sat at a table. For a few moments there was an uncomfortable silence.

"You know I still can't believe that we ran into each other after we both went to visit the same person … who wasn't there. Gone; no message, nothing."

Tara nodded in a non committal fashion. "Yeah I know. I saw her a few times last week, but then when I visited over the weekend she was in an isolation ward; she'd caught some bug or something?"

"But I was…" Geoff stopped. He had heard no mention of isolation wards or illness.

Tara managed to attract the attention of the single waitress, who was busily chatting to Geoff's taxi driver.

"Let's order. Do you want anything to eat?"

"I'll have coffee and cheesecake if they do it," he replied, looking over to a chiller cabinet behind the bar, which still contained some dessert portions, "for the second time today."

"So how *did* you know about me then?" she asked.

Geoff faltered for a moment. "Err, Christine said someone called Tara had been to visit her and I just put two and two together." He fidgeted awkwardly. "I mean it's not exactly a common name, is it?"

Tara didn't look convinced.

"But beyond that," he added, "I don't know anything about you at all. Are you one of her buddies from work?"

"Yeah, yeah that's right; I've known her for a couple of years." Tara swallowed hard. If Geoff hadn't heard about her association with Christine, there was no way she was going to admit to it.

Geoff seemed to accept this, and she saw him looking over to the TV where a baseball game was underway.

"So, err, what did you want to tell me?"

At this point their order appeared, and both set about putting cream and sugar in their coffee. Geoff took a sip, and then another, and then another. He had a strange expression on his face, almost enigmatic.

"Geoff, you've come all this way to talk to me and you've gone quiet. Are you ok?"

"Yeah, sorry, I'm still here. I'm just wondering where to start, that's all."

How to tell her; sentences flashed past in his mind like destinations on an airport departure board. And why tell her? Suddenly he questioned the wisdom of springing this sort of information on someone he hardly knew. But it would be awkward to back out now. Oh well.

He took a deep breath and looked her straight in the eyes. "Tara, I killed someone once."

"What?"

He sighed. "Yes, you did hear me correctly."

There was silence for a moment; she looked away and stirred her coffee while surreptitiously checking how far she was from the nearest exit.

Eventually she spoke. "How? With your car? A road accident? What happened?"

"With a gun, I shot someone."

"Oh my God!" Her voice was trembling now. "Was it an accident? Were you out hunting or something?"

"No, I shot someone on purpose."

"You murdered someone? You've been to jail? Oh my God, oh my God, I don't know what to…"

She stood up. "I think I'd better go, and I think you'd better stay here until I'm gone."

Geoff resisted the temptation to reach out and grab her.

"Tara, *please,* sit down and listen to me for five minutes. Honestly, there is an explanation; a reason. Please…"

She sat cautiously.

"No, I haven't been to jail, because I was only a child and I was protecting my mom."

She shook her head in a daze. "But…"

"I'll tell you what happened, and then feel free to go if you want to, but it doesn't change my offer of you coming to LA with me."

She didn't reply, so he told her the story.

"Ok, I was eleven years old, nearly twelve and I came home unexpectedly one afternoon in the middle of summer. I'd been out playing in some fields nearby, but my friend cut his foot open and went home early. As I got close to the house I could see that someone was arriving in a car. I couldn't see it directly, but there was a big old cloud of dust on the road out front."

He laughed. "In fact that was a great way to tell if anyone was coming to visit. You could see the dust cloud about five minutes before they got to the front door."

He ate a forkful of cheesecake and swigged his coffee.

"Anyway, as I went in to the back of the house I heard my mom's voice. She sounded upset, like she was crying, so I crept over to a slightly open door and I saw this guy holding her up against the door post. She looked scared. In fact I couldn't even see her face properly, but she sure sounded scared. I didn't know what to do, but then he grabbed her hair and ripped her clothes, and she screamed, so I tiptoed into the utility room out back and got my daddy's rifle from the cupboard. He always kept it loaded. Then I walked back."

He stopped, his voice faltering.

"And I remember even now how heavy the gun was as I lifted it up. I'd shot it quite a few times out in the garden, so I knew what to do, but I just felt like I was frozen to the spot. You know, I didn't even know what shooting someone would actually do! Can you believe that? I knew you could kill a fox or a deer, but I didn't know what it would do to a person."

As Tara stared at him with unblinking eyes, he relived the film clip of the incident again in his head. It was etched as a permanent memory, one that could be summoned up at will and still caused his stomach to coil up and make him feel like retching.

"So, I had the gun pointing and I tried to shout. I tried to threaten him, to make him stop. And I thought I was shouting, but I guess I couldn't have been, because he didn't stop! And then he reached down and ... and ... And then I must have shouted for real, because he turned and saw me."

Geoff looked down at the table.

"I shot him in the shoulder and at the same time I realized it was one of my dad's best pals, Danny Stanley. He went down and my mom screamed. He was shouting out and struggling on the ground, but he managed to get up a little way and grab my mom's ankle. He was begging for help, but I ran over and aimed the gun and shot him again, while my mom was screaming hysterically. I didn't know; I thought he could still hurt her. My dad had always told me, if I ever needed to use the gun to use it good, and don't give second chances. But this time my aim wasn't right and instead of hitting him in the arm I shot him in the neck. I've never seen so much blood, it just pumped out of him and he died right there with this crazy grin on his face."

Tara put her hands to her face in horror and whispered quietly, "Oh my lord..."

"My mom dialed 911 and I just curled up in the corner. You know, from that minute on she never looked me properly in the eye again. Anyway, before the police or the ambulance got there, my dad turned up and he was drunk, for God's sake! He wasn't expecting anyone to be home, so when he got in I ran and hid in the utility room, still holding the gun. I could hear them arguing; she was trying to explain that this guy was attacking her, and that she'd managed to break free and shoot him in self defence. And then I heard sirens. My dad came racing through to find me when my mom told him I was in the house, and he grabbed the gun from me just before the ambulance guys came in.

Picture the scene. My dad, drunk, with a gun in his hand; my mom, clothes ripped off, covered in blood; and some guy dead on the ground with his pants around his ankles. And then there was me, of course, dumbstruck in the corner. The police arrested him. He couldn't really protest his innocence with way over the legal limit of alcohol in his blood stream. The next day he was moved to a larger prison before his arraignment and a big riot broke out in his cellblock. A couple of people died, it even made the national news, I think. One was burnt alive in his cell. And my dad died too. He bled to death after being stabbed with a kitchen knife."

Geoff went quiet, and eventually Tara managed to respond. "Geoff, please, I don't know what to say."

"Don't say anything. I'll ask you one thing though. Try, if you can, to see it from my perspective, and don't see me as some cold blooded murderer, because I'm not."

Tara was still dumbstruck. "I … I'll try…"

"And if you think I'm being matter of fact about this then, yeah, perhaps I am, but I've had plenty of time to come to terms with it. But don't think that it doesn't haunt me every single day. Most times when people see me, I'm happy. I am a happy person. But every morning when I wake up, I open my eyes and for a split second everything seems fine. Right up until I remember that one day when I was a kid I murdered someone. And my dad took the blame and died as a result. And my mom also lost her husband and pretty much lost me too. I'm telling you, it's not always easy to smile when you've got a huge cloud hanging over your head like that."

Tara whispered, "Geoff, I'm…" But she stopped. Being sorry was the best she could offer, but it sounded so pathetic and irrelevant. A hundred questions had already formed in her head, but she didn't know what to say.

Geoff looked over to where the cab driver was sitting and raised his hand to indicate five minutes.

"You know I said my mom's ill in hospital? Well, assuming I see her tomorrow it'll be the first time in twenty years; the first time since the accident." He paused. "We lost touch, you see."

"*Twenty years!*" She gasped in horror, "Jesus, that's awful! How come, I mean how did it get to be that long?"

Geoff was matter of fact. "The family separated us. I was raised by my dad's parents, who were convinced my mom was the cause of all this by having an affair, which she was, I suppose. They didn't even know the truth of what happened until I told them years later."

He stopped. "Look, this is a long story and I've got to split. But the thing is, now my mom's got cancer and I have to go and see her. She sent me a letter a couple of weeks ago. I thought I'd never speak to her again, but now I want to see if I can make things right with her. It must have been hard for her to write to me, so I suppose it's the least I can do to go and see what she's got to say."

His voice tailed off to a whisper.

"I guess I'm glad I told you all this, but I'd better go. My cab driver is looking pissed off; he probably feels he's in the middle of nowhere out here."

He downed the rest of his coffee, pushed another few pieces of cheesecake into his mouth, and fiddled in his pocket for some money.

"What I said earlier still stands, by the way," he said, placing a ten dollar bill on the table. "I'm heading back to LA tomorrow, so you need to think hard about this. I'm a nice guy, really I am, and sometimes that surprises me, considering how screwed up my childhood was. But I've kept this from almost everyone in the past." He laughed briefly to himself. "I never even told Christine."

Tara's eyes met his, but she didn't know what to say.

"So, anyway, I'm not going to keep it a secret anymore. My past is fixed; it's me and I can't change it. I don't want to see this barrier every time I'm with someone."

He reached out and grabbed her hand. "I hope you understand."

Tara sat back and ran her fingers through her hair.

"I'll call you when I get back to LA, which will be after I've been to Austin, so it'll be a couple of days. And then you can let me know what you want to do, ok?"

He got up. "I'll speak to you soon."

"I hope your mom's ok," she replied, but he was already walking across the room.

She sat and watched him go over to collect the cab driver. Then he put a note of unknown denomination on the table and they disappeared through the door and out of sight. She sighed and finished her coffee in one gulp before getting up, paying the bill, and pushing her way out of the door and into the warm night air.

On her brief walk home, it began to sink in just how much her life had changed over the last few weeks. Before meeting Gerhard and Becky things had been relatively normal, apart from the obvious embarrassment of not having her own apartment yet. She worked long hours, she commuted, and at the weekends she rested. She read books, she slept late, she consumed the Sunday papers, and every so often went out with her old girlfriends from school and came home staggeringly drunk. But now her whole existence had taken on a dark and somewhat sordid aspect. She had not seen any of her regular friends for nearly two months; her attitude to work had downgraded to almost apathetic, and her previously nonexistent sex life had become sleazy and perverted. And now she had met someone quite by chance who had thrown a completely new level of uncertainty into the situation. And, to top it all, he had killed someone. Murderer or not, could she really contemplate giving up her life here to move to Los Angeles on a whim? Ok, the world was a smaller place these days, but California was still a heck of a long way away. Somehow she knew that she would go, but part of her desperately wanted her old life back.

Without even noticing her well trodden route home she was suddenly at the front doorstep, and her mother was out on the drive putting some rubbish bags by the garage door.

"Hey Mom."

"Hey, I didn't hear you go out."

"I've only been gone half an hour. I met someone down at the bar near the train station."

Tara and her mother had not actually spoken properly since the previous evening.

"And how was work today?"

"Oh it was ok; same as usual. You know what, Mom, I'm going to bed. I'll see you in the morning."

"Goodnight then, honey."

"Goodnight Mom."

Tara took her shoes off in the hall and plodded upstairs, closing the bedroom door behind her with a sigh. Her mother, Rachael, was nearly sixty and her dad, Vince, was a year older and still working as an area manager for a chain of small supermarkets that were spread over most of northern New Jersey. On the face of it, both of them were as healthy as carthorses; her dad hadn't had any time off sick in over five years and her mom constantly boasted that she hadn't caught a cold in twenty years. Now would be a good time to leave, Tara decided. She didn't want to wait until one of them got ill and they started to depend on her. Selfish, but she needed her own life and, up until very recently, it didn't seem like it would ever amount to much. The dream of making it in movies or television in Hollywood was a truly remote one, but she needed to give it a try and would probably have never done so otherwise. She methodically took off her clothes and walked naked into her en suite shower room, switching on the powerful jet and waiting a moment before stepping under the cascade. As she directed her face upwards, the water heated rapidly and gently pummelled her face and upper body. Her eyelids felt it, her earlobes felt it, and her shoulders felt it. This was a chance to do something that had spirited itself out of nowhere and she absolutely *had to* seize it.

She decided to go with Geoff. After all what did she have to lose?

30

Wednesday

When Geoff turned the ignition key in his rented car at Austin's Bergstrom airport, he realized that he didn't actually know where his mother was at that point in time. The only information he had was from her letter and the phone call a few days ago, so he drove for nearly an hour out to Georgetown, only to find that she had been transferred to a hospital in Central Austin the day before.

Currently he was making his way across the parking area of this hospital, gradually wilting in the dry, baking heat. The temperature was nudging 105 degrees and he had forgotten just how hot it could get down here in the south when there was no cooling breeze coming in off the ocean. Los Angeles seemed mild in comparison. But somehow this still felt like home to him, and there was a tangible feeling of hospitality here that LA could never hope to emulate.

He stepped inside into an icy blast of air conditioning and spoke to a staggeringly pretty receptionist, who informed him that his mother was now being monitored in their dedicated cancer unit after seemingly minor surgery to remove a malignant melanoma from her shoulder. The procedure had been carried out in Georgetown several days ago and went well, but the doctor expressed concern that the disease had spread into the lymph nodes and suggested further surgery, which could better be carried out at this more specialized facility. Geoff followed her directions and eventually entered a fairly small ward and asked the duty nurse for Lizzie Dealer. The room was almost silent, save the minor hum of electronic equipment and the occasional beep from a monitor or intravenous drug pump. She pointed to the bed on the left at the far end, cautioning him that his mother was still very tired from her operation, and also from the drugs being administered to her on an almost hourly basis. Geoff nodded a respectful thank you and approached the bed cautiously, his alarm growing when he saw how old and frail she looked.

"Ma," he called out gently, trying desperately to convince himself that he hadn't seen her for twenty years, so perhaps she would look like this anyway.

"Ma, are you awake?"

She didn't stir.

"Ma, can you hear me? Ma, are you awake, are you ok?"

He stood at her bedside for a few moments, lost in thought, and wondering how it could be possible not to properly remember what his own mother looked like.

"Ma, can you hear me?"

He tapped her very gently on the arm and she stirred and opened her eyes.

"*Son?*" She blinked and tried to focus.

"It's me, Ma, it's Geoff; it's JJ. I came as soon as I could. How are you doing?"

Her voice was hoarse and gravelly. "Oh, I'm ok; at least I think I'm ok. I thought you weren't going to come. I didn't think you wanted to see me."

"No Ma," he urged, "honestly, it wasn't like that."

She struggled to swallow. "Hell, my mouth is so dry and I feel like every part of me hurts. I wish they'd tell me what they've done. I wish they'd tell me and then let me go home. I don't like it here. Georgetown used to be nice, but it's gotten so big now."

"You're in Austin now Ma, in a specialized unit. You were transferred here."

She didn't seem to hear this, and as she blinked her eyes filled with tears.

"Damn it," she muttered, "I don't want to be crying around people all the time. I've done enough of that to last me a lifetime."

Geoff quickly poured her a beaker of water. "Here Ma, drink that, it'll help."

She tried to lean forward and raise her arm, but didn't seem to have the strength, so he gingerly placed the rim against her cracked lips and tilted the glass until the water reached her mouth. She sipped once, and then again, sighing with relief as the cold fluid bathed the harsh dry surfaces of her throat.

"Ah, that's good, thank you Son."

She settled back, and for a moment Geoff thought that he should quit while he was ahead and leave now. But then she reached forward and gently grabbed his hand.

"Sit down JJ, we need to talk about some things."

Geoff hadn't even noticed a nearby chair, so he dragged it forwards and immediately winced at the unpleasant grating sound of the legs on the hard linoleum floor. He mouthed the word 'sorry' as a nearby patient stirred from her drug induced slumber. His heart was beating fast, and now he found that his mouth was dry too.

She sighed, but then turned her head and stared at him intensely, her left eye masked by a veil of wispy hair. Lizzie's hair used to be so thick and strong and way down past her shoulders, but now it was cropped quite short and looked thin and out of condition.

"Lean forward Son, let me take a look at you."

He shuffled to the front of his seat and returned her gaze, feeling slightly silly as she stared. It was as if she was trying to imagine how his face might have changed through all of the lost years as he grew into adulthood. Most mothers had scrapbooks bulging with pictures of their kids, but Lizzie hardly had any photos at all. For some reason they were never a family who took pictures, and suddenly this seemed like a real tragedy to her. Her heart ached at everything she had missed; high school and college graduation ceremonies, his first girlfriend, his first car, his first pay cheque. His wedding? This was her only child and she had been robbed of the most precious thing he could have given her – his childhood.

He waited, but gradually felt less uncomfortable as the seconds ticked by. At length she sighed again.

"You know, families shouldn't be apart like this. It isn't right."

He nodded gently. "No Ma, it sure ain't."

"I feel cheated by it. I feel that there's a huge hole in my life where you should have been. And I feel there's another huge hole where your daddy should have been."

Geoff nodded imperceptibly in agreement again, but didn't know what to say.

"But what can I do? I argued with your Aunt Sarah about how she was raising little Janie. It was nothing serious to begin with, but that blew up into a feud that lasted nearly five years. I don't know what to do; I can't just sit back and let people ruin their lives or the lives of their kids. That poor girl; nobody should have to get rid of a baby if they don't want to."

Geoff didn't know anything about this. The last time he'd seen Janie she was a young child. Lizzie seemed to doze off momentarily but then her eyes opened again. She looked desperately tired.

"JJ, I feel so drowsy right now and I'm real sorry because you've come a long way to see me."

"No Ma, it's ok, you need to rest."

"I want to know how you've been," she continued, "I want to know if you're working, if you're married; if you've got a nice house somewhere. But I'm just too tired. I can hardly keep my eyes open. Just tell me one thing right now and I'll find out the rest another time. Have you got a family?"

Geoff laughed to himself as he remembered his last response to the same question.

"No, I haven't got any kids, but I'll be sure and let you know if it happens."

She smiled. "That's good, I'd love to be a grandmother some day and I'd hate to have missed out on it."

The duty nurse passed quietly by. "Is everything ok, Lizzie?" She asked gently. "I'm going to be stopping by with some more medication directly."

Lizzie looked up. "I'm fine; just give me five minutes, ok?"

After the nurse had gone, Lizzie turned to Geoff. She seemed to be summoning up her strength, and after a few moments she spoke.

"You know JJ, it took me quite a few years until I figured that what happened to your daddy, and what happened to Danny…" she hesitated, "none of it was your fault."

Geoff's heart pounded through the wall of his chest. He never thought he would hear these words. He opened his mouth to speak.

"To begin with I thought we'd done something wrong. Perhaps we'd been bad parents or something. But then I realized we hadn't. Guns are something we all grow up with in rural Texas, and no state governor or president is going to change that. It's part of the constitution, it's something we've created, and it's something we've got to live with every day as citizens of this country."

She blinked hard, and her voice faded.

"But you did the right thing, Son. You saw someone who looked like he was attacking me. And you did the right thing. You did what your daddy taught you."

She gently squeezed his hand and sank back into the depths of the pillow.

Geoff moved to speak again, but she wasn't finished.

"You know, I've been over that day so many times. I've been over it and over it."

She stared at him again. "And do you know what? It all came down to laundry."

Her shoulders rocked gently in silent laughter.

"I remember it as if it were yesterday. I wasn't expecting Danny to stop by. He never did let me know when he was going to show up. But I was planning to go into Georgetown and meet up with some of the girls."

She stared at him thoughtfully and then seemed to doze off for a few seconds. Geoff sat helplessly, turning to stare at the heart monitor, half expecting to see it flatline at any moment. Then she woke again.

"And do you know what?" She repeated, "It all came down to laundry."

"Laundry, how?" he asked.

"I was going to go into Georgetown to meet up with some of my girlfriends; Millie, Jane, and..." She stopped to think. "But it doesn't matter who they were, of course. Never saw any of them again. Anyway, I was planning to head on out there early in the afternoon, but I had a huge, and I *do* mean huge, pile of laundry to do. I never used to let it get that bad, but for some reason it had gotten way out of control. But your daddy would never help me with it. He'd do all sorts of other stuff around the house, but laundry was out, and ironing, and cleaning the toilet for some reason. I always seemed to end up doing that."

She stopped again, gently biting her lower lip, and Geoff felt helpless again as he saw tears start to form in her eyes.

"So, I thought to myself, damn it, I'm going to get that laundry out of the way and then I'm going to go to Georgetown. So I'd done the first load, and I was just about to put it into the dryer when I heard a truck pull up outside..."

Her voice broke up and she reached for a tissue to dab at her nose.

"You know, I don't want to talk about the whole thing with Danny; that's private business. It was then and it is now. It shouldn't have been happening at all but, well..." she looked away dismissively, "you're a man of the world; you know what goes on."

Geoff wanted to ask how long she'd been seeing Danny Stanley. He also wanted to know what was wrong between her and his dad, because, from a child's perspective, they seemed to be very happy together.

"The thing is though, Son," she started to cry, "the thing is I never had a chance to speak to your daddy again before he died in jail. They moved him the day after he was arrested and then it all happened so fast. I kept wishing that I'd demanded to see him before he was moved, but they were questioning me too. And I so desperately wanted to protect him and you. I was going to tell the police he was covering for me; that it was me who shot Danny, in self defence, and that you and your daddy were both innocent bystanders. But I never had the chance and he died a murderer; and that's been so very hard for me to accept, when I know it isn't the truth."

She sniffled loudly and wiped the tears from her cheeks.

"But Mom, I..."

"I know, I know," she interrupted, "and what I said earlier still stands. You did do the right thing. It's just that I need to tell you how I feel. Well, how I felt. My whole world collapsed on that day, but..."

She took a deep breath and exhaled slowly.

"The thing is, it's done. Nothing can undo it; not then, and not now. No amount of speculation about me not doing the laundry, or me cheating on your daddy, or you coming back early and finding us can change it. The past is fixed, fixed for good. And we have no choice but to live with it."

Geoff closed his eyes and concentrated for a second.

"It's affected me too, Ma." he whispered. "I lost everything too, and I was just a kid."

He stopped. It was a difficult road to tread, to try and decide who was most affected by this tragedy. But he wanted to find out why she was screwing her husband's best friend in the middle of the day when her son was out playing nearby. And he wanted to know why she was being pushed up a wall like she was about to be strangled.

"I know you did, Son. You had to grow up without your parents and with a terrible burden on your shoulders. It wasn't your fault; you acted in what you thought were my best interests. But it wasn't all my fault either. Sometimes things happen for a reason, but most times I think people say that as an excuse when it's something bad. Stuff doesn't happen for any reason at all if you ask me. It just happens, and it's only afterwards that human beings spend hours agonizing over why. What I did was wrong. I was cheating on your daddy, and if I hadn't done it then things would have been a whole lot different." She struggled and raised herself up slightly, "but I want us to be friends again. I want us to be in contact. Not all the time, not every day. I don't think either of us could stand that. And maybe not even every week, but let's stay in touch, ok?"

He nodded. "Yeah Mom, definitely; life's too short and I'd pretty much resigned myself to not seeing you again, so yeah, we'll stay in touch. I'll make sure of it."

She grabbed his hand and squeezed it as hard as she could manage.

"You are going to get well, aren't you?"

"I don't know," she replied. "I think so. I hope so. Anyway, I've just rediscovered my family, so I can't go dying yet."

Geoff's voice trembled. "No, you'd better not."

The nurse appeared discreetly in the background with a small tray, carrying an assortment of medication, but Geoff spotted her in his peripheral vision.

"How are things going?" she asked quietly. "Now, you need to take your medication Lizzie and then you need to rest. You need to sleep, and sleep, and carry on sleeping to get your strength back, but it'll come, don't you worry."

"Ma'am we need to exchange numbers and stuff," Geoff said politely as he stood.

"Ok," the nurse replied, "we'll do it at the main desk. Your momma needs to rest now, so you say your goodbyes and I'll be right back."

The nurse evaporated into the background, leaving Geoff standing awkwardly by the bed.

"Right then, I have to go back to Los Angeles, but I'll leave my numbers with the nurse and we'll speak soon. And if you need me, I can be over in a couple of hours."

She nodded, but her eyelids were drooping. "It's been good to see you again, Son. I thought it wasn't going to happen. Give your mom a hug before you go, but watch out for my bandages."

He leaned in and put his arms around her shoulders and she did the same back, although the effort of reaching up was considerable. He felt her body shaking slightly as she tried to stop herself from crying. He could feel the bones jutting out through her skin and nightdress.

He stood back up. "I'll be seeing you then, Ma. You'll get better. I know you will."

"I love you, Son," she replied softly. "You made a man's decision when you were only a boy and I admire and respect that. You did what you could to protect me. A mom couldn't ask for any more than that."

Geoff's eyes filled with tears, but he willed them not to break free. All he could do was smile and nod to indicate that he loved her too. The words just wouldn't come out. He touched her arm, then turned and left.

31

As he emerged from the air conditioned chill of the hospital, his thoughts still raw from what had just happened, Geoff decided on the spur of the moment that there was something he urgently needed to do. So, after stopping off at a diner for a hamburger and a strong cup of coffee, he headed north on route 183 again, in the direction of Leander. He had only visited his father's grave once, a few days after the funeral, when his grandparents took him. After that, somehow, the thought of visiting never really came up again. In his head there was something inherently wrong with him going there to pay respects to someone, the death of whom he had so needlessly caused. But today things felt very different. He was tired and weary from the events of the last few days, but he felt an internal momentum pushing him forward and so, approximately one hour later, his car pulled up into the dusty parking area of the tiny rural cemetery and he got out, stretching and blinking in the heat of the afternoon sun. As he walked through the gate he casually acknowledged an old man who was sitting on a bench under a solitary tree, and then started to scour the assemblage of, mostly well-tended, graves.

Frank Dealer's headstone was the last on the back row, just short of a token barbed wire fence to divide the property from adjacent farmland, and Geoff stood for a moment in scared silence; still somewhere in the back of his mind thinking he shouldn't be there.

"Dad, it's me, it's JJ. I've come to see you, at last." Eventually he crouched down in front of the polished stone, which was too hot to touch in the afternoon sun, and half heartedly rearranged some of the faded plastic flowers that half filled a sunken pot.

"I've been to see mom," he said softly. "She's doing ok, I think. She's had an operation for cancer and now she's been moved to a special unit in Austin. They seem to be taking real good care of her." He paused, feeling slightly foolish. "She's going to be ok, isn't she, Dad? See what you can do, huh?" He tapped the headstone gently and sat down on the scorched dusty ground, catching a quick glimpse of a tiny brown lizard as it scuttled behind a small rock to hide from the sun.

"Dad," he said eventually, "I've done some really stupid things, and I hope it's not too late to put them right. I guess you wouldn't even be here if it wasn't for me shooting Danny Stanley. So I just want to say I'm sorry, ok?" His voice cracked. "For ending your life and for ruining mom's. You know what, mine doesn't even matter. It was you two who brought me into the world and look how I repaid you."

He blinked and swallowed hard, shifting position slightly to get more comfortable. Yet despite his emotional state, somehow he felt at peace. For the first time the constant video loop of Danny Stanley collapsing to the ground, his mom screaming, and then the gushing blood and the convulsing, gasping body, was somehow pushed into the background. He paused for a while as the wind rustled and two birds fought briefly in the nearby tree.

"I've messed up in other ways too, Dad," he continued. "There was a beautiful girl called Christine. We met in college. I remember when she came up to me in the cafeteria and sat at my table. We were together for five years, but I never paid her enough attention. I never cared enough; something kept stopping me from opening up to her and I couldn't explain what it was. She left me and now she's been in hospital in New York. I went to see her; I tried to help, but I think it's too late." He sighed in desperation. "I've *got* to change. I've got to turn things around. Will you help me?"

He placed the palm of his hand on the headstone, wincing as the granite surface started to burn his skin. "*Please, will you help me?*" He withdrew his hand and blew on it in a vain attempt to cool it down.

"I was hoping you'd come visit one day, Son." A voice from behind made Geoff jump, and he turned and squinted upwards.

"Pardon me." It was the man he had nodded to on the way in.

"You're obviously JJ; I knew it as soon as you got out of your car."

"I am, yes, can I help you with something Sir?" Geoff stood.

"I'm George Stern, Reverend George Stern. I know your family well. I know you. I married your mom and dad, I blessed you soon after you were born, and I baptized you when you were a few weeks old." He paused. "And I know what happened after that too. I went to Huntsville with your mom to fetch your daddy's body home, and I buried him. I talked to your mom before she left town, and I've talked to her in the last few days."

Geoff stared helplessly into the man's eyes. His voice was so soothing, and his face was so kind.

"Yeah, I've just been to see her too; first time in twenty years."

"And how did you two get along after all this time?"

"It was ok, I guess," Geoff replied. "She was so sleepy and she looked so frail that I really didn't say too much. She said she wanted us to stay in touch though, so that's got to be good, don't you think?"

"It sounds good to me," the man said, and fell silent for a moment, seemingly deep in thought. "You know, what happened that day sent shockwaves through this little town," he continued, reaching out to touch Geoff's shoulder, "but everyone knows it wasn't your fault. You witnessed something you didn't understand, but you knew you had to act. And you did. Now, I've never agreed with guns in the hands of normal citizens, but hell, this is Texas, and nobody blames you, Son. That's what I'm saying. You were a small child facing up to a fully grown man. You saw danger and you didn't stand a chance of fighting him off any other way."

Geoff shook his head and looked down at the floor.

"It's ok, Son, I can see you need to be on your own with your dad here."

"No, no; stay a while, please."

The man smiled. "You know, I feel I can tell you this now because you're an adult. But your mom tried to kill herself with sleeping pills after it all happened. And she came so very, very close to succeeding. I sat with her in hospital when she eventually came round. She felt she was to blame. She thought that if she'd spoken out straight away and told the authorities what had happened, then things would have been different. It wouldn't have saved Danny, but he was taking a risk anyway. If your dad had come home ten minutes earlier he might well have shot him instead! It was a tragic set of circumstances. Nobody could have foreseen it, and nobody could have predicted the aftermath."

Geoff sighed and nodded gently. "Thank you, Sir, that means a lot, really it does."

"Ah, it's nothing. Now I'm going to go, because it's too hot for me in the afternoon sun, but I'll say one last thing. I'm a man of God, and I believe it is fundamentally wrong to take the life of another person, but … but you acted in a split second. And I couldn't ever say that I wouldn't have done the same thing; either as a young boy or now."

He turned to leave. "You look troubled Son, and I know the words of an old preacher man probably don't mean that much, but I think you've suffered enough. Now spend a little more time with your dad, but then you move on with the rest of your life. There's plenty of it still to come so, you make the most of it."

They shook hands briefly. "I'm glad to have met you, Son." The man said, and walked back towards the gate.

"You too Sir, and thank you for the things you said," Geoff shouted back. He remained at the grave side for another ten minutes before returning to his car and driving back to Austin.

Later that evening Geoff was sitting in his motel room, staring at the phone. He felt tired from the heat and the driving, tired from the emotional strain of seeing his mom so seriously ill, but yet he felt exhilarated. Exhilarated because he had finally heard her side of the story; exhilarated that years and years of separation had come to an end, and exhilarated that he had been to visit his dad and had spoken to the preacher. An immense weight had been lifted from his shoulders and his mind was clear and focussed for the first time.

He called Tara's mobile phone. "Hi Tara, how are you doing? Can you talk?"

"Hi Geoff," she replied, sounding pleased to hear his voice, "what fantastic timing, I just got out of a review meeting this second."

"Are you ok?" he asked.

"I'm doing good thanks. Did you see your mom?"

"I did, yeah, I only flew in today"

"And did it go ok?"

"I guess. It was pretty intense; she was hooked up to a machine and on all sorts of drugs, but she was ok. She was talking and she was making sense."

"And did you guys make up?"

Geoff laughed to himself. This wasn't a petty argument over what time he used to come in at night. "Yeah, we did. I think we did; kind of anyway. We're going to keep in touch, which is the important thing. I could just tell it was so hard for her after all this time but…" his voice waivered, "but let's say I heard some stuff that I needed to hear."

"Well, that's fantastic news Geoff," she replied softly, "really it is. I'm so pleased for you. I mean, I know it can't change the past, but at the end of the day, family is all we have and…"

"Yeah well, you can't just wipe away years of silence with one conversation, but I think we both said what we wanted to say." He decided at this point not to mention visiting the cemetery.

"It's a step forward Geoff, and that's fantastic after all you've been through."

"Anyway," he needed to change the subject, "do you still want to come out to Los Angeles with me? I'll understand completely if this whole thing is too much to take on right now." He hesitated. "You know what I mean; however much time we spend together, and that might be none at all if you want, I just don't want you to be concerned about anything."

"I have been thinking about it a lot," she replied, "but, to be honest, the main thing that freaks me out is how we even met in the first place."

"I know, that was pretty spooky meeting up like that. I think it was meant to happen. Although that's not something I'd usually say."

"You could be right," she replied. "Out of all the benches in all the parks you had to sit on mine."

There was a pause. He half expected her to turn him down.

"So?" he asked expectantly.

"So..." she replied eventually, "so I've decided I've been living around here far too long and I think it's about time I moved on."

Geoff's heart pounded heavily. "You'll come over then?"

She took a deep breath. "Yes, I will."

"Great," he said. "That's great."

"Now, are you sure? I mean, well this is a big step for me, I've always lived here and I've never been further west than Philadelphia."

But Geoff couldn't possibly back out now. "Yeah, I'm sure. It'll be a blast, you'll see. I reckon you'll have landed your first acting role within a month; six weeks tops. I'm sure you'll love it over there."

"I'm hoping so Geoff, I'm really hoping so."

"You will, I almost guarantee it. Look, it's been a long day and I need to crash, but I'll be back there tomorrow night, so I'll call you then and we'll make some proper arrangements, ok?"

"Ok, tomorrow then." Tara hung up, excited. She had done some of her packing in anticipation; all she had to do was tell her parents that she was going on vacation with a friend at short notice. For now she had planned to wait a few weeks and then let them know she was going to stay a little longer. And then a little longer, and a little longer. She couldn't possibly tell them she was leaving home on a whim to shack up with a stranger on the other side of the country.

And as for work, she would just have to phone in sick to start with, and then, and then. She hadn't properly decided yet.

Later that night, when Geoff went to bed he decided to banish any worries or concerns over the immediate future. Both he and Tara were adults and if things didn't work out then he'd ask her to leave. Simple. He'd even pay to fly her home. On the other hand, fate might have caused their paths to intersect for a reason. They might be perfect together. But one thing was for certain; nothing would be assumed.

Then he slept for eight solid hours, having almost forgotten what a good night's sleep was like.

32

Saturday

Nearly two months had passed and it was now 9am on a fine September morning as Geoff drew up outside an anonymous building in the Century City district of Los Angeles. He'd dropped Tara off here about an hour ago to attend a screen test for an extra in a popular daytime cable TV series. In the meantime he had driven downtown to visit his now almost redundant P.O. Box, and was surprised to find a brief handwritten letter enquiring about his services. It was from a guy called Greg who had seen the ad in an old newspaper. He wanted to set the record straight it said. His wife Lucy had left him and taken their child. She was not currently in a new relationship and Greg wanted to find out if Geoff could be of any assistance in this matter. Money was no object, it added as a postscript, and Greg had thoughtfully included a small photograph of Lucy. She looked gorgeous, reclining on a lounger in the smallest of swimsuits. Despite Geoff's promise to himself that there would be no more setting the record straight, he had kept the letter, which was now in the glove compartment awaiting transfer to his lockable document box. He would keep it for a week or so, because things had been a little uncertain recently and all options needed to be left open.

For Geoff and Tara's first couple of days together he couldn't resist them staying in Benedict Canyon, even though he knew he was setting Tara's expectations stratospherically high. He told her that their stay would only be short-lived, but that didn't stop her buying into the lifestyle almost immediately, and while she spent her time floating from room to room, and from deck area to poolside to gazebo, Geoff agitated and cajoled to expedite the process of moving to his new agreed residence on Mulholland

Drive. But in the end, nothing could be arranged before his lease ran out and so they had to downsize dramatically, leaving Tara to settle for the cramped second bedroom in Geoff's West Hollywood apartment.

Thankfully, during this period there was no attempt at contact by Hannah, the possibility of which had worried Geoff to the point of not being able to sleep properly. Playing the genial host was difficult when he was absolutely on a knife edge worrying that his mobile would ring when he wasn't next to it, or that men in suits would ambush him by his car. A fair amount of money was at stake here, principally the ten thousand dollars of her money that was currently growing in a speculative currency deal; and he had racked his brains trying to remember what else he had told her about himself. Something was nagging in his head, saying that once when they were both drunk he had told her about his crash pad in a downbeat apartment block in West Hollywood, just off Sunset. There could be people waiting on street corners looking for him! And his neighbour, ex-marine Corporal Bill, who was always out in the parking area attending to his car, would no doubt delight in the chance to be of service in a surveillance capacity.

Hannah had actually tried to contact him on several occasions while he was coast hopping, but his phone was either not switched on or left ringing, and no one answered the bell on the two occasions when she stopped by at the only address she knew. Geoff had actually been very successful in only giving her very restricted access to him as a person. She had his mobile phone number, which theoretically meant she could speak to him anywhere, but when that was left unanswered she realized that she knew virtually nothing else that could be of use. There wasn't even an employer to contact, because he seemed to somehow make his living sitting at home in front of a laptop. She didn't know where he shopped, where he banked, where he ate and drank, or who his friends were, and she certainly didn't remember anything about a crash pad in West Hollywood. She also knew he worked out at a gym, but she didn't know which one. To all intents and purposes he had vanished, and her only option was to stake out his house herself or pay someone to do it. For two days she cruised up and down Benedict

Canyon Drive, stopping on the apron of his driveway for nearly an hour at one point until the Beverly Hills police spotted her for the third time in the same place and asked her to move along. By the end of the second day it dawned on her how much of a long shot this was. The property was unassailable from the outside, totally shielded by dense foliage, a high wall, and solid gates. He was either in there for the duration and watching his entrance on CCTV or he had skipped town. So she decided to leave too, for the time being. Maybe she could get her head together and think of a plan. No way was he dumping her *and* stealing her money. But for the time being her life was a mess. Predictably, her employers hadn't been too impressed with the anonymous video clip, and currently she was suspended from her job without pay. But she wasn't sure she could even go back for the disciplinary hearing in seven day's time. How could she walk into the building knowing that, in all probability, everyone including the cleaning staff, had seen her sprawled naked across the boss's desk?

For Geoff, all in all it had been a very successful first assignment, and within another week he had received his payment from Ken for services rendered, plus a brief note saying that Hannah had left town to live in Cupertino with her sister.

After their acute drop in living standards, Tara and Geoff's fledgling relationship hit a rough patch. They found themselves bickering pointlessly about silly things; eating arrangements, him lending her money until she found a job, what TV station they should watch, who should go to the store to buy groceries, and who left the most hair in the plughole after using the shower. Also, his apartment was too small for two people living separately and this caused many additional arguments, mainly around the subject of bathroom occupancy. For a while the whole arrangement seemed tenuous. Tara had been attending a string of screen tests and auditions to no avail, and Geoff was secretly becoming concerned over a number of bad decisions he had made in recent trading. He lost nearly twenty thousand dollars over the space of two days and his frustration was hard to conceal. Normally when a losing streak happened, and they had happened before, he would console himself with a bottle of bourbon and a few hours at his favourite strip joint on Hollywood Boulevard, but now he felt he had to be a model house mate and cook dinner, perhaps keep the apartment a little cleaner, and maybe spend some time shopping for soft furnishings. Suddenly he had become stifled, and his former life as a bachelor seemed both remote and very appealing.

He was expecting Tara to emerge from the doorway directly in front of him very soon so he cut the engine and lowered the window, letting a pleasant warm breeze drift in and across his face. He smiled and briefly contemplated the somewhat bizarre chain of events over the last few months that had led him to this point.

He remembered the day when it had all started. He had so much to do that week that he almost wrote himself a list. But then the letter from his mother appeared, followed a few days later by Christine's unscheduled reappearance in his life, the combination of which sent everything into a tailspin. But something still nagged at him occasionally, like a dull headache. Somehow he still felt responsible for Christine's current position, and that it should be him who was looking after her if she couldn't work; both physically and financially. And he would have done too, he was almost sure of it, if she hadn't left the hospital without telling him. He couldn't believe she had done it intentionally; something unavoidable must have come up. But she hadn't answered either of his messages, so there was little else he could do.

Suddenly the door across the street opened and Tara came jogging out.

"So, what's the story?" Geoff asked urgently, "Did you get it?"

"Don't know yet," she replied, "I need to go back in about ten minutes. *God, I can't stand this part!*"

"Get in for a minute," he said, "talk to me."

Tara climbed into the truck and sat, nervously fidgeting with her fingernails.

"You know what, Geoff?" she said, "I'm sorry for the way I've been the last couple of weeks. As much as I complained about my job in New York, I *hate* not having one over here. So I'm sorry for being grouchy. It will all stop as of Monday, I promise."

Two days previously Tara had received a phone call saying she had been offered a job as an administrator in a nearby tax attorney's practice, after an interview only an hour earlier.

"But I've decided something. I'm going to keep on auditioning for the rest of this month and into October, and then if nothing comes up..." she hesitated, "I'll probably head back to New York for Christmas."

She touched his arm. "I mean, I know there's nothing, really, between us, but I just wanted to check. Is that ok with you?"

Geoff shrugged. "That's cool; you do whatever you think is best."

"Right then, I'm going to go back over. Wish me luck!" she said as she climbed out and ran back across the road.

"Good luck!" he called out and she turned and waved briefly before disappearing through the door.

Then Geoff's phone rang, it was his estate agent Juanita, and she sounded in a terrible rush.

"Geoff, hi, good news. I can't stay on the phone as I'm supposed to be somewhere else, like now, but I'm just letting you know that the folks you're waiting on at Mulholland Drive have finally left and, subject to a thorough inspection, you can probably move in within the week."

"Hey Juanita, that's excellent news, now can I..."

"Sorry Geoff, gotta go. I'll speak to you Monday, first thing. I'll be at my desk at eight."

And with that she hung up.

Since returning to her apartment back in New York City, Christine had been recovering steadily and could now get around in short bursts with reasonable speed and not too much discomfort, although standing for anything longer than a five minute shower was still somewhat of a trial, as she was suffering some quite serious, but as yet undiagnosed, back pain. She visited the outpatients' ward for occasional checkups, and had received one or two visits from the police regarding the ongoing case of the missing Don Borello. He still had not reappeared, and the effort being dedicated to the case appeared to be dwindling. But apart from this limited human contact, she felt desperately alone. She had spoken to her parents, but only to give them the very briefest overview of her situation. The last thing she needed was for them to decamp to her apartment for an unspecified time frame, and her relocating down there also wasn't an option. Somehow she felt a need to speak to Geoff; to tidy things up and maybe to apologize for inviting him back and then vanishing. To her, there was still a tenuous link between them, and it seemed that as long as he was involved in her life, even if only in a peripheral sense, then there was no way for her to close the door and truly move forward. She had toyed with the idea of calling him many times, but none of the scenarios she played out in her head gave her the outcome she wanted.

Several thousand miles east in London, Paul and Helen were sitting at a pavement café sipping cappuccinos in the late afternoon sun. It was unusually hot and sunny for the time of year and Paul was leaning forward on his plastic chair to prevent the rivulets of sweat running down his back from staining his shirt. A large percentage of the sweating was due to nerves. Helen, though, seemed unflustered by the heat. In contrast to what was said over the phone, she had moved out of the apartment by the time Paul had returned and was currently staying with a friend in nearby Greenwich, while she considered what to do. They had met several times since, and Paul felt that he was definitely close to getting her back. He had freely admitted that his trip to visit Christine was stupid, and that he wasn't even sure what he wanted to come of it; although deep down, of course, he was. Helen didn't believe this, and she held all the cards. She wanted to know why he felt the need to deceive her, knowing of course that she would have gone ballistic if he had asked first. And she wanted to know why, at the very, *very* least, if this trip was so important to him, and it was for a purely innocent reason, she couldn't have come along to sightsee in New York while he went hospital visiting. She knew that she didn't want to hear a truthful response to these questions, but was determined to keep asking them for as long as they continued to make Paul sweat and squirm. From her perspective, he was nowhere near getting her back, and she had started seeing Mark from her office following their communal night out before Paul returned. He seemed like a nice guy, very up front and honest. They were seeing each other again tonight, and she would let Paul know her final verdict on their future together soon. That is, that there almost certainly wasn't one.

Around ten minutes later, Tara came bursting out of the door and ran across the parking area with her arms waving, she looked immensely excited and Geoff climbed out of the truck to meet her.

"So, yeah, tell me, tell me…"

"I got it! I got it … I got it, *I got it!*" she screeched.

She jumped into his arms and they twirled around, Geoff staggering momentarily from the impact.

"Oh my God, that's fantastic!"

She dropped from his arms and jumped up and down. "You should see some of the lines I've got. Come on, I want to go back to the apartment and rehearse."

"When do you start on it?"

Tara was very excited. "End of next week. Oh Geoff, I can't believe this. Thank you for spotting the ad, I went through that magazine twice and never even saw it."

"It was just lucky," he shrugged, "either of us could have found it."

She put both hands to her head and ran on the spot. "I have an acting job! I've been out here two months and I've already landed an acting job. I can't believe this, I'm so happy I could *scream!*"

"Hey, hold on though, what about your new secretarial post?" he asked seriously, "You'll have to ask for time off on your first day."

But her expression conveyed the response far better than words ever could.

"Are you glad you came to the west coast with me?" he asked.

"Shit, yes! I'm freaking out here, big style." They hugged.

"Hey, and don't forget you need to call your mom later. Isn't she due out again today? You know, I'm so pleased she's on the mend and that you guys got back together again."

Geoff's mother had been given a provisional 'all clear' over a month ago, but had recently been in hospital again for yet another battery of tests.

"Me too!" he replied, "I'll have to take you to Texas next time I visit."

She beamed. "Yeah, that'd be fabulous! I need to see more of my own country, for God's sake."

But then she theatrically put her hand to her brow. "If I get a break in filming that is."

"Come on then," he said, smiling, "let's go rehearse, as long as I can be the leading man."

They both laughed again. Geoff opened the passenger door and escorted her into the truck, then ran around, climbed in himself, and pulled away with a massive amount of wheel spin to celebrate the moment.

As they drove, Tara bubbled relentlessly about her new role and Geoff couldn't find a gap wide enough to announce the news about Mulholland Drive. But when they passed the turn off for their apartment she stopped.

"Hey, where are we going? Oh c'mon, I need to get back and start rehearsing a.s.a.p."

"I've got some good news too," he replied.

She looked round. "Tell me, but I don't know how much more good news I can deal with in one day."

"Ok," he said, "Ma'am, we're heading back for some more canyon living. I surrendered the lease on Benedict Canyon before I even met you, but I just got a call from my realtor five minutes ago, so we're heading higher into the hills; to Mulholland Drive!"

Tara screeched with excitement.

"And now with you being a bona fide Hollywood actress," he continued, "we might even be able to make the rent every month."

He let out a bellow of celebration. "*Result!*"

Tara screwed up her face in amazement. "Shit, Geoff that is just *so* fucking cool! Oh man, that is awesome! Are you sure we can afford it, I mean…"

"Of course we can! I'm going to trade my rear off, you'll see. It's gonna be great Tara absolutely great; totally copasetic."

"Stop the truck Geoff." She said suddenly. "I need to do something."

They were now driving through Beverly Hills, so Geoff quickly signalled and pulled over onto the apron of the driveway of a very expensive looking house.

"Excuse me a minute," she said, before getting out and running over to a superbly manicured lawn, where she turned two successive cartwheels before running back to the truck, vaulting onto the flat bed behind the cab and letting out a huge high pitched holler to the neighbourhood. Then she jumped down onto the road, climbed back in and refastened her seat belt.

"Cool," she said, slightly out of breath. "Drive on."

Something clicked inside him as they drove away and he saw how happy Tara was. Suddenly everything seemed ok. Suddenly it seemed like a 'future' had materialized out of the murk that had clouded his vision ever since Danny Stanley. His relationship with Tara was still very much at the 'just good friends' stage, but there was a definite hint of promise floating on the breeze. He reached over and retrieved Greg's letter from the glove compartment.

Tara was still buzzing with excitement, but she saw him screw it up into a ball and throw it out of the window.

"Hey, what's that you litter bug?"

"Oh nothing," he replied, "just some junk mail."